IMPALED

A gruesome murder sparks a manhunt

RAY CLARK

THE
BOOK
FOLKS

Published by The Book Folks

London, 2024

ISBN 978-1-80462-172-1

www.thebookfolks.com

IMPALED is the eleventh book in a series of mysteries by Ray Clark featuring DI Stewart Gardener. The full list of books is as follows:

Impaled: *1.* *Transfixed or pierced with a sharp instrument.*
2. *Fixed in an inescapable or helpless position.*

I would like to dedicate this book to two people who did more for me than I could ever imagine, and asked nothing in return.

Michael Allen 1942 – 2023
Mark Eyre 1986 – 2023

Lives of great men all remind us
We can make our lives sublime,
And, departing, leave behind us
Footprints on the sands of time.

Henry Wadsworth Longfellow (1807 – 1882)

Prologue

The Yorkshire Gazette
Beware Omega Man

People in the north of England have been warned to be vigilant if wearing high-value watches or jewellery, following a spate of thefts.

Several expensive watches have been stolen in a number of locations including the car parks of golf clubs, supermarkets and, most recently, the railway station in Leeds.

Travellers have described a man posing as a charity worker with a clipboard who has stolen watches from his victims without them realizing as they sign a petition, waiting in queues for food and, in one instance, shaking hands with him.

Described as Omega Man, he is believed to have been operating all over West Yorkshire in the past few months.

PC Ray Thompson, based in Bradford, said, "We have had a number of incidents of a similar nature and I would again remind people to be vigilant. Be particularly careful if you are wearing any high-value watches or jewellery and are approached in suspicious circumstances."

One theft occurred in the car park of the Bradford Golf Club while another happened close to a golf club in Headingley.

Mr Ethan Parks, who lost his £14,000 gold Rolex, described the man as a "highly trained professional". Twenty-eight-year-old Ethan, an accountant, was at the rail station in Leeds in September when he was approached.

He told the *Yorkshire Gazette*, "The man had a clipboard and was making out he was deaf. He wanted signatures for a petition for a new deaf centre. I signed it with my left hand, which was the same hand my watch was on. He was highly delighted and hugged me. It wasn't until ten minutes later, about to board the train to London, that I noticed it was missing. He was the only person I could remember being in contact with. It was too late to do anything about it."

There have been many more incidents across the county, including several thefts in cinemas where seventeen people lost their watches in one night.

Several descriptions of the man lead police to believe he is using a number of different disguises, one of which was said to be a female, approximately 5ft 9in tall, with long dark hair and an eastern European accent. There is a possibility that more than one person is involved.

Chapter One

Early December

Glancing across the restaurant and out of the window he could see that York Place appeared to be deserted.

Only to be expected, thought Detective Inspector Stewart Gardener, given the location – rather than the time of year.

He was having a meal with the botanist Vanessa Chambers, whom he had met on his first case following his wife's death. Fitz, the Home Office pathologist, had introduced them, and he had not seen hide nor hair of her until quite some time later when they had bumped into each other in the town centre of Leeds, pretty much in the middle of a crime scene; more recently still when he and his sergeant, Sean Reilly, had been investigating a body in a van fire.

December wasn't a good month for Gardener. Three years ago, his wife, Sarah had been killed on the streets of Leeds, following a romantic evening in an Italian restaurant. Which was exactly where he was tonight – albeit a different venue.

A number of times during the evening, Vanessa's expressions reminded him of the first time they had met, in her office; she appeared to enjoy life and, perhaps not take it too seriously. She was in her early forties, blonde and bubbly, with a figure to die for – not unlike Sarah.

Vanessa was dressed in a black, figure-hugging dress that finished a little above the knees of her long, slender legs. She spoke with a confident upper-class accent, wore very little make-up, and throughout the night he had often caught a faint odour of her perfume.

White Linen, if he wasn't mistaken. And he wasn't. It had been Sarah's favourite.

Vanessa lifted her cup to her mouth and toasted to a wonderful evening, most of which they had spent talking, perhaps not confidently, more testing each other out – as you would on a first date.

Vanessa had booked the table, and had then called *him*. He'd had no desire to offend her; so against his better wishes, and at the insistence of his father, he'd finally agreed to go.

The Da Vito Ristorante offered a range of dishes, with vegan and gluten-free options. The building sat in the centre of the business district, opposite the Leeds Hypnotherapy Clinic and next to City Smile Dental; three floors high with bay windows, a Georgian brick façade and black railings at street level. Gardener suspected it may also be listed. He knew it was possibly one of the oldest buildings in the area, dating from the early nineteenth century.

The interior had frosted-glass-topped tables, high-back leather chairs and parquet flooring. The atmosphere was romantic, with light background music that he couldn't name but he'd bet Fitz could. They were sitting in one of the corners at the rear of the room, which was quieter. The front, lower section was pretty full despite being Saturday. Then again, it was December. The service had been superb.

Strangely enough, both had chosen the same starter of fresh king prawns in their shells, finished with white wine, garlic and chilli. Even stranger was that they both went for the same main meal of baked sea bass fillets, with potatoes, shallots, cherry tomatoes, black olives and rosemary. A French Chardonnay was recommended to wash it down. They were now on coffees.

"It's been a lovely evening," said Vanessa. "Thank you for coming. I wasn't sure you would."

"Neither was I," replied Gardener.

"I can understand why."

"Can you?" Gardener could have kicked himself for his reply, it was a little sharper than he had meant, and he was so obviously out of practice.

"Your wife," she said, after taking a sip of her coffee. "From what you've told me, it sounds like you had a really good relationship, and you appeared to have built a rather special family."

"Aren't all families special?"

"They should be," replied Vanessa. "Although, I reckon in your job, you meet your fair share of ones with special problems."

"You can say that again." He lifted his coffee and sipped it. He rarely drank coffee. In fact, he could only think of two occasions when he would; one was from the percolator in Fitz's office, and the other would likely be in a restaurant, where it always appeared to taste different. He had no idea what they did to it, but it was always mellow, the way he liked it.

"Anyway," said Vanessa, "didn't we promise we would not talk about work this evening?"

"I remember one of us making that concession."

Gardener felt guilty; as if perhaps he shouldn't feel at ease in another woman's presence in a romantic setting. The music changed, but he still couldn't tell you what it was.

"There is one question I've been dying to ask you all night," she said, sipping more coffee, and staring at him so intensely that it made him feel like he was not simply the only man in the restaurant, or Leeds, but the entire planet. His stomach lurched.

"Perhaps you'd better ask it," he replied.

She leaned forward. "What do off-duty policeman get up to in their spare time?"

Gardener smiled. He had no idea what she was going to ask but he wouldn't have bet his last fiver on it being that question.

"Us in general?" asked Gardener. "Or just me?"

"Just you."

Butterflies in his stomach again. The lady was obviously interested. He'd known that from the odd occasions they had met, and the fact that some of her comments were borderline flirting.

"Motorbikes," said Gardener. "Well, one in particular."

"Really?" She smiled. "*Which* one in particular?"

"A Triumph."

"Go on," she said. "Tiger Cub, Speed Twin, do tell." She finished her coffee.

"You sound like you know a bit about bikes."

"I'll tell you if you tell me."

Gardener laughed. "Shouldn't that be, I'll show you if you show me."

"Later, maybe."

Gardener sensed he was going to have trouble with her. She wasn't frightened to say what she thought, and it didn't take a genius to know what she was thinking right now.

"A 1959 T120 Bonneville."

Her eyes lit up. "Where in the world did you find that bad boy?"

"I didn't. My father did, in a breaker's yard. He'd been searching for spare parts for a friend. When he got back home, he told Sarah."

"And she bought it for you?" asked Vanessa, her eyes melting and her expression softening. "How lovely."

Gardener reflected. He would rather not tell her the story but he didn't think it was fair to Vanessa if he didn't.

"It was the last thing she *did* buy for me."

Vanessa put her hand to her mouth. "Oh, how awful. I'm so sorry. I shouldn't have asked the question, or pushed the point."

"You weren't to know," he replied. "She knew I'd wanted a Triumph Bonneville for as long as she'd known me. I'd never found the right one, or the right time to buy one. Once Sarah had made an offer, my father picked up the bike…"

He paused but she didn't say anything.

"He waited until we had gone out before smuggling it into the garage. Sarah never saw it. She died the same night."

There was an awkward silence, but Vanessa broke it. "Did it need a lot of work?" She was possibly trying to keep him on the subject of the bike itself as opposed to dwelling on something so sad and painful.

Gardener laughed. "It was wrecked. The tyres were bald. The exhaust was hanging off. The seat had been chewed by something, probably mice or rats. Badges were missing; the fuel tank was worn down to bare metal. No front number plate – a smashed headlamp."

"Now that does sound like something worth spending your time on."

Gardener paused, finished the last of his coffee, and then said, "There's a lot more to you than meets the eye. Your turn."

"My brothers were responsible for turning me into a biker. All they ever talked about was their bikes, and they spent every weekend on them. And because they did, I did. They said I had to help them, but I got all the dirty jobs; changing oil, or worse still, rubbing the bloody paintwork down so they could respray. If there was a dirty job to be done, I got it."

Gardener laughed. He knew that feeling. He was pretty sure his father had done the same thing.

Suddenly, his phone interrupted any further conversation. He reached into his jacket pocket and checked the display. It was neither his son, Chris, nor his father.

He knew the number. Desk sergeant David Williams from Leeds Central was after him. It had to be something serious.

"I'm sorry," he said to Vanessa. "I have to take it."

"Of course you must, don't worry."

"Dave?" said Gardener, into the phone.

"I'm really sorry, sir. You're the last person in the world I wanted to call. I realize you're not on the list."

"Must be a good reason," said Gardener.

"We've come across something nasty in Beeston."

"Beeston *is* nasty," said Gardener.

"Very nasty," said Williams. "If there had been anyone else, I would have called them, but we are so strapped, and crime just seems to be increasing to such a point that it's becoming a bloody hobby."

"Okay," said Gardener. "I understand." And he did. It went with the territory.

"I'll send a car round," said Williams. "Are you at home?"

"No," replied Gardener. He told Williams where he was.

The desk sergeant sounded even more embarrassed. "I'll have your sergeant pick you up as soon as possible."

"Okay," said Gardener, "but I need a favour."

"Name it," said Williams.

Gardener explained who he was with, and that he wanted a car round at the restaurant to take Vanessa home before he left to attend the scene.

"Consider it done."

Gardener ended the call and put the phone on the table.

"You don't have to do that for me," said Vanessa. "I can call a taxi."

"You could," said Gardener. "But I'm not going to let you."

The Lord only knew where the panda car had been when he'd requested it but he saw it roll up outside on the street in front of the restaurant window within a minute. As the officer came through the door, the front of house approached him. Everyone glanced in Gardener's direction.

Gardener rose, approached the waiter and paid the bill, with Vanessa following. He turned to the officer and told him they must take her home; that she is not allowed into the city on her own under any circumstances.

Much to her embarrassment, she was escorted from the building, perhaps feeling like a convict if her expression was anything to go by.

He didn't care. He had never forgiven himself for Sarah's death, and he did not want another on his conscience.

Chapter Two

The documentary wasn't long, a little under an hour, like most. It was very interesting, if railways were your cup of tea. He imagined Michael Portillo would have been in his element.

It wasn't the railway however that had him sitting forward and taking notice. Out of sixty minutes' worth of footage, there were perhaps only two that had *really* piqued his curiosity.

One week following the airing of the documentary, a telephone call from the producer proved very lucrative.

Chapter Three

"Jesus," said Detective Sergeant Sean Reilly, as he drove the pool car into Noster Terrace. "What the hell's this, *Gunfight at the OK Coral?*"

"If I know anything about this place," said Gardener, "it's more likely *The Texas Chainsaw Massacre.*"

The street was dark, a few of the lights were out and a slight eerie mist hung low, as if afraid to drop to ground level. Gardener figured they were not seeing the place at its best, but then again, even in daylight, it was unlikely to have a best.

Washing lines hung between the small, terraced houses, as if they were still in the 1940s, signifying possibly a close-knit community. Could be interesting. At the end, Gardener saw the flashing blue lights.

A lot of the buildings had bars at the windows and doors. From what he could see, as they continued, most of them likely needed some work here and there; a bit of pointing between the bricks, possible roof slates missing, windows needing replacing. He'd seen it all before. People lined the street, huddled together in whispering groups, like nothing ever happened here, but he knew otherwise.

As they reached their destination, the road came to a dead end, which then gave way to a field. That was something he didn't like.

Reilly killed the engine and the pair of them left the vehicle. It was pretty chilly, compared to where he had been a short while back. As he found himself wondering if Vanessa Chambers had reached home safely, his phone pinged. A text told him she had. She also thanked him for a wonderful night, before wishing him good luck. Something told him he was going to need it.

"Seems like a good start to Christmas for someone," said Reilly, as he came around to the passenger side of the car.

"Probably not us," replied Gardener.

A young PC was standing at the end of the short front path leading to the house. He was short and stocky, around five feet five. His uniform was well kept and underneath his helmet, the SIO noticed what appeared to be ginger hair, but it was hard to tell due to a lack of light.

Gardener approached him, displaying his warrant card, and introduced himself and Reilly.

The young man nodded. "PC Andrews."

"How are you?" asked Gardener.

"Been better," replied Andrews. "And warmer."

Gardener glanced past him. The house was an end of terrace. The front was red brick, with an extension built onto the roof to provide an extra bedroom, and a small front yard with a broken front wall.

He turned and glanced behind him. The view for the owner was a graveyard, which had a path to the left, leading to possibly another road. Also to the left, he stared out across a darkened field. The only thing he noticed was a "No Tipping" sign, which was only because it was quite close, and lit by the final streetlamp.

Reilly strolled across to the cemetery, studying the view.

Gardener turned back and faced the house. A narrow path led to the front door, which was uPVC with a glass window above.

As he faced Andrews, Reilly returned, blowing into his hands.

"What time did you receive the call?" Gardener asked Andrews.

He consulted his notebook. "Around eight forty-five."

"What time did you get here?"

11

"About twenty-five minutes later, ten past nine."

Twenty-five minutes, thought Gardener, glancing once again at the field; plenty of time and room to leave with little trace.

"Did *you* see anything suspicious?" asked Reilly.

Andrews shook his head. "Nothing I can remember." He turned, and pointed across the street to the first house on the right after the graveyard. Two women were standing outside the front door in big parka coats and jeans, both clasping what Gardener took to be hot drinks. One of them was smoking a cigarette.

Andrews continued. "When I arrived, Janice Portman, the one on the left, was standing by her front door, talking to her next-door neighbour – her on the right. By that time, a few of the residents were starting to appear."

"And it was Janice Portman who rang it in?" asked Reilly.

"Yes."

"How did she describe what was happening?" asked Gardener.

"She said she heard screams and shouts," replied Andrews, turning and nodding toward the property he was guarding. "Apparently he's known for watching his TV quite loudly, but she didn't think it was the TV this time."

"What *did* she think?" asked Reilly.

"Sounded to her like a disagreement, suggesting that there was more than one person in the house."

"Did she actually see anything?" asked Gardener.

"No," replied Andrews.

"Who does live here?" asked Gardener.

"A man called Steven Sutton, and his family."

"Are they all in there?" asked Reilly.

Andrews shook his head. "No. Just one victim – male."

"Did she see anyone come to the house, or leave?"

"No," said Andrews, clasping his hands to his mouth. "Well, not between the times she called. She did see someone walking across the field, very near to the house, at around six-thirty."

"Did she recognize him?" asked Reilly.

"No, it was dark."

"And *you* didn't catch sight of anyone around the house, or leaving it?" asked Reilly.

"No, sir."

"Is the house empty now?"

Andrews nodded. "Apart from the victim."

Gardener glanced at the field yet again. "The obvious escape route must have been via the back door and across there." As he peered further into the distance, he could see the outline of Elland Road, Leeds United's football ground. Luckily there was no evening match.

"What did you do when you arrived?" asked Gardener.

"The two neighbours were outside so I quickly spoke to them first, to try and get an idea of what might have happened."

"I take it the shouting had died down by then?" said Gardener.

"Yes, it had been quiet for a while."

"What next?" asked Gardener.

"Went straight into the house in case he was still alive and needed further assistance."

"Where exactly have you been in the house?"

Andrews stared at the front door, which was open. The light in the hall was on. "I glanced into the living room – everything looked okay. I went upstairs. The first door on the left is the bathroom, the next is the bedroom he's in."

"Did you see anything untoward in the house, as if perhaps it had been burgled?" asked Reilly.

"Or anything to suggest a disagreement had taken place downstairs?" added Gardener.

"No, nothing. It's pretty tidy by rights. Clean, smells fresh."

"Okay," said Gardener. "Is he alive?"

"No," replied Andrews. "If he was, he wouldn't want to be."

"As bad as that?" asked Reilly.

"You need to see it."

"I think we do," said Gardener.

"She mentioned something else," said Andrews, nodding toward Janice Portman. "Something she thought very odd."

"Go on," said Gardener.

"It was like a cracking sound. At first, she thought it might have been a whip."

"Oh, Jesus." Reilly rolled his eyes. "This isn't some kind of sex game gone wrong, is it?"

"I doubt it," replied Andrews. "He's got a strange circle on his chest."

"A circle?" asked Reilly.

"Yes," said Andrews. "I've no idea what it is. Fucking weird, if you ask me." He glanced at Gardener. "Sorry, didn't mean to swear, but whatever it is, it weren't caused by no whip."

Gardener turned, scanning the crowd, which appeared to be a diverse mix of colour and fashion. There were perhaps twenty people stretching the length of the street, but judging by the expression of the nearest, the police may well be an everyday occurrence.

"Have you spoken to anyone else, yet?" Gardener asked.

"One or two," said Andrews. "Most of the residents are Eastern Europeans. Not many of them want to speak to us."

"Great," said Reilly.

Gardener turned back to the house, spotting a small portable bin that had been set up with scene suits. He asked Andrews for the scene log, and he and Reilly signed it, before suiting and booting.

Gardener turned to his partner. "Let's have a look, shall we?"

Chapter Four

They entered the hall. The stairs were on the left. A passageway on the right continued down to a kitchen but the door nearest to them led into the living room. The SIO glanced inside. As Andrews had said, everything was neat and tidy, with pale green wallpaper and a wooden floor. A gas fire was fixed to one wall, which was lit. He noticed a large-screen TV and Sky system, a three-piece suite, and items of furniture including a Welsh dresser that were all in good condition.

Gardener turned and leaned back outside to PC Andrews. He requested a vehicle with stepping plates be brought to the scene.

He turned to his partner. "Shall we?"

"Might as well," replied Reilly. "Let's see what we're dealing with."

Climbing the stairs, Gardener noticed the colour green was pretty popular. The wallpaper was dark, the carpet light. A couple of coastal scenes in oils were hung on the wall as they ascended. He was struck by how quiet it was; no background noise – no radio or TV playing, and no voices from outside on the street. No sign of pets in the house.

At the top of the stairs, he slowly pushed open the bathroom door. The space was tidy, with items placed neatly on shelves and the windowsill.

"If he's in such a bad way," said Gardener to Reilly, "why isn't there more of a mess around the rest of the house?"

"Just what I was wondering," replied Reilly.

They turned and headed for the bedroom. Gardener pushed open the door, which squeaked on its hinges. When it opened all the way and they were satisfied the room was clear he stepped in before turning to his partner.

"Sean, just before we get into this, would you do me a favour and check the other bedrooms? Make sure we *are* clear of people."

Reilly nodded, disappeared. Gardener waited until he returned.

"All clear, boss."

Gardener nodded and they proceeded further in. The victim was sitting in a chair in the middle of the room, with his back to the door, facing the only window, which was open slightly, creating a chill.

His arms were tied very tightly together behind his back with a rope, which had chafed against his skin, to the point of drawing blood.

"Looks to me like he was in quite some pain," said Reilly.

"Judging by the blood around the wrists, he fought pretty hard to try and free himself."

Gardener leaned in toward the rope. It was old, perhaps contaminated by oil or grease or something similar, judging by the colour.

It was then that he noticed the victim's hands were actually missing. Glancing at the floor however, he would guess by the lack of blood and the way it had pooled that they may have been severed after death, but what with, and why?

He studied the room.

"What are you looking for?" asked Reilly.

"Either his hands, or some evidence of what was used to remove them."

"I don't think we're going to be that lucky, boss," said Reilly. "It's quite a clean crime scene."

"That's what I thought," said Gardener. "Someone has been rather meticulous."

"And no doubt done a lot of planning," said Reilly.

"If they're that good," said Gardener, "it's possible they were wearing a scene suit like we are. I reckon we'll struggle with evidence."

Gardener stepped around the front of the victim in order to ascertain whatever the circle might be that Andrews had mentioned.

Reilly joined him and stared on.

"What do you make of that, Sean?"

Reilly knelt down for a closer examination.

Steel bolts had been driven into the victim's chest, to form a circle. The heads of the bolts were flat, level with the man's torso, which left Gardener wondering how that was possible, as they almost appeared to be a bolt within a bolt. The colour was silver and they were small and round. There were twelve of them. The pattern on the victim's chest was indeed a circle. He was very pleased to see that it was not a perfect circle. That would have worried him.

Reilly stood back up. "If I didn't know any better, I'd say they were nails."

"Nails?" repeated Gardener.

"Yes. My guess is this pattern has been made by a nail gun – a heavy-duty one. It's the only thing I can think of that would give the killer the speed or the accuracy in a short time frame."

"Makes sense," said Gardener. "The neighbour mentioned the sound of what might have been a whip."

"A nail gun could fit that description," said Reilly. "Would have to be pretty powerful to drive its way through the body like this one has – especially as we know there is some bone in the area."

Perhaps the most disturbing aspect of the scene was that two fingers, almost certainly severed from the victim's hands, actually pointed to two different nails, inside the circle.

Gardener leaned in. Again, there was very little blood around the severed digits. Both of those had been fastened using the same style nails, going right through the middle of the finger and into the chest, once again indicating something very heavy duty. "Do you think they're his?"

"Doesn't make sense if they're not."

"So where the hell's the rest of his hands?" asked Gardener.

"Trophy?" suggested Reilly.

Gardener nodded. "Possibly. What do you make of the circle, and where the fingers are pointing? Any ideas?"

"Could be anything," said Reilly. "Although the first thing that comes to mind is a clock."

"Maybe," said Gardener. "If the circle represents a clock, that could mean those fingers are pointing to the numbers three and five."

"They could be telling us that it's five-fifteen," said Reilly.

"Or three twenty-five," said Gardener.

"Maybe it's nothing to do with the time," offered Reilly. "Might be his age."

Gardener studied the victim. He was dressed only in a pair of blue boxer shorts, which he had soiled, indicating a high level of fear. His body had sustained other cuts and bruises, all of which suggested a level of torture. The victim's throat had also been cut. That, once again, appeared to be after death, because the blood had dripped and pooled. There was no spatter.

"Thirty-five might well fit," said Gardener. "Because he doesn't look fifty-three."

"Is it anything to do with where he lives?" asked Reilly.

Gardener shook his head. "Not sure, did you notice a number on the door?"

Reilly nodded. "Forty-two, so it can't be that."

"If we find out more about the man," said Gardener, "are we likely to find out more about why the fingers are pointing to where they are?"

"Probably," said Reilly. "If not, God only knows what we're examining."

"Could it be a ritual killing?" said Gardener. "A reference to a stone circle?"

"Is it something to do with the occult?"

"I hope not," said Gardener. "I don't fancy delving into anything connected to black magic."

Reilly rolled his eyes. "That's all we need, all that Aleister Crowley shit."

Gardener glanced around the bedroom, which wasn't strictly a bedroom as there was no bed. It was really only a box room at the side of the house, with one small window facing the open field with a view of Elland Road.

"If that was the way the killer came in, it is unlikely they'd be seen," said Gardener.

"Makes a lot of sense," said Reilly. "If I was them and it was dark, it's perfect for arriving and leaving."

"What did you find in the other rooms, Sean?"

"They're both bedrooms," he replied, "suggesting a family lives here. One was a master bedroom and the other belonged to a child. Judging by the photographs on the walls of the child's room, I'd say it was a boy."

"If that's the case," said Gardener, "where *are* the wife and the child?"

"That's the sixty-four-thousand-dollar question," replied his partner.

"Have they been abducted, or killed?" asked Gardener.

"Are they a part of this?" asked Reilly.

"That would have been some argument – bit brutal if it was."

"Maybe they're separated," said Reilly, "but come and stay on occasions."

"She might simply be away on holiday and he couldn't take time off?"

"It is close to Christmas," said Reilly. "Depending on what he does, that might be the case. Won't be a very good one, will it?

Gardener glanced at his watch. "Let's call the team, have some actions rolled out. This is really nasty."

Chapter Five

The team finally rolled up pretty much together, with most of them bringing hot drinks. They huddled in a circle, arms around themselves, thin mists of breath seeping from their mouths, speculating at what their boss had found.

Gardener stepped out from the hallway and walked down the path. Both he and Reilly had used the time well to further search the house. Although every room appeared to be lived in, it was clean. They had found letters addressed to the occupants, confirming the name of Sutton. They had also found bills and other personal documents indicating Steven Sutton's wife's name was Kerry, and his son was called Paul.

As Gardener gathered everyone around in order to explain what he and Reilly had found, the SOCOs entered the street in two vans.

Before he started, DS Sarah Gates passed him and Reilly cups with warm drinks. Steam rose through the small holes in the lids.

When he'd finished talking, the team naturally had questions but for now he only had basic answers.

"A nail gun?" asked DC Dave Rawson, dressed in a thick outer coat and stout walking boots. "Who the hell walks around with a nail gun in their pocket?"

"A joiner," offered DS Colin Sharp.

"And the nails form a circle in the victim's chest?" asked DS Bob Anderson, cupping his hands and blowing into them. "Have you any ideas on that one?"

"What are we looking for?" asked DS Frank Thornton. "A joiner who's into black magic on the side?"

"A lot of what we've found," said Gardener, "we can concentrate on in the incident room once everything's been photographed." He checked his watch. "Judging by the time, all we can do now is the usual: house-to-house, speak to all the neighbours, ask as many questions as they'll allow and see if we can form a picture of the man's last movements."

"Do we know who it is?" asked Gates.

"We haven't had a positive ID," said Gardener. "But the neighbour across the road gave us the name of the people who live here, and we've found a number of personal documents that back up her statement. Identification of the victim is needed as quickly as possible, starting with the neighbours. What do they know about the family? Can we further confirm who else lives in the house, how long they have been here?"

"What about the wife and child, sir?" asked PC Julie Longstaff.

"We don't know, Julie," replied Gardener. "ID will be imperative so we put out an APB on them. At the moment we have no idea where they are; whether or not they're involved, or if the killer has taken them. Once we confirm it's the Suttons, we'll be able to see if there is any immediate family living in the area."

"Last known movements are going to be a big help," said Reilly. "That way, we can start to interview all the extra people we come across."

"As soon as it's light tomorrow, concentrate on the shops, pubs, and takeaways in the local area," said Gardener. "There will not be a shortage of them."

"There's one at the end of the street," said Rawson.

"If we can find out where he works," said Reilly, "we can speak to colleagues. They might help with his last known movements."

"Someone definitely wanted this man dead," said Gardener. "The crime scene is clean and meticulous. Nothing we've so far seen or found suggests a robbery. Whoever did this came in quickly and cleanly, with one thing in mind – destroying the victim."

"So once again, we're looking at revenge for something," said Rawson.

"Probably," said Reilly.

Gardener glanced up and down the street, some people were still standing on doorsteps; others had left. "This is Beeston, I really can't imagine there being much CCTV in the area but if there is, we need to check it."

"Does the victim have CCTV?" asked Anderson.

Gardener glanced up but saw nothing at the front of the house. He strolled around the side facing the field. There were no cameras there.

"It doesn't look like it," he said upon returning.

"I don't like the idea of that field," said Anderson, pointing to it. "That could be hiding anything."

"Any idea where it leads to?" asked Thornton.

"Not yet," said Gardener, "other than somewhere down near the bottom we have Elland Road."

Sarah Gates glanced at the graveyard. "That's a bit like the field, it could be hiding anything."

"Either one would make a great escape route," said Longstaff.

"I've also put a call in for a PolSA team to do a fingertip search," said Gardener. "Luck might favour us with that one."

"Wouldn't hold my breath," said Rawson.

Gardener found his comment amusing – negative, but probably correct. Glancing across the street, he couldn't see CCTV on any of the houses. "This will be old-fashioned, time-consuming legwork. And the quicker we start, the quicker we can get out of the cold."

Gardener finished his little speech as the Home Office pathologist, Dr George Fitzgerald – otherwise known as Fitz – rolled up. The elderly pathologist stepped out of the car to greet them.

"I thought it might be you two."

"Don't give us that," said Reilly. "You'd only be bored at home."

"I wouldn't mind finding out."

Gardener mentioned what they had found but asked if Fitz would mind waiting while the SOCOs put out the stepping plates, as they were now all suited and booted and ready to go.

Once done, Gardener led Fitz up to the room where the victim was still seated. It seemed eerily quiet; he couldn't help but feel that death had a silence of its own – almost suffocating.

Fitz was positioned in front of the victim. "All looks rather interesting."

Gardener explained that he thought the hands had been severed and the throat had been cut after death because of the blood pooling.

Fitz agreed, and following a basic examination he told them there was very little he could do there, and was happy to sign the scene over to the SOCOs and have the body removed and taken to the mortuary as soon as possible.

Back outside, Gardener addressed the SOCOs. He asked if he could have any and all electronic equipment – phones, computers, and iPads – as soon as possible so he could start the team on the social media sites.

As he was about to leave to set up an incident room, he turned back to the crime scene manager, Steve Fenton, asking if he would pay particular attention when searching the scene to see if he could find the victim's hands.

Before leaving, Gardener glanced at his watch, shocked to find it was a little after one in the morning.

Chapter Six

"Hello, Archie, love," said Dora, with a high-pitched voice. "How's your mother? She must be getting on now."

"She is," replied Archie. "My fucking wick."

"Oh, that's nice," said Dora. "You're a lovely lad, you are. Looking after her like you do. There's not many sons would see their mother right, like you. And mine, of course."

Archie Figgs glanced at his watch. It was a little before ten o'clock. He was early, which is how he liked to be. The setting was a small tearoom at the side of the canal in Rodley, not far from the Railway Inn. A small plot of land had been given over to benches, which offered a terrific view of the boats in the summer; it was equally as good in winter providing you were on the inside.

Old Dora ran the café. Archie didn't actually know her surname. She had to be ninety if she was a day, deaf as a post, couldn't hear a word you said, despite the hearing aid. Customers had long since given up shouting their orders at her, they simply pointed at the menu – which wasn't very extensive – or the items they wanted, which were inside glass cupboards, or below the glass-topped counter. That didn't help either, because Dora's eyes were no better than her ears. But she was lovely and the food was to die for.

Dora cared about people and she was always nice to them because she wanted to be, not because she was serving the public. Rumour had it she had been doing the job for seventy years and she simply did not want to retire. The tearoom was something to live for, something that made her leave her bed in the mornings. She wore a blue flowered apron and her grey hair was tied in a bun. She was plump, and Archie always remembered you should never trust a skinny chef, so Dora would do for him.

The room had about six Welsh dressers that incorporated everything Dora needed including teapots, tea, sugar and coffee, and a variety of other kitchen implements. A large counter in front of Dora had glass enclosures for all the pastry, sandwiches, and the chocolate items. The tables and chairs were wooden and had all been handmade by her sons and grandsons over the years, so the styles often changed; no one cared, it was different. As Dora was from a completely bygone era, most of the music was swing and jazz and war stuff.

"What you having, Archie, love?"

Archie scanned the shelves and could quite happily have ordered one of everything. "I'll have a cup of tea and one of those pork pies."

Archie was British through and through; meat and two veg, none of this foreign shit. Give him steak and kidney pie, mash, peas and gravy, or sausage and chips, and he was happy; sausage rolls, pork pies, pasties – stuff we won the war on, as Archie used to put it.

"Pardon?" shouted Dora.

Archie simply pointed to everything, and then shouted at her to turn her hearing aid up.

"I haven't seen your mother for ages, Archie, does she get out much?"

"Only her mind," said Archie.

"Pardon?"

"Fine," he replied. "She's fine. I'll tell her you've been asking after her."

"Good lad. Go and sit down I'll bring your stuff over."

As she said that she turned to face the counter but then turned back quite quickly.

"There's a bloke been looking for you," said Dora, grabbing Archie's pie and sliding it on to a plate. No tongs and no gloves but that was how it was. It never hurt us years ago so why should it now?

"Me?" replied Archie. "Who is it?"

"No idea, love."

"Where is he?" asked Archie, glancing around.

"Don't know that, either," replied Dora, swivelling her head as well.

The place wasn't that big so whoever it was couldn't be that far away. "What's he look like?"

"I wouldn't like to say," replied Dora.

"What does that mean?"

"Let's put it this way, if he were two-faced he certainly wouldn't be wearing that one. I know looks are only skin-deep but he must have been born inside out."

Archie laughed. He knew who it was; it could *only* be one person. He picked up his pie and chose to sit at the table near the door, watching the boats. The music in the background was Vera Lynn – the forces' sweetheart. He didn't mind her, she had a nice enough voice.

Dora suddenly appeared, putting his tea in front of him, and as she walked away, Harry Pinchbeck took her place, as if by magic, making Archie jump.

"Where the hell did you come from, up through the floor?"

Harry had thinning black hair that he swept to one side in an effort to disguise his baldness – and a large forehead. He squinted quite a lot, and he fidgeted when he was talking to you. His lips were so thin that Archie thought they were a pair of elastic bands. A nervous tic in his left eye didn't help either him or you because that's all you tended to concentrate on. He had old-fashioned jam jar glasses that made his eyes appear twice their normal size.

With a long, pointed nose and small teeth, Harry didn't really have much going for him.

He wore a leather jacket and jeans and boots that didn't appear to have been manufactured in the current century. Rumour had it he lived in a flat in a Victorian house in Beeston but Archie wasn't too sure, nor did he care – he certainly wouldn't be visiting anytime soon.

Harry danced around a little before taking his seat and staring intently at Archie's pork pie. Archie felt guilty and shouted loud enough to wake the dead in Dora's direction to repeat the order.

"Fucking hell, Arch," said Harry, squinting. "You auditioning for the Quo, or what?"

"What do you mean?" asked Archie.

"Well they must have heard you in Leeds."

"She's deaf, isn't she," said Archie, pointing toward Dora.

"Who is?" asked Dora.

Archie jumped because he hadn't seen nor heard her. *She'd* also materialized as if by magic, with Harry's order. Without waiting for an answer, she simply slid back to the counter.

Harry demolished the pork pie almost in one go, pulling more faces than Phil Cool as he was chewing, as if he hadn't eaten for a month; leaving Archie gobsmacked, because he hadn't touched his. But he did, in case Harry had other ideas.

"Still living with your ma, Arch?" asked Harry, eventually.

"I *don't* live with her," replied Archie, adamantly and quietly, but with enough force to push home the warning that the subject was dangerous territory.

"What, you just rent a room, like?"

"Look, big nose, if I've told you once, I've told you a dozen times. *She* lives with *me*, got it? *She* lives with me!"

"No need to get personal."

"You started it," said Archie. "I do it out of the goodness of my heart."

"I didn't know you had one, Arch."

"Are you asking for a dry slap?" Archie took another bite of his pie. He'd never tasted anything like it. It was so good he closed his eyes and moaned.

"Good, aren't they?" said Harry.

"How would you know?" asked Archie. "I don't think yours touched the sides."

Harry Pinchbeck leaned in for the kill. "I've got some stuff, Arch. You interested?"

"Depends what it is."

"All good stuff. Not knock-off."

"Fuck off, Harry," said Archie. "I wasn't born yesterday. Nothing you have is yours. What have you got?"

Harry slid a bag from under the table, which surprised Archie, because he hadn't seen him carrying anything. He pulled out a Sony PlayStation and an Xbox. "Samples, Arch. Got quite a few of these, all in good nick."

"Not new, though."

"I never said they were," defended Harry. "I said they weren't knock-off."

"Oh, of course, Harry, they're all yours. What else have you got?"

"You don't want these?"

"No," said Archie.

Harry reached back into a bag that Archie was beginning to think was Doctor Who's Tardis. It couldn't possibly hold everything he was pulling out.

He drew out a couple of laptops. "These are nice. Fire-damaged."

"Fire-damaged?" repeated Archie. "Why are you trying to sell me stuff that's been fire damaged? Put them away."

Insulted, Harry reached back down to the bag. "What about a nice phone?"

Archie backed away. He avoided technology like the plague, and he particularly hated smartphones.

"I have a phone." And to prove it he pulled it out of his pocket. It was small and grey with black edges with a blue stripe running down the sides, and a screen so small that a stamp would have covered it. It even had a small wheel on the left-hand side.

"The fuck's that?" asked Harry, blinking and dancing as if he had been plugged into the mains.

"A phone."

"A what?" said Harry. "That's a phone? Who made that, Moses?"

"What's wrong with it?" asked Archie.

"Give us a few hours and I'll tell you. What the hell is it?"

"It's a Sony CMD J5."

"I should sell it back to them, then, they'll be looking for museum pieces."

Harry then produced a phone from an inside pocket so fast that Archie thought it was an illusion: *now you see me, now you don't*. "This is what you want, Arch. No self-respecting businessman would be seen dead with that. What do they think when you turn up to meetings with that thing?"

"Meetings," shouted Archie. "Where do you think we are, *Dragon's Den*? We're not in fucking London, for Christ's sake, we're in Rodley at the side of a canal doing some dodgy deals – or trying to."

Harry ducked. "Keep your voice down, Arch. Don't mention the 'D' word, I have a reputation."

"You're not wrong there," said Archie. "You make Fagin look like the pope."

"Never heard of him. Is he new on the patch? Anyway," said Harry, without waiting for an answer, "are we doing the business or what?"

Archie glanced at the phone, all flashing lights and symbols and sliding screens. "Not with that thing we're not," said Archie. "They can track you with them things, you know. They know who you are and where you are every second of the day, mate. They know everything about you, where you spend your money *and* how much. No, you can stuff them. I'm a cash man, and they can't trace me with this phone."

"NASA couldn't trace that bastard."

"Do you have anything worth buying this morning, Harry, or have I wasted my time?" said Archie, standing up.

"Wait a minute," said Harry. "Don't be so hasty."

On the point of giving up, Harry pulled a small, grey velvet bag from an inside pocket. He slipped it on the table in front of Archie.

"What is it?"

"Open it and see."

Archie leaned in, grabbed the bag, and slid out a pocket watch. He sat down immediately, almost drooling, eyes like saucers. Harry was talking Archie's language now.

Archie knew immediately what Harry the Shard was trying to offload on to him, because he knew all there was to know about watches. He had here a classic open-face silver-tone pocket watch, with a very thin polished brass case suitable for engraving. Archie longingly stared at the rich white railroad-style dial with black twelve, and red twenty-four-hour markers, and a fourteen-inch silver-tone curb link chain with a belt clip holder attachment.

It's the perfect addition to anyone's timepiece collection, thought Archie.

"Where did you get this?"

"Why do you want to know?" asked Harry.

"Because it isn't yours."

"That's rich," said Harry. "You're the biggest fence this side of the county line. Do you tell people where you get your stuff?"

"County line?" asked Archie. "What the hell have you been watching, *Bonanza*?"

"Do you want it, or not? If you don't, I know someone who will."

Archie knew that Harry would never tell him where the watch was from, or of its history – and it certainly had one, but he knew Harry had something special in his greasy little mitts, and Archie was going to have to work bloody hard to relieve him of it.

But if anyone could, Archie could. He started the bidding at five pounds.

"See you around, Arch," said Harry, holding his hand out for the return of the watch.

Harry may have appeared to have fallen off a Christmas tree, and was generally regarded as thick as treacle, but he knew a deal when he had one.

After a seriously lengthy discussion, Archie reluctantly bunged Harry seventy-five pounds because he knew the watch was worth a lot more, and if he played his cards right, he could make some real money.

Chapter Seven

Phillip Walker left the kitchen and stepped down into the living room of his small cottage. The building was very old-fashioned, and although he had never actually undertaken any research, he believed the whole row of cottages dated back to the eighteenth century, retaining a number of original features, such as the ceiling beams and wooden-framed windows.

He reached a table and four chairs, nestled in a small alcove at the back of the room, and placed his tea and biscuits in the only clear space he could see amidst a mountain of paperwork.

He stepped back toward the fireplace and checked the Parkray central heating unit for coke. It was fine for now, no need for a fill-up. It should last until he decided to leave for the station. If he topped it up then, it should last until he returned home later in the evening.

A hi-fi unit stood in the corner of the room, something he'd bought forty years ago, and it still served him well. He placed a vinyl record on the turntable, listening to the sound of stylus settling on plastic, with all the little crackles that followed; a rich sound that today's modern, clean digital stuff could not compete with. There was something satisfying about it.

He sat down as Barbara Streisand's voice filled the room.

Phillip removed his glasses, breathed on them, and used the polishing cloth in the case to clean them. As he put them back on his head, he studied the mess on the table.

Where does one start?

With a digestive, thought Phillip. He broke it in two, popped one half in his mouth and took a few sips of tea. He did not dunk biscuits; never had, never would. It was a disgusting habit – especially if you overdid it and the bloody thing fell into the cup. You could never remove it all, and then you were faced with a layer of sludge at the bottom.

He picked up a sheet of paper, studying the legal jargon. It appeared that there was still a problem with the will.

Phillip was forty-seven and currently alone. He had very few people he could really call friends – never had. He had no girlfriend, nor did he have any family, as they had all passed – his mother, Brenda, only quite recently.

Phillip had no idea what had happened to his father, Jack. His mother had never talked about it. All he had managed to cobble together was that Brenda and Jack had gone through a rough patch. Jack's own father, Jed, had been killed, shortly after Jack had turned twenty-one years of age. Jack suspected he knew who was responsible for the incident and couldn't let it lie. Following a series of arguments on the subject, Brenda went to stay with her own mother for a week, over in the Lakes. Even over that distance, they had continued to argue.

Eventually, Brenda returned home to find Jack had upped and left and was never seen again.

Phillip was born a month later.

He reached out and popped the other half of the digestive into his mouth and crunched away, studying the document.

He'd attended the reading of his mother's will, and he'd found out a number of things – in particular the mention of something special being left to him, a family heirloom. Problem was, no one actually knew where it was – including the solicitor.

Someone must, thought Phillip.

As his mother had passed away, he was unable to bring up the subject with her. Not that it would have done any good. Whatever had happened between his mother and father had left a really nasty taste in Brenda's mouth and she had flatly refused to talk about it. To him, or anyone else, it would seem.

It had clearly been stolen. But when? And by whom?

Phillip, however, was a very determined person. He was going to find out. If he said he was going to do something, he would, and he would see a job through to the bitter end. He was a real believer in right is right, and wrong is no man's right.

Justice should prevail.

Phillip started his second digestive.

Chapter Eight

At a little after two o'clock the following day, Gardener checked his watch as Reilly drove the pool car back to Noster Terrace. They had taken a call from the officer in charge of the scene to say that Kerry Sutton had returned to the house with her son, Paul. The officers had left the incident room immediately.

As Gardener had suspected, the terrace was no better in daylight. If anything, it was slightly more hostile. At the end he could see a squad car and forensic vans parked outside the house, in front of and opposite what he now knew to be Holbeck Cemetery and Holbeck Park. No people lined the streets today; the excitement had obviously died down, the interest having waned.

Reilly pulled the car to a halt and they both jumped out. In the distance he could see PolSA officers conducting a fingertip search of the park. He seriously doubted they would find anything useful, because he also now knew that Leeds United had played at home the previous day. Lord knows how many people had used the park before and after the game. The weather had not improved. If anything, it was colder. The sky was dark grey, threatening rain, or something worse; a chill wind blew in from the east.

He walked toward the house and noticed a young, Asian PC whose name was displayed on her badge as Velma Patel. She was dressed in uniform with a police-issue quilted jacket over the top, and woollen mittens and chunky boots. He introduced himself and Reilly and displayed his warrant card.

"Are you okay, Constable, it's pretty cold today?"

She smiled. "I've had worse, sir."

"Were you on duty when Kerry Sutton arrived home?"

"Yes, sir."

"How is she?" asked Gardener.

"She has a lot of questions, sir."

"Did she say where she'd been?" asked Reilly.

"On a small break with their son, visiting her mother down south," said Patel.

"That would certainly explain her absence last night," said Gardener. "I take it you haven't said anything about what's happened?"

"Nothing, sir," replied Patel. "More than my job is worth, but she knows something is wrong."

"I'm afraid it will still come as a serious shock for her," said Gardener.

"Where is she?" asked Reilly.

"Next door." Patel pointed. "A Mrs Elsie Reid."

"Thank you," said Gardener. "Is everything okay here?" he asked, nodding to the house.

"As far as I know. The SOCOs have been in and out all day, putting things in the van."

Gardener and Reilly left Patel, slipping down the path to the house next door, where Gardener rang the bell. The lady who answered was plump, with her grey hair tied up in a bun, and tortoiseshell glasses on a chain that disappeared behind her neck. Gardener tipped his hat and had his warrant card ready.

"Ooh, come in, love," she said.

She led them down a dark hallway with wallpaper that appeared to have been up for years, and a brown carpet that may have been down even longer. Despite the dinginess it smelled fresh and appeared clean. He could hear a radio playing in the background.

She stopped before entering the kitchen. "I'm Elsie Reid. Kerry's in there, love. I haven't said anything, because I don't really know anything. Would you like tea?"

"Yes, please," said Gardener. "How is Mrs Sutton?"

"She has a lot of questions," said Elsie, almost as if she had heard PC Patel use the phrase.

"Has she had some tea?"

"Yes, but I think she'll need another."

"Is her son with her?" asked Gardener.

"No, he's across the road at a friend's house."

Thank heavens for small mercies, thought Gardener.

"Before you go, can I ask if my officers have taken a statement from you, Mrs Reid?"

"Yes, love, but I couldn't tell them anything. I was out at the bingo last night with a friend."

He nodded, before pushing the door open. The pair of them stepped into a modest parlour with a blue Dralon three-piece suite, a dark blue carpet and pale blue walls. Elsie had a TV in the corner but it wasn't on. There were countless ornaments, a magazine rack, and a small table next to one chair with a number of dog-eared paperbacks, suggesting Elsie Reid spent a lot of time in the room.

Kerry Sutton stood up immediately.

Gardener gestured with his hands. "Please, Mrs Sutton, you don't have to get up." Once again, he introduced them both and held up warrant cards, and removed his hat.

Kerry Sutton was almost as tall as Gardener. She was dressed in a pair of tight blue jeans and an orange and black quilted jacket, despite the room being warm. She had black hair that fell around her shoulders, and a long, angular face with green eyes – currently red-rimmed – and white teeth. She clutched a handkerchief in her right hand. As she sat back down she blew her nose.

"What's happened?" she asked, her voice on the verge of breaking. "Why can't I get in my house, and where's my husband, Steven?"

"Mrs Sutton, I'm really very sorry to have to tell you that there was an incident in your house last night."

"An incident? What do you mean?"

Before he could address the situation, Elsie Reid slipped in through the door with a tray, containing three teas and a plate full of Cherry Bakewells.

"I realize you might not want to eat but I think it's only right to offer guests a little something with a drink." She placed it on a coffee table in the middle of the room.

Kerry Sutton may not want anything but he was sure his partner would make a large dent in the small mound of cakes.

When Elsie Reid had left and everyone had tea, Gardener resumed his explanation. This had to be the hardest of jobs in his line of work. No matter how many times he had done it, it was never any easier.

"I'm afraid that a man was attacked and killed in your house last night."

"Killed?" repeated Kerry.

Gardener nodded.

"And you think it is Steven?" she asked.

There was simply no easy way of breaking it, but he didn't think she would have any doubts by now. She arrives home from holiday and finds her house a crime scene, she's not allowed in and her husband is nowhere to be seen.

"We believe it is. I know this is going to be very difficult for you, but we are going to need a positive identification. We thought it might be a little easier if we showed you a family photograph and maybe you can confirm it is your husband in the picture."

"A photo? Christ, man, what's happened? How bad is it, like?"

Gardener detected a very slight North East accent. "It isn't pleasant, Mrs Sutton."

She blew her nose again and her eyes started to fill up. She sobbed, and her body stiffened up. She covered her face with her hands. When she managed to regain some composure, she asked, "Is he still in the house?"

"No," said Gardener. "The Home Office pathologist has taken the body to the mortuary. We will have to ask you to come and make a positive ID, but we would prefer to make him a little more presentable."

"Presentable?" shouted Kerry. "What in God's name has happened?"

"Perhaps we can show you the photo."

Reilly had brought with him a small brown paper bag. From the inside he retrieved a family photo in a frame and passed it over.

"Is this your husband, Mrs Sutton?" asked Gardener.

At that, Kerry Sutton broke down, nodding her confirmation very slightly.

"Are you okay?" asked Gardener. "I know how terrible this must be for you."

To start with, she never answered. Gardener took a sip of his tea and waited patiently. After some time, she glanced up at him. "I'm sorry."

"Please," said Gardener, "don't apologize. If you feel up to it, we would like to ask a few questions."

"What do you want to know?" Her voice was flat and lifeless, as if she knew it had to be done, so the quicker the better.

"Firstly, can you tell us how old he was?"

"He was born in 1975, which makes him forty-eight."

"How long have you lived here?"

"Steven's been here years. He was born in Armley."

"Can you remember where they lived in Armley?"

"No," she replied, sniffing loudly. She suddenly reached to the side of the chair that Gardener couldn't see, pulled a bag forward, and fished out another handkerchief. "It was near a graveyard somewhere, but that's about all I know. I don't think he had a very good childhood. His mum and dad split up when he were young. His mother met someone and they moved here, which suited him perfectly."

"Why was that?" asked Gardener.

"He's only a stone's throw away from his beloved Leeds United." As she said it, she glanced out of the window, not that anyone could see the football ground from here. "He'd loved 'em forever, right from the word go. He even met and remembered some of the big names like Billy Bremner and Peter Lorimer and Paul Reaney."

Gardener changed the subject, asking more about when Steven had moved to Beeston.

"Like I say, I don't know a great deal because he never really talked about it. I think it was a bit better than when he was in Armley, but it still wasn't a picnic."

"What makes you say that?" asked Reilly.

"Like I said, he wouldn't talk about it; as if he was embarrassed, or maybe trying to hide something. His stepdad seemed okay at first, but from what I've read between the lines, things in that relationship turned sour. It's a surprise he turned out to be as good as he did. Brilliant husband and father, that's all I can say. God, our Paul's gonna miss him. He'll be devastated."

Kerry struggled with her composure, which was understandable, especially with their mention of their son.

After a pause, Gardener asked, "When and how did you two meet?"

"At a cup-tie, would you believe? My brother was a fan as well. He didn't have anyone to go with so he dragged me to the match, kicking and screaming. We met Steven in the bar afterwards. Leeds had won, convincingly, and he was buying a drink. We all got talking and one thing led to another as they say."

"How would you describe your relationship?"

"Same as anyone else's. We had our ups and downs, didn't agree on everything but we had one thing in common that kept us going. Our son. Steven would have done anything for us. We were well loved and we knew it."

Gardener understood that one.

"It wasn't easy, believe me," Kerry suddenly said.

"How do you mean?" asked Gardener.

"We tried for kids for years. Nothing happened. We went to the doctors, had loads of tests and they said we were both fine, that all we had to do was stop worrying and things would take a natural course. And they did, we finally had Paul. We never gave up trying but no more came. We'd have loved a little sister for him."

Gardener sensed a good family life and, on the whole, a good relationship. "Where did he work?"

"National Rail. He worked at the station in Leeds. I managed to secure him a job servicing and maintaining the tracks, with our Aaron, my brother. Steven was out of work, struggling to find something, and our Aaron felt that it was only right to help Steven support his family. He knew National Rail were desperate to find people for the jobs on offer. The rest is history."

"When did he start?" asked Reilly.

"Sometime around 2001. He's been there ever since."

"I'm going to ask you a really delicate question, now," said Gardener. "But do you know of anyone who might want to harm him?"

Kerry immediately started crying. After a short period, she eventually she said she didn't. "He pretty much got on with everyone."

"Had he spoken of any recent arguments or disputes, at work, maybe?"

"Nothing that I can think of. I'm sure if there had been, our Aaron would have mentioned something."

"And he gets on well with all the neighbours?" asked Reilly.

"Mostly," she replied.

"What do you mean by mostly?" asked Reilly.

"Most of them keep to themselves. They're nearly all foreign, as you'll notice when you go and take your statements, or whatever it is you do. We don't speak much, not because we don't like them, but because they have a different culture and we just don't have a lot in common."

"Does Steven have any family?"

"I don't think so," said Kerry. "His dad passed away years ago, and his mum's not around anymore."

"Was he an only child?"

Kerry appeared to hesitate at that question before answering. "No. I know of a half-brother's existence from a passing comment – but I have no idea who he is, or where he lives. I've heard the name Roy mentioned."

"I take it *they* didn't get on," said Reilly.

"Doesn't sound like it. I only ever heard this half-brother talked about on two occasions and neither of those went well. From what I know they knew very little about each other and Steven never had anything good to say about him."

"Do you know his name?" asked Gardener.

"No." The answer was a little too sharp.

"And you don't know where he lives?" asked Reilly.

"No."

Gardener wanted to know more about that situation. He suspected something must have happened in the past between them; or maybe nothing happened between them, perhaps whatever it was had only happened to her husband, and maybe even she didn't know about it.

Gardener decided, however, that now not the right time. So he continued with his questioning. "And there is no more family that you know of?"

"No."

He changed direction completely. "Did he have a daily routine?"

"Pretty much," said Kerry. "He was always up early for work, around six o'clock. In the summer he'd pushbike to the station, or wherever else it was, if they were working close by. In the winter he would often get lifts off friends, or Aaron. He'd be at work for eight and usually home by six. Most of the time he stayed in."

"Did he have any hobbies?" asked Gardener.

"Only Leeds United. He lived, ate, and breathed them blokes. He liked the odd pint down the pub, but not often."

"Does he have any close friends?" asked Reilly.

"The two closest that I can think of are Tony Petter and Robert Smith. Tony lives round the corner in Marley Terrace, number seventeen; and Robert also lives close by in Noster Street, number four. They often went to the game together, and if he went drinking and playing darts or pool it was usually those two he would go with."

"Do they work for National Rail?" asked Gardener.

"No," replied Kerry. "They both work for an engineering firm in Leeds called Dawson's."

Reilly made a note.

"When did you last see your husband, Mrs Sutton?" asked Gardener.

She was about to answer when grief took over, and forced a moment's silence.

Finally, she said, "That would be last Saturday. I took our Paul down to see my mum. She lives in Whitstable in Kent, retired there a few years back. We don't get to see as much of each other as we'd like, so when she asked us all to come over, we jumped at the chance. Only Steven had no holidays left. I said we could go another time, but he insisted. Said we hadn't had a proper holiday for a year or two, what with Covid and everything going sky high. We were just making ends meet."

"When did you last speak to him?"

"Friday night, about five o'clock. He phoned me, said he'd had a hard week, he'd missed me, and he was going down to the pub with Tony and Robert." She stopped talking and started crying, before adding, "And that was the last time we spoke."

"Do you know which pub?" asked Reilly.

She shook her head. "It'll be one of them down on the main road near the ground. There's two or three; I've not known the lads use anywhere else."

Gardener gave her a few more moments whilst Reilly made notes, before asking, "Do you know anything of his movements yesterday?"

"I know for a fact that he went to watch Leeds play yesterday, another cup-tie, would you believe? A home match – you should be able to check that easy enough. They're all members of the supporters' club so they'll all be on record with the ground. Kick-off would have been three. Match would have ended around five. You'd have to ask the other lads for what happened afterwards. I could guess, but you'll need more than that."

Gardener didn't think there was much more he could ask, so he checked if there was anyone she could stay with.

"I have a sister who lives in Bramley."

Gardener asked if she would write down the details.

"Thank you, Mrs Sutton. We'll leave it there for now but we may have to come back and ask you some more questions. This is going to be a very difficult time for you and you will need a lot of help with things. I realize you have your sister and your mum, but if you need anything at all, please don't hesitate to contact us."

Gardener stood up. "Would you like us to arrange a visit from a family liaison officer?"

Kerry nodded. "Maybe when I get settled in with my sister. I'm sure it would be very helpful." She stared at Gardener and then at the floor. "God only knows what I'm going to tell our Paul. It's going to kill him. He loved his dad so much."

Gardener stepped forward. "Would you like us to be here when you do?"

"No, thank you. You have enough to do, catching whoever did this." Kerry grabbed his arm. "Just promise me one thing."

Gardener nodded but he didn't speak.

"Please catch him. I wouldn't like to think there's a nutter out there who can get away with doing things like this. God knows it's bad enough I should lose my husband, but I wouldn't like anyone else to lose theirs."

"We intend to catch the killer, Mrs Sutton," said Gardener. "And thank you for speaking to us during what must be a very difficult time for you."

The pair of them left. As they did so, Elsie Reid was close by, in the kitchen, ready to take over and help her neighbour. They bade her goodbye and thanked her for the tea.

Outside, Gardener asked, "What do you think?"

"Hard to say," said Reilly. "I think there's something in his past."

"Which he hasn't told her about?" asked Gardener.

"I don't think so. The trouble is, what *has* he been up to, when, and does his death have anything to do with it?"

Gardener replaced his hat. "Let's go and fire up the incident room."

Chapter Nine

It was early evening before the team had finished their initial inquiries in connection with the scene at Beeston. As they filed into the incident room for the first full catch-up, Gardener could see how cold they were. The temperature outside had dropped somewhat; the weather forecast threatened minus figures with a possible overnight snowfall. Inside was little better due to recent budget cuts and soaring energy prices.

Eyes lit up as most of the team spotted an urn on a table to the right of the whiteboard that was full of hot soup, and a tray of bread rolls. Gardener wasn't sure how Reilly had managed it but he was pleased he had.

Once they were all seated, Gardener recapped on what they had found in the house in Beeston the previous evening, with a number of photographs all pinned to the whiteboard.

"We had a call from the PC guarding the scene earlier today to let us know that Kerry Sutton had returned home, with their son, Paul," said Gardener.

"Well, that's something," said Longstaff, "at least *she's* okay."

"She was," said Gardener, "till we tore her world apart."

"*Is* it her husband?" asked Frank Thornton, both his hands wrapped around his mug of soup.

Gardener nodded, standing beside one of the whiteboards. "We showed her a family photo. She confirmed it was her husband, and we, of course, know that the very same man is now in the mortuary. So, the victim is forty-eight-year-old Steven Sutton."

"Was she up to talking?" asked Sharp.

Gardener nodded. "Steven was born in Armley but we're not sure where. His parents parted when Steven was quite young. A stepfather came on to the scene a little later, but he didn't appear to be much better."

"So he's had a tough life," said Rawson, one hand around his mug of soup, while he was dipping bread in it with the other and throwing it down his throat at an alarming rate. "Did she say how tough, or what the problem was?"

"No," said Gardener. "She felt there was something in her husband's past but he didn't appear to want to talk about it. Maybe he was embarrassed by something, or maybe his stepfather abused him, or treated him really badly, but whatever it was, he wouldn't talk about it."

Gardener noticed an interesting change of expressions between Thornton and Anderson, suggesting that maybe they knew something he didn't. He was sure all would be revealed when he gave them an opportunity to speak.

He continued. "Kerry told us he was a big Leeds United fan. She mentioned that he was going to the game yesterday so perhaps that's something we can check on. I'm sure the ground has CCTV, which will almost certainly be a nightmare to trawl through."

"Did he belong to the supporters' club?" asked PC Patrick Edwards.

"Yes," said Gardener.

"So he would have had a ticket, and he'll be in their files," said PC Paul Benson. "It should be easy enough to check if he made it to the match."

"We can probably find out easier than that," said Reilly. "Kerry told us that he almost always goes to matches with two of his friends."

Reilly pulled out his notebook and checked. "We have the addresses of both of them. One is Tony Petter and the other is Robert Smith. We checked the area out this morning, it's a bit like a maze. There are six or seven streets all with similar names, all joined by one main street. These mates live around the corner."

"So if you two want to check that one out for me," said Gardener, staring and Edwards and Benson, "I would appreciate it."

Gardener checked his watch. "By the time we've finished tonight it's going to be too late to do anything about it, but first thing tomorrow can you two also check an engineering firm in Leeds called Dawson's and pay them a visit? That's where Petter and Smith work."

"Did Sutton work there as well?" asked Sharp.

"No," replied Gardener. "He had a job with National Rail. Kerry Sutton's bother, Aaron, secured a job for him about twenty years ago and he's been there ever since. So maybe you two could check that one out. See what *they* can tell us about him, and speak to Aaron Butcher, Kerry's brother. Between his friends and those people, we might be able to build a picture of his life and his last movements."

"I'm assuming the marriage was okay?" asked Sarah Gates. "No problems?"

"None that she could bring to mind," said Gardener. "It was like most marriages – good and bad times. She thought he was a very good father and husband despite the problems he may have had in his early life. She couldn't think of any recent disagreements, either with her or anyone else."

Once again, Thornton and Anderson exchanged glances. They knew something. As soon as Gardener had told them everything, he was going to pursue the glances.

"Any family?" asked Rawson.

"This is where it gets interesting," said Reilly.

"How so?" asked Rawson.

"The only family that Kerry Sutton knew of," said Gardener, "could be a half-brother, but she doesn't know his name and she doesn't know where he lives. They didn't get on by the sound of things, so that's something we need to look into."

"That won't be so easy?" said Anderson. "Especially if we don't know much."

"You're right, Bob," said Gardener, "but we need to find out. I'd like his full name, where he lives, where he works and most of all, what happened in the past to cause a rift; and does it have anything to do with what's happened to Steven."

"Wouldn't be the first time," said Reilly.

"Maybe not," said Sharp. "But if the rift happened years ago and if they've had nothing to do with each other, it's not likely he's waited this long before killing him."

"Maybe he's a patient man," said Gardener. "We can also tell you that Kerry last saw Steven the previous Saturday, before the trip to see her mother, and she last spoke to him on Friday night on the phone, sometime around five – we can check that if the SOCOs find his phone. He seemed okay, said he'd had a hard week but was looking forward to the game on Saturday."

"So he had every intention of going," said Edwards.

"Definitely," said Gardener. "Hopefully, we'll find out that he did, which will narrow the window that we have to operate in."

Gardener turned, writing notes on the board, fully intending to interrogate Thornton and Anderson over their expressions.

When he faced the front again he asked if anyone had anything from the house-to-house and the witness statements.

"These were pretty hard to come by, boss," said Rawson. "The street has a lot of Eastern Europeans living there. They didn't want to speak because they don't trust the police."

"Or they were out," said Sharp. "Those that did speak claimed they didn't really know the family at the end of the terrace and only spoke occasionally when walking the dog around the field."

"One of the Eastern Europeans thought they saw him near the Chinese takeaway sometime around six o'clock," said Benson. "He was walking in the direction of his house."

"Was he seen leaving the Chinese takeaway?"

"No," said Edwards. "But he looked like he'd been in because he had one of their little white bags in his hand."

"In that case," said Gardener. "Will you call on the shop and find out?" He made a note on the board and then said, "And we'll have to check with the SOCOs to see if they found any remains amongst the rubbish."

"He was also seen by his neighbour, Janice Portman, at six-thirty," said Bob Anderson.

"He was entering the front door of the house with said carrier bag in his hand," said Thornton.

"Okay, Bob," said Gardener. "So we know he was alive and well at six-thirty. Right, time to spill. Judging by your expressions, you've discovered something interesting."

"She's quite astute is Janice Portman," said Anderson. "She doesn't miss much."

"Does she live on her own?" asked Rawson.

"For Christ's sakes, Dave," said Reilly. "She's old enough to be your mother.

The team laughed. Rawson blushed. "I didn't mean that, you pillock. I just meant that women on their own never do miss much."

"We know what you meant," said Reilly, still smirking.

Gardener raised his hand and calmed the banter down. "Go on, Bob."

"Janice Portman reported seeing someone near the house at around six forty-five. She had no idea who it was, and even though it was dark, she said she didn't know him from the shape or the walk."

"Leaving the house?" asked Gardener.

"Not really," said Thornton. "He was on the field at the side of the house, as if he'd approached from the back and was walking toward the cemetery."

"We could do to find out who that was," said Gardener. "If only to eliminate him, or see if he saw anyone else. It does seem a little too early for what happened to Sutton. He was alive and well at six-thirty. What happened to him couldn't have been done in fifteen minutes, but whoever that was could be a very important witness."

Gardener wrote it on the board. He turned back to the team. "We might need to rely on a press release with that one. Anything else from Janice Portman?"

Anderson nodded. "She actually heard what she claimed were screams at around eight-thirty. She had no idea what it was about but it wasn't unknown for Sutton to watch films late into the night and have his TV louder than it should be."

"Interesting," said Gardener. "But not a crime. His wife was away, he'd had a takeaway and a beer, or two. If it *was* the TV, could the neighbour ascertain whether or not the sound was from upstairs or downstairs?"

"We never asked that," replied Anderson. "But we did ask her if she could clearly hear what was being said. She claims she could hear a man's voice shouting 'where is it?' The other voice was screaming that he didn't know what the first voice was talking about."

"What she does remember," said Thornton, "is the man's voice who was asking wherever *it* was, sounded a bit unusual; sort of gravelly and rough sounding, but she knows no one like that, possibly backing up the point that it was a film he was watching with the sound turned up."

"Did she listen, or stay outside for any length of time?" asked Gardener.

"No," said Anderson. "She'd only gone outside to put some rubbish in the bin when she heard it. But it was cold so she went back in to her fire."

"But she must have come back out," said Gardener, "because she rang it in."

"She did," replied Anderson. "About ten minutes later. It was preying on her mind."

"Did she hear anything different?" asked Gardener.

"No," said Thornton. "Pretty much the same thing, so she came back in and checked her TV channels but saw nothing like what she could hear at the Suttons' house. That's when she decided to ring it in."

Gardener thought about that. "It might be worth having a look at what was on TV last night but I doubt we'll have any luck with that. He might have had Sky, or any number of streaming services."

"Or a DVD," said Rawson.

"Good point," said Gardener, glancing at Longstaff and Gates. "When the SOCOs have finished and you guys have his electronic equipment we might have a better chance. Otherwise, we might have our first clue."

Anderson continued. "Something else she said was that rarely did anyone have a go at him over his TV was because he was a big bloke and known to have a nasty temper."

"Really," said Reilly. "She ever have any trouble with him?"

"We asked that," said Thornton. "She said he'd always been okay with her. She reckons he's a rough diamond, better for knowing. He'd helped her on a number of occasions and would take nothing for it."

"Why does she think he's a rough diamond?" asked Reilly.

"Here's the interesting bit," said Anderson. "She knows he's done a bit of bird but she has never held that against him."

Chapter Ten

"Pardon," said Gardener.

"He's been inside," said Thornton.

"Doesn't happen to know why, does she?" asked Gardener.

"No," said Anderson. "What she's picked up is local gossip. Apparently, it was years ago, before she went to live there."

"I wonder what Kerry Sutton knows about this?" asked Reilly.

"Does she know anything at all about it?" asked Gardener.

"I'd bet she does," said Reilly. "I'd guess that she was holding something back."

"Maybe she didn't want us digging too deep," added Rawson.

"Too late for that," said Reilly. "Her old man's been tortured to death for something."

"Okay, Bob," said Gardener. "If Steven Sutton has done time, we must have something on record. And we'll probably have a DNA match as well. I'd like you to really go to town on that one. If we can find out why, it opens the field up a little more."

"How long has Janice Portman lived there?" Reilly asked Anderson.

"About fifteen years."

"We know the Suttons have been there longer than that," said Gardener. "Kerry Sutton told us that her brother found him a job with National Rail and he'd been there twenty-odd years. He'd been finding it hard to get work. If he had a record and was fresh out of prison that might be why. So we need to be looking back to around the turn of the century."

"I wonder if it was drug-related?" asked Reilly. "Judging the state of him, I'd say he was tortured."

Gardener nodded. "Torture can mean a number of things. It's usually a very personal killing for some kind revenge."

"Or to extract information out of the victim," said Rawson.

"All of which *could* be drug-related," said Gardener. "I still find it very odd that he's been left alone for twenty years or more before extracting revenge. What's happened here suggests something more recent."

"If it is a drug-related offence, is it likely he was *still* selling them?" asked Gates

"I wouldn't have thought so," said Longstaff. "Judging by where he was living and what we know so far, it doesn't look like the Suttons had a lot of spare money."

"It could be any number of things," said Gardener. "But until we find out why he had a record and went to prison, we're not really going to know where to start looking. We need to go and see all these people that have cropped up tonight to see if we can establish a bigger picture, and his last known movements.

"We know he was alive and well on Friday night. Presumably he went to the game on Saturday, which would have finished around five. Let's assume he had a pint with the boys, stopped off at the takeaway on the way home and stepped in through the front door at six-thirty. Someone was seen in the area at six forty-five, and by eight-thirty he was in serious trouble. A two-hour window for us to investigate more thoroughly."

Gardener changed subjects. "We have no results at the moment from the fingertip search. The field they are searching is in fact a park – Holbeck Park. The graveyard opposite Sutton's house is Holbeck Cemetery. Does anyone know what's at the other end of the park, apart from Elland Road?"

Benson nodded. "That leads to Hoxton Mount, which is a small group of houses facing a waste ground, or possibly a car park at the side of the football ground."

"Okay," said Gardener. "We need to speak to the people who live there. That could be awkward because it was the day of a football match. There would have been thousands of people milling around."

"Whoever did this," said Gates, "was pretty much hidden in plain sight."

"Yes," said Longstaff. "It wouldn't have mattered what he looked like, I doubt he'd stand out."

"And what's at the other side of the cemetery?" asked Gardener.

"That's Fairfax Road," said Edwards, "with more houses."

"Which means a lot more legwork," said Gardener. "More house-to-house calls needed. Whoever this man is, he could have approached from any number of directions."

"We don't even know how he got there," said Reilly. "Was he in a vehicle, or on foot?"

"Judging by what he did to Steven Sutton," said Gardener, "he would have had to carry a bit of equipment around, so maybe he has used a vehicle. I take it no one has mentioned seeing a strange vehicle parked around the area."

Most of the team shook their heads.

"They appear to be very close-knit," said Gardener. "I would assume they'd know most people coming and going, so a strange car might stand out. Have we come across any CCTV?"

"Not from the people we've spoken to," said Sharp. "Maybe when we widen the search to Hoxton Mount and Fairfax Road we might find something, but it's not a very affluent area."

"No," said Rawson. "These people want to keep a roof over their heads and food on the table, and it looks to me like that's a daily struggle."

"That said, a lot have bars at the windows and doors," said Reilly.

"Which suggests a certain level of crime," said Gardener. "You never know, someone somewhere might have some hidden cameras. Keep trying. The timescale suggests that our killer was in and out fairly quickly, and they knew what they wanted. I think it's been well planned, so something from the past would be a good bet."

Gardener glanced at the photos in order to raise another action.

He turned and said, "The rope. This looks pretty interesting. It isn't new so maybe we can take it over to forensics to see if they can offer an explanation for what that rope is contaminated with, which might give us somewhere else to look. There might be something on that rope that's very specific to a particular industry.

"We need to try and ID where it's from, what it's off, what its original purpose was. Mostly, what are the stains in the rope?"

"Another thing that might be worth looking at is the knot," said Reilly. "What type of a knot is it?"

"If it's something specific, it could point us in another direction," said Gardener, glancing at Sharp and Rawson. "Can you guys look into that one for me?"

"It's that circle on his chest that I find interesting," said Anderson.

"Didn't someone say they thought it was a nail gun?" asked Thornton.

"I thought it was," said Reilly.

"I think this is going to be really important," said Gardener.

"There are a lot of nail guns on the market," said Gates. "We've spent a bit of time googling these things."

"It's a big area," said Longstaff. "Some are gas, some are electric, some are spring-operated, all kinds of different ones."

"I thought that might be the case," said Gardener. "We might be able to rule out a gas one. Surely that would need some specific equipment to operate it, and I can't imagine our killer is carrying that kind of stuff around."

"No," said Reilly. "He'd hardly go unnoticed if he was dragging a bloody great gas cylinder around."

"The nails themselves are likely to tell you what type of machine it is," said Rawson.

"Maybe even the manufacturer," said Sharp.

"Some nail guns only accept their own make of nails," said Benson.

Gardener appreciated the excitement the nail gun had caused. "Well worth an action to ID the gun and then look at local suppliers who may have sold one recently. Bob, Frank, can I leave that one with you?"

Anderson nodded, making a note.

"Well, that's you lot sorted," said Gates. "I'd hate to think what the boss has lined up for us."

Gardener pointed to the photos on the board, in particular, the fingers inside the circle of nails, and where they were pointing.

"Steven Sutton's arms were tied around his back, and his hands were missing. Around the front, we *think* he has been attacked with a nail gun. The patterns of the nails form a circle, and there are twelve of them. Two of his fingers point to two different nails. Any ideas?"

Gardener caught Sharp staring at the photo. "What are you thinking, Colin?"

"That if the circle represented a clock, the fingers would be pointing to the number three and the number five."

Gardener told the team what he and Reilly had discussed about the numbers at the scene, relating to age or where he lived. Nothing stacked up. But he still felt that they played an important part somewhere, indicating that if they found out more about the man, they may find out more about the numbers.

"Almost certainly," said Longstaff. "It's a puzzle. Maybe it's something personal to the killer not the victim."

"In which case," said Gates, "it could be anything."

"Is it a ritual killing?" asked Rawson. "A reference to a stone circle, maybe?"

"If it is, it could be really deep," said Longstaff. "Does this have occult connotations? Are we going to have to delve into anything concerning black magic?"

"God forbid," said Gardener, "but it's as important as everything else we have to figure out, if not more so. This is perhaps the only thing we have that makes no sense to us, but probably does to the killer. So, I'd like you two ladies on this, please. Look into everything we've suggested, in particular the meanings of numbers. I know there are sites out there that suggests numbers have meanings, maybe we could pay some attention to that."

Gardener glanced at his watch. It was late, the team had put in a long day and he knew the first twenty-four hours were the most important, but people also needed to rest.

"Okay, guys, go home, get some sleep and let's blitz the place tomorrow. Meanwhile, I will go and see DCI Briggs and ask him to arrange a press release for witnesses. We definitely need to speak to whoever was passing the house at six forty-five. Why was he there? Where did he go *from* there? More importantly, did he see anything useful?"

Chapter Eleven

Archie Figgs rolled into Bramfield along Main Street on his recently acquired e-bike. Slipping into Market Place he jumped off and chained it to a lamp-post behind the police station, chuckling to himself. Normally, he would not be seen dead near a police station, but the shop he wanted was directly opposite.

The Crusher XF900 was totally top of the range, with a motorcycle-inspired frame, full suspension, fat tyres, and a high-capacity battery, it was the perfect all-terrain e-bike: 1200 watt motor, 48v, 17ah, lithium-ion battery, giving him between 35 and 62 miles on a full charge. The manufacturer had also added an easily accessible USB charging port right on the battery, which was of little use to Archie. All he knew was that it must have cost someone a fortune.

Archie rounded the corner, thinking about the day he had acquired the bike. What a cracking day that had been, when an absent-minded commuter had flown into the station in Leeds, no doubt in a real rush. He'd parked the bike in one of the specially modified cycle racks, before pulling out a chain and padlock to secure it. But then his phone had distracted him. Following a heated conversation, he'd simply walked off without locking the bike.

It was still there ten minutes later – still unlocked.

The fact that there was no charger didn't bother Archie, he could soon pick one of those up; in fact, he did, the very next day. Problem was, the bike was reported stolen to the police very quickly, which meant he had to cease trading and lie low for a week or two.

That was why he had found it funny parking at the back of the police station. All and sundry had been searching for the bloody thing for a while. Now it was under their noses.

As Archie approached the road at the front of the police station, he noticed the nosey old desk sergeant standing on the steps, blowing into his hands.

"Morning," said the desk sergeant, whose face had to have been modelled on the moon, thought Archie, which was the only place that had bigger craters. "It's a fresh one."

"You're not wrong there," said Archie, mimicking the sergeant and blowing into his own hands.

He ended the conversation quickly, slipping across the road. "What the fuck are you out here for, then?" said Archie, to himself. "Get back inside, you daft bastard."

Why did people – especially smokers – do that? thought Archie. They'd spend ages outside, dancing around on their feet, rubbing their noses and blowing into their hands, all the while moaning about how fucking cold it was.

Archie clocked the family-owned traditional jeweller's, A.R. Browne's, established by a man called Benjamin Browne in 1888. The board at the side of the shop informed everyone that his father, Alfred Browne, had founded a tinsmith's in 1818, and some of the original tools remained, as did most of the cabinets on the inside. The shop had a massive selection of gold and silver jewellery, watches, clocks, sterling silver and silver-plated giftware, pewter and crystal.

Perfect for Arch.

It had a long-fronted double window with wooden frames and blue-painted woodwork. There was a second level, which Alan Browne lived in because he was too tight to pay for anywhere else.

As Archie stepped in through the door, the interior was all glass and wood, consisting of counters and tall, standing units, with long, thin chairs that you only ever saw in wine bars, the ones that were so uncomfortable that you decided to stand all night rather than risk crippling yourself.

Alan Browne was behind the counter. He was well over six feet, as thin as a rake, with a bloodless complexion worse than Count Dracula's. He wore thick tortoiseshell glasses that he can't have cleaned anytime in the last century, so how the fuck he ever saw anything was beyond Archie. Browne must have worked from voice alone.

He had a habit of leaning over the counter as close as he could without hitting you, and then spoke so forcefully that he ended up covering you in spit, not that he could see he was doing it. His suit had to be older than him but to give him credit, it was immaculate. Rumour had it, Bluebeard Browne was as bent as a nine-bob note. If you wanted something, he would find it. Another rumour said he slept on his money – that his mattress was stuffed with it.

The only other person in the shop was standing in front of the counter, a little further back from Browne, and was the spitting image of Elvis, with his jet-black hair and thick lips. His voice was deep.

"I had to laugh the other day, Alan. My little lad came into the room and he said, daddy, what's a transexual? I said I have no idea, but go and ask your mother, he'll know."

The pair of them burst out laughing before Browne turned his attention to Archie Figgs, who was also laughing.

Browne leaned forward and boomed into Archie's face. "Can I help you, young man?"

Young man, thought Archie, drying his head. Then again, everyone was probably young compared to Bluebeard.

"Do you value watches, sir?" Archie thought he'd tag the word on, show a bit of respect. Not that *he'd* been shown any.

"We do everything here," said Browne.

I'll bet, thought Archie.

"What do you have?" asked Browne.

Archie removed the carrier bag from inside his jacket pocket and placed it on the counter. Browne squinted at it.

Elvis leaned in forward as well. Archie glanced at him.

"Don't mind me," said Elvis.

"I won't," said Archie.

"He's a friend of mine," said Browne.

That was a new one on Archie; he didn't think Bluebeard had any. He placed the two velvet bags on the counter.

Browne leaned in close. Any closer, thought Archie, and the chances were his back would crack and he'd end up face first through the glass cabinet – might be an improvement.

Archie decided to let the jeweller remove them. The first out of the bag was a silver Rolex. Browne removed his glasses and shoved a monocle on his right eye and brought the watch up so close to his face that Archie thought he was going to push his eyeball through the back of his skull.

Browne made a few noises. "Interesting."

"How interesting?" asked Archie.

"Are they yours?"

"My late father's."

Browne pulled the watch down a little. "Oh, I am sorry. Has he passed long?"

"A long what?" asked Archie.

"No, did he die recently?"

"Oh," replied Archie. "Sorry. Yes, not so long back, that's why I'm still a little unsettled."

Browne returned to the watch without passing comment. Elvis still had more than a passing interest.

"These are a very common watch from Rolex," said Browne. "They made thousands of them."

Really, thought Archie. You can't kid a kidder. Archie had probably forgotten more than Browne knew about watches.

"Not worth a great deal, then?" pushed Archie.

"I could probably give you about thirty pounds. Fifty at a real push."

Archie knew that was utter bollocks. The watch was worth a grand of anyone's money.

"Oh," said Archie. "What about the other one? I think that's much older."

Browne put the Rolex on the velvet cloth, before lifting out an ancient Seiko, also silver, very slim, with a silver handle.

"Oh, now this is interesting," said Browne. "This your father's as well?"

"Was."

"How did he come by that one?" asked Elvis, as though it was a double act. If it *was,* they'd be fucked on *Britain's Got Talent,* thought Archie. Cowell would send them through the mangle.

"I believe his father actually brought it back from World War Two. The family rumour was that it was stolen from the Nazis"

Browne nearly dropped it. "Are you sure?"

"Not completely," said Archie, lying through his teeth. The only true word about that statement was the fact that it was stolen.

Browne mumbled something.

"Sorry," said Archie. "Didn't catch that."

"If we could authenticate this, you may be on to something."

"How much?" said Archie.

"Well, it's very difficult to put a price on it yet," said Browne, obviously hedging his bets.

"Roughly," said Archie. "You see, these have sentimental value, but my late old father wouldn't have wanted me to hang on to them forever. I mean, one day, they won't be worth anything."

"Very true," said Browne. "Well, if it's what I think it is, we might get four figures for you."

Fucking vampire, thought Archie. It was worth five figures – without a decimal point – and they both knew it.

Browne put the Seiko back on the velvet cloth as his phone rang. Whoever it was, he binned them off quite quickly, and returned his attention to Archie, who had now packed the watches back up under the watchful gaze of Elvis, who had actually written something in a notepad.

"If you want to leave them, young man," said Browne. "I'd be happy to get a proper quote on the Seiko."

"Let me have a think about it," said Archie.

"As you wish," said Browne, quickly losing interest.

Archie was about lay a depth charge on the counter. As he put the watches back in the carrier bag, he suddenly removed the pocket watch he had bought from Harry Pinchbeck.

"I don't suppose this is worth anything, is it?"

Browne had now returned his attention to Elvis, although he still had the monocle in his right eye. He turned and stared at Archie, as if he was something he had stepped in outside the shop.

Then he gave the slightest glance at the pocket watch, which was open in front of him. Browne did a double take and the monocle fell out of his right eye and nearly went through the glass in the cabinet.

After realizing his mistake, he quickly recovered, replaced the monocle and grabbed the watch all in one fluid movement.

That was enough for Archie. Now it was time to turn up the heat.

Browne did not actually say anything for a full five minutes. He simply made a series of noises that were a cross between a fart and something you might hear in the middle of Jurassic Park.

He suddenly placed the watch back on the counter and consulted a number of publications from a drawer in a cabinet behind him that had to be even older than he was.

Finally, he straightened up and asked. "Where did you get this?"

"Where?"

"Yes, where?"

"Why?" asked Archie.

Browne leaned in close and actually whispered. "I've never seen anything like it."

"Can't be worth anything then, can it?"

"Please tell me where you got it."

Archie had him. Whatever Browne claimed would be complete twaddle, and he would rip Archie a new one to own it.

"It was in with a box of fire-damaged timepieces I recently bought at an auction."

"Where?" asked Browne, his eyes having narrowed to slits.

Elvis had almost stopped breathing.

"Where what?" asked Archie.

Browne blinked rapidly, as if he couldn't understand or evaluate the scroat standing in front of him.

"Where was the auction?"

"Oh, I see. I can't remember now."

Archie quickly collected his items before leaving the shop in a hurry. He crossed the road and slipped around the back of the police station, only to find his e-bike missing.

"Oh, for Christ sake," shouted Archie.

"Can I help with something, sir?" asked a voice behind him.

Archie turned and jumped when he saw the moon-faced sergeant from the station.

"No, no," he said. "Just missed the bus home."

"Oh, dear. Far to go?"

"No," said Archie. Fuck that, he was telling the coppers nothing.

"Not lost anything, then?" asked the sergeant.

"Only the bus."

The sergeant nodded, tipping his cap. "I'm sure there'll be another soon."

Chapter Twelve

The Executioner's Arms was located at the back of the prison in Armley, a spit and sawdust establishment that should have been closed years ago. In fact, it was, and has been several times since. The place had been reopened so many times that the police had given up. It would be easier to shut the prison down. Only someone with a warped sense of humour could have so named it.

It was also the sort of place where people spoke in hushed tones, and if you were unknown to the locals, you did not step one foot through the front door, unless you wanted your teeth removing and your face reshaping and you were happy to suck your meals through a straw for a while.

Roy Sutton was in the toilets, which accessed through a narrow tunnel at the back of the pub. When you stepped through the door at the end thinking it would lead you into the toilets, you were wrong. It actually led you outside into a yard – the urinal was in another brick-built tunnel with no roof.

If you wanted to keep dry whilst standing and pointing you had to lean in as far as possible so that you were almost touching the porcelain; someone else's idea of fun. Behind you, there were four cubicles, which luckily did have a roof but it was old-fashioned, corrugated wavy tin, that leaked. As you exited there was a mirror but you'd have to have the eyes of a golden eagle to see anything in it. No one was brave enough to ask what the stains were.

Roy Sutton peered into the glass, trying to do something with his hair, but he had no idea why. It wasn't as if he had anyone in his life. He was short and squat with wild ginger curls sprouting up in patches, most of which was matted because he couldn't be arsed to wash it.

Roy also knew he should wear glasses but he was too proud, not to mention the fact that he saw it as a sign of weakness, especially considering the way he earned his money. Roy smiled and ran his fingers across his teeth, which had also seen better days. The cemetery he lived near was cleaner, with tombstones straighter than his teeth. He wasn't in the best of his terrible health, which he put down to a very bad diet, excessive smoking and drugs; the latter, both as a user and a seller. But he couldn't be bothered to do anything about that either. Life was too short.

As he was leaving the toilet he blew into his hands. Someone on the way in nearly barged into him in an effort to empty his bowels.

"Watch where you're going, you," said Sutton, glaring at the man. Apart from any other problems Roy had, a very short temper with an even worse attitude were at the top of the list.

The man quickly turned, causing Sutton to jump back, as he had already started what he was visiting the toilet for. He was a good foot taller than Sutton, with eyes so black they were near invisible in the poor light, and features which suggested to Sutton that his face had been set on fire, before being put out with a shovel, and then set on fire again.

"The fuck are you gonna do?" said the man.

Sutton thought better of it. Anyone with that kind of attitude and balls wouldn't be worth tackling. Besides, he had better things to do. He simply turned and walked away.

"Thought as much," said the man, still using the yard as a toilet.

Sutton slipped through the door, down the narrow tunnel and into the bar, which was little warmer than outside. He returned to his table and took another swig from his drink, which tasted awful. He suspected the cellar must have been in the sewers.

The bar was pretty much one long room and the choice of drinks and snacks was very limited: mild, bitter, lager, and crisps. No one touched the bowls of peanuts on the bar for fear of having their fingers bitten off by the rats, who were in fact friendlier than the clientele, and definitely more approachable than the landlord. Big Jim was an ex-con covered in tattoos, with so many studs and rings in the rest of his body that a man with a metal detector once walked past him on a beach and the bloody thing lit up like Blackpool illuminations. Most people left Jim alone, with good reason.

In the distance, at the end of the bar, Sutton heard the clack of high heels approaching his table. He stopped drinking and glanced upwards. Walking towards him was a lady of the night, perhaps the only one in Armley that would dare use the Executioner's. She was well known.

Ellie was dressed in a long red trench coat. Underneath, she had the tightest leather skirt Sutton had ever seen, with a black low-cut top, revealing a pair of breasts that were well past their sell-by date and closer to her navel than her chin, and long black leather boots up to her thighs. Her skin was so tight it couldn't have been far from splitting;

apparently that was due to a number of facelifts. If she had another she would have to start shaving.

"Anything I can do for you tonight, my friend?"

"Fuck off," replied Sutton.

Affronted, she stepped backwards. "Just trying to be friendly."

"Tell that to someone who cares."

"You want to watch your attitude, sunshine, before someone watches it for you."

Sutton left the table. "That going to be you?"

"No, but it might be me," said Big Jim, pulling a pint of mild.

Sutton immediately backed down. People who knew Jim well said he had earned his reputation through boxing, bare-knuckle fighting and even wrestling. As if to back that up, there was a photo on one wall of Big Jim in the ring with Giant Haystacks.

To avoid any further confrontation, and luckily for Sutton, his contact walked through the front door – well, walking would be putting it a bit strong. Cracker had long brown hair underneath a baseball cap. With small wire-rimmed glasses, a stick-thin frame and crooked teeth, he painted a pretty picture, especially as his legs and arms wouldn't work the way he wanted them to; Pinocchio was better on his feet.

Apparently, Cracker had crossed his previous supplier by trying to evade payment. He actually managed invisibility for six months before they caught him. The nickname was down to the sound his bones had made in the toilets when they had held him captive for twenty minutes.

Cracker pretty much passed straight through the pub and into the yard outside.

Sutton finished the dregs of his pint and left his table, approaching the bar.

"Another," he said.

"What else?" asked Big Jim.

"Crisps."

Big Jim grabbed Sutton by the throat. "You know what I mean."

Sutton squawked the word 'please'. Jim let him go, poured his pint and threw the crisps on the bar.

Sutton returned to the table and left everything on it before slipping outside, feeling into the pockets of his jeans and jacket to make sure he had everything Cracker needed.

In the yard, a view of the prison loomed over the building. With its dim lighting and large façade in the shadows, it should have been enough to put you off wrongdoing.

Cracker was standing in front of the urinal, and he was anything but straight.

Sutton approached him, making sure there was no one else around. In all honesty, he doubted it would have mattered. He suspected Big Jim knew everything that was going down, particularly if he allowed Ellie Partridge onto the premises, though he suspected she was servicing Big Jim.

"What have you got?" Cracker asked.

"The usual," replied Sutton.

"Nothing else?"

"What do you want?"

"Something different, give me a better trip. I'm bored of this shit."

Truth be told, Sutton was bored as well, but he liked the money too much to ever give it up. "Leave it with me. Anyway, don't want to be here all night, other people to see and all that. Got your money?"

Cracker reached into his pocket, which was no mean feat, given his shape. Still, if he ever needed a new career, Sutton reckoned that any circus would have been proud to have a contortionist of his ability.

"Bad do about your brother," said Cracker, his hand full of notes.

"I haven't got a brother," replied Sutton.

"You haven't now."

Sutton stared at him. "The fuck are you on about?"

"Don't you read the papers?"

"Do I look like I read a newspaper?" shouted Sutton, his patience diminishing. "What am I? An academic?"

Cracker reached inside his jacket and extracted a tabloid. It was thin, which suggested most of the sheets were missing. "Look at this."

The story about a death in Beeston was front page news. He speed-read what it said, flinching when it mentioned Steven Sutton, and what had happened.

He gave Cracker the paper back. "So what?"

"It's your brother, man. Why has someone done him in? Who do you think did it? Do you think he was still mixed up in this shit, and crossed someone? There's some nasty people out there."

"You'd know," said Sutton.

"Don't you?" asked Cracker. "You wanna be careful. Might be you next."

Sutton doubted it. "He got what was coming to him."

It was Cracker's turn to flinch after that comment. "I know you didn't like him but..."

"Stop right there," said Sutton, raising his hand. "To like or dislike someone shows emotion. Let's get this clear I had no feelings whatsoever towards that shitsucker. He was nothing to me after what happened."

"But..."

"Look," shouted Sutton. "Do you want this shit, or don't you? I'm not standing here all night. I have plenty more customers."

Chapter Thirteen

Phillip had finished watching the local news and weather broadcast and had decided to make himself some tea, as it was something close to approaching ten-thirty in the evening.

After finishing in the kitchen, he took his drink and a couple of digestives into what most people would call a man cave. He wasn't really keen on the name. For him it was simply another room, one that was set up to cater to his needs.

As Phillip was a lover of films, pretty much of any kind, he had had an extension built at the rear of his cottage, which he kitted out with a log burner, and had converted into a small cinema so he could spend the winter evenings watching them.

The room was still warm because he'd spent most of the evening there already. To say it was a cinema was perhaps incorrect because it didn't have rows of seats like normal ones, there were only two large comfortable armchairs in there, with a table between them. Phillip bent forward and shifted the board on the table a little, placing his tea and biscuits on it.

Along the front wall, he had a large pull-down projector screen; on the back wall, his projector sat permanently on a purpose-made shelf. Across the sides was a huge collection of DVDs – possibly one thousand of them, the majority of which were old Universal and Hammer productions, all on shelves and in alphabetical order. How anyone could do otherwise, he didn't know. If he wanted to watch a film he didn't want to spend all night searching for it. Underneath one shelf he also had a cabinet with drawers, in which he kept a rather large collection of memorabilia from those studios.

He'd met a fellow enthusiast on the Internet some years back, who lived somewhere in California, and who had actually worked for Universal Studios. The material he'd sent to Phillip was probably worth a fortune to collectors: photos of Lon Chaney from *The Phantom*, some of which were deleted scenes, and others pertaining to an alternate ending.

There were also a number of foreign film posters, and photos of a derelict Stage 28, where they filmed both of Chaney's biggest films, *The Phantom* and *The Hunchback*. It was very rarely used and said to be haunted.

Phillip had also collected a lot of material from Hammer, and had made numerous visits to Bray Studios and, as such, had also picked up rare material from the Amicus studio as well. The Lord only knew what would happen to it all when Phillip passed on.

Why should he worry about that? It was giving him a lot of pleasure now, and it wasn't harming anyone. He was single, had no family. There was a lot to be said for it. You could do what you wanted, when you wanted and where you wanted.

As he sipped his tea, he turned his attention to the problem of the will, the missing heirloom, and what had really happened to his father, all of which were puzzles that needed to be solved. And he believed he had the right equipment to do that.

Phillip glanced to his right, picked up and broke a digestive in two, placed one half in his mouth and the other on the table next to his Ouija board.

He'd been introduced to the board through a friend who had later died suddenly due to a serious accident. The board, however, was something Phillip kept to himself, for fear of ridicule; he'd suffered enough of that throughout his life – particularly in his school years.

For as long as Phillip could remember, his father's disappearance had unsettled him; it had left him feeling incomplete, and one should never be incomplete. He couldn't accept that it had simply happened, and that he had never been seen or heard from since – not that Phillip had ever met him, as it had happened before he was born. He'd spent his life wondering what had gone on, and why, but no matter what he did, he could find no answers.

As Phillip entered his forties, still plagued by the incident, he'd started attending church in order to try and find answers, but still, none came. He questioned the local priests with the usual questions; if there is a God, why do bad things happen? Surely God would understand Phillip's grief, and help out. The clergy had no answers, could only offer comfort. Only one he had spoken to had known his father, but like everyone else, he had no idea what had happened, nor did he know anyone who did.

Following a service one Sunday morning, one of the parishioners had overheard the conversation. He'd watched Phillip slip into the graveyard, taking a seat on one of the benches. Phillip had with him a flask and a lunchbox, and often spent his time after church with the same routine.

The parishioner's name was George South. He'd asked Phillip if he could join him. He, too, had a sandwich. Phillip had a spare cup and had poured a drink for them both. They'd talked for around thirty minutes before George had broached the subject. He'd said he lived locally, and every Thursday night he held a spiritual meeting with friends, who often talked and helped each other. Phillip didn't think anyone could help. George explained about the board and invited Phillip, explaining that *it* might have an answer.

Phillip mulled it over, liked the idea, and had agreed. He turned up and spent a month with them, and really liked them. They were good company. He was fascinated with something called the talking board, as they referred to it; no one called it a Ouija board. He was completely overwhelmed by some of the things they had discovered, so much so that he came away and purchased his own board, to try at home.

That was when he started to ask pointed questions. To his surprise, he finally received an answer... of sorts. Phillip believed that his father had actually made contact. He asked if he was still alive, but all his father had said was that, wherever he was now, it was dark and confined.

What did that mean; dark and confined? If his father was making contact through a spirit board he simply could not still be alive, so where was he and what had happened?

Phillip was blown away by the message, and for a short time, became completely obsessed with the information. Determined as he was, Phillip needed to sort the matter out to his satisfaction. He needed to find answers.

In order to do that, he felt he needed to check his family tree, and he had to start asking questions of the people he knew in the town, and where he and his father had worked. What did they remember about him, and the night he went missing? Had anyone *ever* seen him since?

He visited the police. Was there anyone still on the force who could tell him anything? He realized he may not be allowed to search through the official documents, but surely someone could tell him something.

There were records concerning his grandfather's death, and what had transpired, and there were rumours about *him* having been involved in a feud of some kind with another man called Cyril but that's all he could find out. No one had any conclusive or definitive answers.

But the board had. And he believed it was the board that had given him his first clue, pointing him in the right direction.

Then came the documentary, and he saw what he believed might possibly be the missing heirloom. He was finally being informed first-hand that it was not the stuff of legends, that it *had* been made, it *did* exist, but no one knew where it was.

Phillip was on to something. He wasn't going to let it go. He had to find out the truth, and possibly find the heirloom.

However, despite the board allegedly putting him in touch with his father, and confirming the existence of the heirloom, indicating a possible location, he had yet to find it.

Phillip finished his biscuits, staring at the board and, for the first time since he had started using it, he began to question it.

Chapter Fourteen

The following morning, Reilly pulled the pool car into Great George Street, and then into the car park of the Leeds General Infirmary. A meeting with Fitz was beckoning.

The pair of them jumped out, Reilly locked the vehicle and as they headed toward the entrance, he suddenly said to his partner, "Why did I pick you up at a restaurant on Saturday night? What were you up to?"

"Having a meal," said Gardener, without venturing any further, though he knew it would be a waste of time. That question was loaded with intent.

They slipped up the path and through the main doors into the building, before continuing their way to the mortuary.

"A meal, you don't say," replied his partner. "Now I'm going to have to try that one, so I am. Who'd have thought you could go to a restaurant for a meal?"

"I'd suggest you try it sometime," said Gardener. "But they're all very civilized. I'm not sure you'd fit in."

"I'll be alright if Laura's with me. She tends to keep me on a tight leash. So how was Vanessa?"

Gardener wondered how long it would take. Even before the conversation had started, he knew his partner would know everything about the night.

"Who have you been talking to?"

"Who do you think?"

"My dad," said Gardener. "He can't keep anything to himself."

"He has your best interests at heart," said Reilly. "And so have I. It's about time you started seeing this girl. Seems to me you've both been skirting around your feelings."

Gardener wasn't sure if that was true. Vanessa was not afraid to say what she thought. "It's early days, but it still feels strange."

"Why?"

"It's hard to say," said Gardener. And he meant it. He had to admit he really liked her. She felt like a breath of fresh air to his normal environment, a release, or an escape from some of the horrors he faced. "I enjoyed myself, and I didn't. It felt comfortable, but then it didn't. Does that make sense?"

Suddenly, they were at the door to the lab.

Reilly turned to face him before they entered. "Of course it does. This is a new direction, and it's the first time, especially after what happened with Sarah. But if you think about Sarah – and I know you do – it's what she would have wanted, to see you happy.

"And come on, old son, it's not as if you've rushed into any of this. You've let the dust settle, you've taken your time and you're still a bit cagey. But anyone can see that this Vanessa one is good for you."

Gardener nodded, hoping Reilly was right. "Thank you." His partner's views meant a lot to him. There was no one he trusted more, both on a personal and professional level.

Gardener turned and opened the doors and the pair of them walked into Fitz's office. As Gardener sat down, Reilly immediately headed for the coffee machine and the filing cabinet, where Fitz was known to keep a stash of chocolate bars.

"Morning," said Fitz, glancing at Reilly. "I see he hasn't eaten."

"I wouldn't bank on it," said Gardener. "He was at the office early this morning, so he'll have eaten something somewhere – more than once."

"A man could get a complex when he knows he's being talked about," said Reilly.

"Not with skin as thick as yours," said Fitz. "I've always said if they dropped the big bomb, the only thing left walking would be the cockroaches and you."

Reilly had poured the coffees and returned to the desk with a Bounty bar in his hand. "I'm not sure I know what you mean."

Fitz collected some paperwork together, folded it and placed it in a desk drawer and then turned his attention to a folder on his desk marked "Steven Sutton".

"What do we have?" asked Gardener.

Fitz opened the file. "Quite a lot. From what you've heard and read in the witness reports he was alive at six-thirty, and very probably dead around nine o'clock, which doesn't leave a lot of room for error. Whoever did it, must have planned it well and watched him carefully for quite some time."

"Or actually knew him," offered Reilly.

Gardener nodded to his partner, and then asked Fitz, "How did he die?"

Fitz rose from his desk and beckoned them to follow him into the lab, where Steven Sutton's body was laid out on a gurney. The pathologist pointed to two small marks on Sutton's chest that were inside the circle of nails, more or less in-between a couple of holes, where his fingers had been attached by more nails.

Gardener leaned in closer but it was Reilly who actually asked the question. "Are they from a Taser?"

"Yes," said Fitz. "As you know, police Tasers fire two small, barbed, metal prongs, which are attached to the weapon via very thin wire cables. When one of these hits you, the prongs puncture the skin. The depth depends on the amount of clothing, which in this case was very little, so they're a little deeper than usual. The reason I never saw them in situ was because one of his fingers covered the marks. Have you found his hands, yet?"

"No," said Gardener. "At least I don't think we have, the SOCOs haven't said anything."

"So he was zapped," said Reilly.

"That would answer a number of questions," said Gardener. "Certainly the one about how the killer managed to manhandle the victim with what looked like apparent ease."

"Exactly," said Fitz. "You get hit with one of these things and every major muscle group will spasm and tense up, to the point you literally cannot move a muscle, which causes you to lose balance and fall over."

"Depending on the amount of charge," said Reilly. "It's a temporary condition; normally wears off after two or three minutes."

"Yes," said Fitz. "I suspect the charge will have been quite powerful, so our killer would have the time he needed to move his victim around. Sutton's not a small man."

Fitz had made a good point. Sutton, in life, had been quite stocky, around five feet eight inches and perhaps weighing around thirteen or fourteen stone.

The pathologist leaned in closer, pointing again to the two small red puncture marks on the victim's skin. "The distance they are apart is relative to how far away they were from the weapon when it was fired. The further away, the more space between marks, because the prongs start to splay out after travelling through the air. These are very close together, suggesting it was at close range."

"So we know he was stunned, making him easier to move," said Gardener, "but we're still not sure where he was in the house. Steve Fenton believes that Sutton was actually in the bedroom upstairs, the front one, which faces out on to the street. They found the remains of the Chinese takeaway and four beer cans – two full, two empty. There is no evidence to suggest that he was dragged *up* the stairs."

Gardener turned to Fitz. "The alcohol in his system, was it just the beer?"

"Yes," replied Fitz. "There wasn't a lot, so two cans sounds about right."

"Any drugs?"

"Nothing I could find," said Fitz, "other than prescription drugs. There was evidence of ramipril, which is often prescribed for blood pressure, and judging by the furring of the arteries, he would have needed it."

"Diet not so good?" asked Reilly.

"Probably not," said Fitz. "Anyway, let's return to what we think killed him. Sutton had been for his takeaway. We know he was back in the house at six-thirty, may possibly have had a quick shower and then lounged on the bed in a pair of boxer shorts to eat his takeaway and watch some TV. At some point between six-thirty and nine, he was surprised by an unexpected visitor."

"Looking at the time slots," said Gardener, "I'm inclined to believe it was sooner rather than later. Let's say the killer arrives at seven, or maybe seven-fifteen."

"How did he get in?" asked Reilly. "Has Sutton left a front or back door open? We've had nothing to say there was any forced entry."

"I'd venture to say it was back door," said Gardener. "If it had been the front, I'm sure the neighbour opposite would have noticed."

"The question then is," suggested Reilly, "did he even *know* the back door was open?"

"Maybe not," said Gardener. "It's possible the killer was even inside the house by the time he got back with the takeaway. Let's return to the timeline. The killer takes Sutton by surprise at say seven-thirty at the latest. He tasers him immediately so there is no resistance, drags him into the room at the side of the house, ties him up and possibly waits for him to come round."

"Sutton has something the killer wants," said Reilly, "because the neighbour overhears him asking 'where is it?'"

"In-between cracking noises that sound like a whip," said Gardener. "Which must have been these nails." Gardener pointed.

He turned to Fitz. "This man must have endured some serious pain. The evidence indicated he was alive through all of it, because there are blood trails from the nails."

"Possibly to the final nail," said Fitz, "which I suspect would be the one positioned at two o'clock. That one appears to have been a longer nail because it punctured his heart."

Chapter Fifteen

It was late afternoon into early evening before Gardener and Reilly had the team together in the incident room. He was eager to share what he had found with them, and equally as interested to see if they had discovered anything to move them forward.

That a Taser had been used to subdue Sutton caused some speculation.

"A Taser?" said Rawson.

"That puts a different perspective on things," said Anderson.

"I can guess what you're thinking," said Gardener. "It opens up the suggestion to a policeman being involved."

Rawson nodded. "Other than the police, it's illegal to own or buy one."

"I agree it's illegal," said Gardener, "but not impossible. I dare say you can buy these things from the dark net, and a dozen other places."

"But given what we've so far discovered," said Sharp, "it's possible. A lot of planning went into the killing. Who better than a policeman? He would have had the opportunity to scope the place out."

"And then you have the Taser," said Rawson.

"And he's managed to get in and out of the place without being seen... so far."

"It's definitely worth considering," said Gardener. "We can't discount anything but this case is still in its infancy. I think we need a lot more meat on the bone before we can start connecting dots."

Gardener went on to mention that Fitz believed Sutton was alive and awake and feeling every insertion of the nails before the final one that killed him. They then had to consider the possibility that the killer might have been successful in finding what he wanted, which could be an end to the matter; if he hadn't, there may be more victims. Either way, the police were still in the dark about a lot of things.

Returning to the subject of nails, he asked Anderson and Thornton if they had made any headway with the gun.

Thornton shook his head. "Nothing much, other than to suggest that the style of the nails appears to be something from the past."

"It's not as easy as it sounds," said his partner, Anderson. "There are so many on the market, but like Frank said, from the people we've spoken to, they think the style of the nails used look like something that was used years ago."

"Brilliant," said Reilly. "If we're not looking for something current, God knows what kind of problems we could run into."

"It's a pretty powerful gun," said Thornton. "Believe it or not, the last place we visited was Screwfix, here in Leeds. One of the older employees suggested we should start consulting the construction industry, or something similar. He thinks that whatever was used to hammer these nails into Sutton's chest was a powerful machine."

"Which is why he reckoned it would have been used somewhere heavy," said Anderson. "The building industry, maybe woodworkers."

"Possibly even engineering," said Thornton. "So, we spent a bit of time looking and listing the places we need to visit tomorrow. With a bit of luck, we might hear something positive."

Gardener thought the comment about engineering was interesting and he would come back to that once he had heard how Edwards and Benson fared with Dawson's Engineering, and Petter and Smith.

For now, he turned his attention to the rope and asked Sharp and Rawson what, if anything, they had found.

"Funny you should mention engineering," said Rawson. "We left the rope with forensics and they've come back with a report."

Sharp took over. "The stains are really dark, and heavy."

"Heavy?" Gardener repeated. "What do they mean by that?"

"Whatever the stains are on the rope," said Rawson, "and they reckon with a bit more time they'll have an answer for us, they seem to be very specific to a heavy-gauge industry."

"Did they offer any suggestions?" asked Reilly.

"They seem to think it's a grease," said Rawson. "It's almost black and really thick."

"A bit like the grease that goes into CV joints on a car?" asked Gardener, having used something similar on the bearings for his bike renovation.

"That kind of thing," replied Sharp. "Only a lot heavier, and possibly thicker."

"Christ," said Reilly. "That must be interesting stuff, so what are we talking?"

"Maybe the commercial vehicle industry," said Sharp.

"Or trains," offered Rawson.

"Interesting," said Gardener. "So this rope could have been lying around in a warehouse, a goods shed, or a garage floor for the last ten years."

"Couple that with a vintage nail gun and we could end up scouring museums," said Reilly. "Or at least the places where they carry out repairs before they go into the museum."

"I'm not so sure on that one, Sean," said Gardener, "but it does fit with National Rail, which then leads us to Sutton himself. He worked for them. Maybe this rope had been lying around in his shed and the killer has simply made use of it. What did National Rail have to say about Sutton?"

"Strangely enough, he was a model worker," said Sharp. "He's worked there for over twenty years, always on time, always did a good job, went where he was sent without complaint. They can't think of a time when they had to have a word with him for anything."

"Why strange?" asked Gardener.

"From what we found out at the last meeting," said Rawson, "Sutton has a record. We asked them about it and they knew nothing – they were surprised. To be honest, because he was recommended by Kerry's brother, Aaron Butcher, and they were desperate for workers at the time, they didn't do much of a background check."

"The rest is history," said Sharp. "He turned up, did a good job and kept his nose clean, so whatever it was, perhaps he had turned over a new leaf."

"I'll come back to his record. Sean and I did a bit of digging earlier and we know what it was. In the meantime, I'd like you two guys to return to the railway workshops, where the repairs are carried out, with the rope. See if you can match it to anything they have lying around, and perhaps check up on any of this heavy grease. Bring some back for forensics and see if they can match it up. It would be really helpful if they can, give us a positive direction in which to look."

Gardener turned to Edwards and Benson. "All the talk of engineering leads us to Dawson's, and Petter and Smith. What did you manage to find out?"

"Those two are devastated by the news," said Benson. "They were close friends, all of them, had been for years."

"Did they know about his record?" asked Gardener.

"No," said Edwards. "They were really surprised, sir."

"Maybe they're not as close as they make out," offered Reilly.

"How long had they known him, and how did they meet?" asked Gardener.

"They've been in the area about fifteen years, so Sutton was there before them," replied Benson. "They met at a match, or to be more precise, in the bar afterwards. All Leeds supporters, all lived in the same area, so they had a lot in common."

"Okay," said Gardener, making notes. "Can they tell us anything more about his last movements?"

Edwards grabbed his notes and gave them the once-over. "After they'd all finished work on the Friday night, they all met for a quick pint in the local pub, which was The Old White Hart on Town Street."

"But," said Benson, "as usual, the quick pint turned into a long one, especially as Kerry was away. They stayed until nine o'clock, when they left for an Indian. They went to Kebabish on Beeston Road. The Indian takeaway confirmed that. Said they were regular customers."

"They all went back to Petter's house," said Edwards, "where they downed a few more beers and talked about the match the next day. Sutton and Smith left around midnight. Both walked home in different directions."

"I doubt they'll have been in any fit state to notice if anyone was following," said Reilly.

"You guessed right," said Benson.

"Which takes us to Saturday," said Gardener. "We know he was alive. Did anyone see him, then?"

"We have statements from one or two of the neighbours who bumped into Sutton at the local shops on Saturday morning," said Benson.

"Then he was seen leaving the house at twelve-thirty by Janice Portman," said Edwards. "She was going to the shops, and *he* was going to the match on Elland Road."

"That's where Petter and Smith come back in. They all met for a pint before the game in The Old Peacock – the one opposite the ground. After the match he went straight home because he said he needed to clean the place up before Kerry and Paul returned from their week in Kent, visiting her mother."

Benson added. "We did speak to the manager of the Marley Chinese Takeaway on Noster Road. He confirmed that Sutton was in there on Saturday night, sometime around six-twenty, where he bought egg foo young, with a portion of prawn crackers."

Gardener was a little disappointed. There was nothing out of the ordinary that they could pounce on. The rest they knew, apart from what really happened between six-thirty and nine.

"What about Dawson's Engineering?"

"Well, here's the really interesting bit," said Benson. "I think we're going to need to pay a return visit to that place in view of what we've learned tonight."

"Why?" asked Reilly.

"Dawson's Engineering actually manufacture parts for trains," replied Benson. "That possibly brings Petter and Smith into the picture."

"It is possible," said Gardener. "When you talked to them, did you have any reason to think that they were even *in* the picture?"

"No," said Benson. "They all seemed like good mates enjoying a common interest; a pint and a game of football."

"But there *could* be something," said Gardener. "You checked how long they had been friends. You obviously mentioned his record that they claim not to know anything about. I take it that you asked about any recent mood changes, or any problems he may have mentioned?"

"We did," said Edwards. "But they didn't know of anything. They pretty much said he was a good mate. He had a good job, he was reliable, and he'd pretty much do anything for you. He loved his football and that was his main topic of conversation."

"Janice Portman mentioned he was a big man with a bit of a temper. Did they mention anything about that?" asked Gardener.

"No," said Benson. "According to them two, they'd not seen that side of him, not at a match, or in the bar afterwards. There had been one or two scary moments in the past with away supporters but most of the time Sutton turned the other cheek."

"Okay," said Gardener. "Can you both go back and question Petter and Smith a little deeper? Find out if there was anything in the past that they could point us to? I also would like you to speak to them individually, one of you take Petter and the other take Smith, we may find out more that way. And then go back into Dawson's and check out any greases they may use, check the stock and bring some samples back for the lab analysis."

Edwards and Benson nodded in unison. Gardener noted the actions on a new whiteboard and turned his attention to Gates and Longstaff and the numbers. He didn't relish what they might have to add, but to be fair, what they had discovered so far was positive.

"It's a bloody minefield," said Gates. "We really have no idea what we're looking for."

"You do surprise me," said Gardener.

"I'd have laid odds that the pair of you would have cracked the case by now," said Reilly.

"Oh, don't you worry about that one," said Longstaff. "We have found something interesting."

"I was afraid of that," said Gardener. He decided to take a seat in front of the whiteboard. "Go on, then, let's have it."

"There's some great stuff out there about numbers to keep our conspiracy theorists going forever," said Gates.

What came next was like a double act in a theatre show.

"Did you know," said Longstaff, "that Lincoln was elected president in 1860, and Kennedy in 1960."

"Both were assassinated on a Friday," said Gates.

"Lincoln was killed in Ford's Theatre."

"Kennedy was killed riding in a Lincoln convertible made by the Ford Motor Company."

"And it just goes on. We have loads more for you on that one."

"Oh, Christ," said Reilly. "We could be here all night with these two."

"Okay," said Gardener. "I like the conspiracy theory angle, but have you found anything pertaining to the numbers on Steven Sutton's chest?"

"What we've found might not have any bearing at all," said Gates.

"The trouble is," added Longstaff. "There are reams and reams of this stuff, and we could be here for days without stumbling on what could be important."

Gates pulled out a file, and for the first time during the meeting, switched on the overhead projector.

"With very little to go on, we concentrated on the numbers three and five, partly because of a rather interesting little grid we came across."

"It seems that numerology is among the oldest of the psychic sciences," said Longstaff.

"According to numerologists," said Gates, "each number possesses a certain power that exists in the occult connection between the relations of things and the principles in nature which they express. All that humans are capable of experiencing can be reduced to the digits one through nine."

"So, this case *might* have occult connections?" asked Reilly.

"Well, everything we've found about numbers seems to have some connection to it," said Gates. "Anyway, those on the number three path through life have discovered the joy of living," said Gates. "They will tend to find their opportunities on the lighter side of life, in circulating and socializing. An artistic environment is best for the three personalities as they are always seeking expression through writing, speaking, or art. The negative polarity for the number three personality is to become superficial."

"That doesn't strike me as describing Steven Sutton," said Gardener.

"Not from what we know so far," added Reilly.

"But go on," said Gardener.

"Those with the number five as their destiny must be prepared for frequent, unexpected change and variety," said Longstaff. "Five personalities do a lot of travelling and learn to understand all classes and conditions of people, and they are generally without racial prejudice. Five people always are seeking the new and progressive.

Number five personalities must guard against becoming self-indulgent."

"That doesn't sound like him, either," said Gardener.

"Just have a look at the graph I mentioned, so you can see how we arrived at what we did. With a name given as an example, it shows how to arrive at the number vibration."

123456789
ABCDEFGHI
JKLMNOPQR
STUVWXYZ

Example:

STEVEN SUTTON
125455 132265

22 19
4 1
4+1 = 5

"Look at the numbers," continued Gates. "Steven adds up to twenty-two. Sutton adds up to nineteen. Two and two make four, one and nine makes ten; so you add those two again, and one and zero make one. Add them both together, and four plus one equals five."

"But what does it mean?" asked Reilly. "What is the killer trying to tell us?"

"Unless he's chosen those numbers through blind luck," said Rawson.

"I doubt there is any luck involved in this," said Gardener. "But the likelihood is he's chosen the numbers for a completely different reason." Gardener thought about it. Nothing that Gates had said married with Sutton or his personality, so what did they mean?

"Whilst I'm not willing to rule out what you ladies have discovered," said Gardener. "I'm tempted to think that there is either a lot more to it, or they could mean something else altogether."

"To be honest, boss," said Gates, "you're probably right."

"But I think we're on to something," said Longstaff. "So we need to give it more attention."

"Agreed," said Gardener. "However, there may be something more in Sutton's past that will point to why the numbers have been chosen, which is what need to try to find out."

A knock at the door halted any further discussion.

Chapter Sixteen

As the door opened, the team was greeted with desk sergeant for Leeds Central, David Williams, a tall and stocky and rather distinguished officer whose short brown hair was rapidly turning grey. Although he was dressed in his uniform, he had chosen to leave the jacket on his chair and sport a shirt and tie. He carried with him a file.

"David," said Gardener. "How are you?"

"I'm well, sir." Williams continued walking toward the front where Gardener was now standing.

"What do you have for us?"

"An interesting witness statement from Saturday night."

Gardener pointed to the middle. "Take the floor."

Williams did, turning to face the team.

"I took a call about two hours ago from a man called Tim Standing. He was walking his dog in Holbeck Park sometime around six-thirty. He noticed a man approaching the houses in the area around Noster Terrace. It was dark and almost impossible to see the man, who had his head down."

"That's a pity," said Reilly.

"But understandable if he's our man," said Gardener. "He probably isn't stupid enough to think he won't be seen by anyone but he'd do his best to maintain a low profile. Go on, David."

"According to the witness, our man appeared to be a professional of sorts – perhaps the best description is of a city gent."

"How so?" Gardener asked.

"He wore a bowler hat, and was carrying what could only be described as perhaps a Gladstone bag."

"Did the man speak, or nod or confirm in any way that he had seen the dog walker?" asked Gardener.

"No," said Williams.

"And the dog walker had no idea who it was?" asked Colin Sharp.

"No, he walks his dog every night but he had never seen the man before."

"Could it have been a doctor?" asked Benson. "I'm only asking because of the Gladstone bag."

Gardener shook his head. "Unlikely."

"What doctor would walk across the field to attend to a patient?" asked Reilly.

Gardener glanced at Williams. "We might be on to something, David. See if you can get one of the lads to pop down and speak to him, see if he remembers anything else. And perhaps some of the operational support officers to scan the witness statements more closely; someone else may have spotted this character."

"Another press release might help," suggested Bob Anderson.

"Standing also said something else interesting," added Williams. "That the man walking towards him actually reminded him of Jack the Ripper."

"Jack the Ripper?" repeated Reilly. "Why the hell would he say that?"

"Because the long flowing coat he wore appeared to be more like a cape. But I think he only said that because he'd been watching a film called *From Hell*, the night before."

The team laughed. Gardener made a note on the board. "Okay, we need more about this character walking across the field. Did anyone else see him, and what time would that have been? We also need to be searching through witness statements that cover the times between eight-thirty and nine-fifteen. Where did he go? Someone somewhere must have seen him. At the very least we need to identify and talk to him, even if he is not our man."

"Does sound a bit odd, though," said Reilly. "A strange sort of look for December. It might have been early but it was bloody cold, you'd think he'd be better dressed."

"He may well have come in a car," said Gardener, "and parked it around the corner from where he was seen. Did Standing say which direction the man approached him from?"

"Yes, sir, the Elland Road end of the park."

"So he could have parked his car on Hoxton Mount," said Gardener. "Check the statements again. There are only a few houses there, so any strange cars would have been noticed."

Gardener updated the whiteboard. "Thank you, David, that's something more to go on."

Williams nodded and then sat down. "Do you mind if I sit in? I'm at the end of my shift but I'd like to hear a bit more."

"If you're sure you don't mind," said Gardener.

He addressed the team. "I mentioned earlier that we found out a bit about Sutton's record. After having gone through everything, Sean and I popped back to see his wife, Kerry."

"How was she?" asked Gates.

"Bearing up," said Gardener.

"*Did* she know about his record?" asked Thornton. "*Was* she holding something back?"

"She either didn't – or claimed she didn't know too much," said Gardener.

"But she was able to give us a bit to go on," said Reilly.

"It was drugs-related," said Gardener, "which seemed to have started back in his later years at school."

"No surprise there," said Anderson. "That's usually where it happens."

"True," said Gardener. "Though you wouldn't expect a parent to get you into it."

"His father?" asked Longstaff.

"Stepfather, actually," said Reilly. "The man his mother met and married was called Brian Shilling. He had Steven selling cigarettes to start with."

"Which later turned to drugs," said Gardener.

"It continued after school," said Reilly, "but, like most drug dealers, he got caught. A spell in prison soon rehabilitated him, and it was while serving that sentence, his real father, Patrick, died, and his stepfather, Brian, left his mother and moved away."

"Christ," said Rawson. "Bit of a double blow. It's a wonder he didn't re-offend and go back inside."

"He *was* allowed out for the funeral," said Gardener. "But maybe all that bad luck worked the other way. Shortly after, he was fully released from prison and decided he needed the straight and narrow if he would ever amount to anything. His girlfriend and future wife, Kerry, saw to that."

"That's when she landed him the job with National Rail," said Reilly.

"Which is where her brother Aaron came in," said Gardener. "So, on the face of it, Steven appears to have been a reformed character."

"Good on him," said Anderson. "Some of them are."

"Agreed," said Gardener. "The thing is, someone wanted him dead. So who was it, and why? That's what we need to find out. Was it an isolated incident, or will there be more? Did anyone find out anything about the elusive half-brother?"

Most of the head-shaking meant no. However, Colin Sharp said that he and Dave Rawson had made a start on checking out all the Suttons in the area, putting together a list that they would narrow to go and speak to. There wasn't, in fact, that many, so they might hit something positive quite quickly.

"Okay," said Gardener. "In that case, we think we can help. Kerry thinks his name is Roy Sutton. She can't for the life of her think why the brothers didn't talk but if Roy is anything like Steven, maybe he went into a life of crime. So we need someone looking into a possible Roy Sutton who may live in the area, and who may be mixed up in drugs like Steven."

"It's a long shot, sir," said Sharp.

"I know, Colin, but at least it's a little something else to go on. And we have another Sutton dropping into the mix. Kerry said his father, Patrick, died while Steven was in prison. Let's have someone looking into a Patrick Sutton, see if there is any background there we can use?"

"Did she say where Roy or Patrick lived?" asked Anderson.

Reilly consulted his notebook. "Patrick used to live in a place called Back Mitford Road in Armley, number forty-two. By the time we'd finished with Kerry there wasn't enough time to check it out."

"But it might be worth a visit," said Gardener. "If he passed away, the house may have sold to someone else, or it may possibly have been handed down to the elusive half-brother. And while we're looking people up, check on this Brian Shilling, he might still be around. And has anyone spoken to Aaron Butcher?"

"He's on our list, sir," said Rawson.

"Okay," said Gardener. "We need to talk to him, at the very least find out where he was on Saturday night."

Another knock on the door disturbed the meeting. The door opened to Steve Fenton, the crime scene manager.

"Thought you might like to hear this, sir."

"Have you got something?"

Fenton nodded. "We've found the fingerprints of one Harry Pinchbeck, otherwise known as Harry the Shard, at the house in Beeston."

"Who?" asked Gardener.

At the same time, David Williams laughed out loud. "Harry the Shard?"

Fenton nodded. "Only in the kitchen, however, nowhere else. But it's a start, and it certainly puts someone at the scene around the time of the murder."

"Surely not Harry Pinchbeck," said Williams, still laughing.

"Who's Harry Pinchbeck?" asked Gardener.

"A career thief who could win awards for stupidity," said Williams. "Trust me, when the Lord was giving out heads, Harry thought he said beds and asked for a soft one."

The whole room erupted in a peel of laughter. When it finally died, Williams said, "I just can't see Harry being your murderer but I can't argue with the fact that the evidence puts him at the scene. He really doesn't have the brains for something like this."

"How stupid is he?" asked Reilly.

"Do you remember that other bloody idiot from Bramfield, Manny Walters?"

No one could forget Manny Walters.

"Well he makes Manny Walters look like *Mastermind* material."

"Fucking hell," said Rawson. "This has to be worth hearing."

"I once remember he needed desperately to sign on to get his giro, and was told he had to provide a passport photo. He went to a machine and printed four photos of himself, and he wrote his name on the back of each like he was instructed to.

"On the way back to the job centre he decided to do a bit of shoplifting, so he went into a corner shop asked for an expensive bottle of whisky and some cigarettes. The shop owner was a bit suspicious of him because he looked like a druggie, so he didn't put the items on the counter.

"He told Harry he has to hand over the cash first. Harry reached into his pocket and pulled out some paper that felt a bit like cash, and he handed it over to her without checking. He quickly snatched the whisky and ran off. The shop owner looked down and suddenly noticed he'd handed over four photos of himself, with his name helpfully written in the back!"

The laughter hit new levels. As it died, Rawson said, "Oh Jesus, that was priceless. Even I could have cracked that one."

"Well, before I go, let me tell you this one. Harry was once arrested for stealing a baker's van. The baker had left it out in his yard with the engine running whilst loading up his bread buns, when Harry jumped in a drove off with the back doors open.

"I got there within minutes because I was just around the corner on another job. There was literally a bread bun trail that I could follow along the road – because the buns had been dropping out the back. I made a few turns into an industrial estate and there Harry was, getting out of the van.

"I jumped out and told him he was nicked, he reached into his pocket a pulled out a pistol saying he had a gun. Well, at that point, my heart skipped a beat, but the silly bugger got carried away and pulled the trigger. The little flame of the cigarette lighter came out of the barrel and he just said 'oh shit'."

The team were beside themselves.

Eventually, Williams said, "They threw the book at him, not only theft of the van, but possession of an imitation firearm with intent to evade arrest. Poor sod got a few years for that one. I realize he's suddenly in the picture but he's not your man."

Gardener put his name on the board. "Someone find him, please."

Chapter Seventeen

The TV news and newspapers were a waste of time, mostly. They were full of rubbish to help them sell.

At least, that's what he thought.

Every now and again however, he came across something interesting; like the article in the morning's *Holbeck Chronicle*, stating that the murdered man in Beeston, Steven Sutton, had a living relative, but not full blood.

A half-brother, called Roy.

Chapter Eighteen

Desk sergeant David Williams informed Gardener that they had Harry the Shard sitting in an interview room, ready and waiting. As it was only mid-day, Gardener was pleased.

After studying Pinchbeck's record, Gardener really didn't think they had Steven Sutton's murderer sitting in the room, but he might have seen *something* of value to them.

He and Reilly spent a few minutes outside, deciding on the best plan of attack. Gardener figured it was pointless beating around the bush, because they had the man banged to rights – they had his prints at the scene. They were not going to waste a lot of time going around the houses, and given the man's total lack of intelligence, a hard and fast routine was the most likely way to unbalance him.

The pair of them entered and Gardener almost flinched at the man's unusual appearance: thinning black hair, domed forehead, a nervous tic, large glasses decorating a nose that needed no help – hence his nickname, The Shard. Having watched him for a few minutes prior to entering, Gardener noticed he moved quite a lot. It would be an interesting interview to say the least.

Both detectives pulled out a chair and sat down. Gardener opened the file in front of him and spread the papers out a little, allowing Reilly a good view.

"Harold Ambrose Pinchbeck?" asked Gardener.

Harry's eyes widened a little. "No one calls me that."

"But it is your name?" questioned Reilly.

Harry nodded.

"Mr Pinchbeck, you're not under arrest," said Gardener. "We've asked you to come in because we'd like a little chat. With your permission we would like to record the conversation."

"Why?"

"So that everyone is covered. You can have a copy, and that way you know that we can't say you said something when you didn't, or vice versa."

"Makes a change," replied Harry.

Gardener went through the preliminaries before asking, "Where do you live?"

Harry gave them the full address in Beeston.

"Do you live with anyone?"

"Who are you – benefits office?" Harry's defensive side had not taken long to show.

Gardener ignored the question. "What do you do?"

"I can't work."

"Can't, or won't?" asked Reilly.

"Can't," said Harry, "on account of my back. My arms and legs aren't so good, either. Body is full of aches and pains. There are some days I can't even get out of bed for the pain."

"I'm surprised the benefits office didn't think it cheaper to pronounce you clinically dead and have a state funeral," said Reilly. "But your record says otherwise, Harry, old son. Your legs and arms seem to work okay when they're full of someone else's property."

Harry remained silent.

Gardener glanced through Harry's records, noticing that there wasn't a doctor in the city that had ever actually found anything wrong with him, including the police doctors who had visited from time to time when he was remanded in custody.

"Do you have family?" asked Gardener.

"No."

"How do you spend your time?"

He never actually answered the question because a knock on the door disturbed them. Reilly answered, taking a tray with tea and biscuits.

Within seconds of them being served, Harry had devoured his with a number of facial expressions that reminded the SIO of a grouper, or a blowfish.

Gardener decided hard and fast was needed. He tapped Reilly's foot under the table.

"Let's talk about Friday night, where were you?" asked Gardener.

"Friday?"

"Stop stalling," said Reilly. "With your health you must know exactly where you were."

"Oh, well, Friday," said Harry. "Yes, I was in The Old Peacock opposite the football ground. A couple of friends called and took me out for a bit."

"Names?" asked Reilly, pushing forward pen and paper.

Harry quickly jotted them down.

"Where were you on Saturday?" asked Gardener.

"In Leeds."

"Where?"

"The railway station."

"All day?" asked Reilly. "What the hell were you doing all day?"

"Keeping warm. It's nice in there, see, saves on heating bills."

"So, you were not in Beeston?" asked Gardener.

"No."

"Are you sure?" asked Reilly.

"I know where I was, I'm not stupid."

"We believe you *were* in Beeston, Mr Pinchbeck," said Gardener.

"Believe all you like," said Harry, a little of his confidence returning. "But with a lack of cameras you'll have a hard time proving it."

That was a mistake. "We don't need cameras," said Gardener. "We have fingerprints."

"Not mine."

"We're not stupid," said Reilly, leaning forward. "You have a record a mile long – remember the bakery? We have your prints and we can put you at a house in Beeston."

"I live there," shouted Harry. "I have friends there. You'll find my prints in most people's houses."

"That doesn't surprise me," said Gardener. "Noster Terrace?"

"I know one or two who live there."

"Last house on the left," said Reilly.

"Don't know him," said Harry, but then he nearly rose from his chair, catching the table in the process. "Here, was he the bloke that's been murdered?"

"You can read, then?"

Harry sat down. "I hear things."

"I'll bet you do," said Reilly. "Mostly without seeing anyone, I'd guess."

"Are you trying to fit me up for murder?"

"Were you at the house or not?" asked Gardener.

"Don't think about lying to us, Harry," said Reilly. "We have your prints."

"Where?"

"Here," said Reilly, pulling them out.

"No, for God's sake, I meant where in the house?"

"You admit you were in there, then?" asked Reilly.

"I didn't."

"You did."

"I'm admitting to nothing."

"You just have," said Gardener. "You asked where the prints where in the house, indicating you'd been in."

"And then buying time while you think of an excuse," added Reilly.

"You were there, Mr Pinchbeck and we have proof," said Gardener. "So why don't you save us all a lot of time and tell us where you were and at what time."

"Do I need a lawyer?" Harry asked.

"Can you afford one?" asked Reilly.

"Pro bono, haven't you heard of that?"

"If you have nothing to hide, Mr Pinchbeck," said Gardener. "You'll tell us and you'll walk out of here this afternoon."

It was obviously a tempting offer, thought Gardener, and to be fair, they knew it very unlikely that he had murdered Sutton, but they needed him to open up, give them something to go on.

Eventually, Harry said, "Kitchen, and only the kitchen. I did not take anything from the house and I was only in there minutes – not even that."

"Why?" asked Gardener.

"Back door was open."

"Why were you there?"

"I live in Beeston."

"We know that," said Reilly. "But you live a few streets away, why were you in Noster Terrace?"

"Walking home, from the match."

It was very unlikely Gardener could argue that one, or prove otherwise. "Why *that* house?" he asked.

"I told you," said Harry. "I was passing, light was on, I thought I heard voices."

"Again?" asked Gardener.

"Not that old chestnut," said Reilly.

"I went to see if everyone was okay," Harry said.

"But you don't know them," said Reilly.

"And then what?" asked Gardener.

"I heard the front door slam," Harry said, "and I legged it."

"What time was that?"

"I don't know."

"Think."

Harry rubbed his head a few times. "It was well after the match. I'd had a pint, so maybe six, half six."

"You didn't take anything?" asked Reilly.

"Not from the kitchen, or anywhere else in the house."

"Did you see anyone?" asked Gardener.

"Like who?"

"Anyone else in the area?"

"As I said, it was well after the match. Not too many people were around at that time. Most had gone home for their tea, or they were in the boozer. I saw a couple of dog walkers."

"No one else?" asked Gardener. "Or anyone who looked suspicious, out of place?"

"No. And I didn't hang around."

"Where did you go?" asked Reilly.

"Home, stopped in at the Chinese on the way. I like their stuff."

"What time was that?" asked Gardener.

"I don't know."

"Come on, Harry, think," said Reilly. "What time?"

Harry actually glanced at his own watch before saying. "About quarter to seven. Had a chat with him behind the counter, left about seven, got home about ten past. Stayed in the rest of the night."

Gardener thought about what had been said. Harry claimed he did not take anything from the house, and he was only in there minutes because he heard the front door slam shut. The times backed up what they already knew. Sutton had returned home at that time.

Harry then went to the Chinese and all it would take to back up his story was one phone call or a visit, which they would do. He would also ask one of the team to pay a visit to Harry's flat, which was in a large Victorian house in Beeston, so there would be other people who could back up what he'd claimed.

Gardener would have to let him go. All he had were fingerprints in the kitchen, and nowhere else in the house.

Gardener rose from the table. "Okay. Mr Pinchbeck, we're going to let you go pending further inquiries. But bear in mind, we might need to speak to you again."

Chapter Nineteen

It might have been an uneventful day; the night, however, was going to be anything but.

Reilly pulled the car to a halt on Back Mitford Road in Armley at a little after ten o'clock. He killed the engine and both officers jumped out. Gardener didn't say anything as he surveyed the area.

Strangely enough, as with the crime scene in Beeston, the house in Armley was opposite the New Wortley Cemetery. The last house in the street was an end of terrace, two-up two-down and, like many, had gates and bars on the front door and windows.

Studying the house, he noticed a basement. Three concrete steps led up to the front door, with a steel handrail on the right, and a small overgrown garden beyond. Overflowing wheelie bins were standing on the street. A small washing line ran from the door to a pole in the postage-stamp-sized garden, with a low stone wall separating it from the property next door.

"Have you noticed something, Sean?"

"I've noticed a lot," replied his partner. "Which bit are you talking about?"

"No CCTV," said Gardener. "In fact, this place is pretty barren. What do these people do if they want anything? No shops here, street corner or otherwise. It just appears to be a maze of houses, much like the scene in Beeston but at least they had local shops."

"That struck me. Another victim killed in similar-style housing, and living opposite a cemetery."

Gardener turned to his right. At one end of the street was a community hall, which connected to Hall Lane and HMP Leeds; peering left, despite the low lighting he could see a path at the other end, following the grounds of the cemetery.

Gardener approached the PC guarding the scene. He was tall and slim, with a young face that had yet to really see some action; there were no worry lines. Over his uniform he had a padded jacket, and he wore fingerless gloves. Gardener doubted they were much use with the weather as it was at the moment.

"PC Johnson, sir," said the young officer.

Gardener and Reilly introduced themselves and the SIO asked him what he knew.

"We had a call into the station sometime around nine. The victim inside was found by a neighbour, a lady called Ann Franklin. She spotted two men running away and the front door open. She knocked and called out. There was no answer. She went inside and found the body and almost passed out. She called us, I came out, saw that, and then called you."

Gardener was amused by the terminology; he saw '*that*'.

"Did she know the victim?" asked Gardener.

"She reckons it's a bloke called Sutton. He's well known around these parts."

"For what?"

"Drugs, a bit of violence; anything that brings in money, really."

Gardener turned to his partner. "Someone's a step ahead of us, Sean."

"He is dead, I take it?" Gardener asked the young PC.

"No doubt, sir."

"She saw two men running away?" asked Gardener.

Johnson nodded. "Yes, sir."

"I wonder what that was all about."

"Drug deal?" said Reilly. "Possible burglary, but if they were running away, could *they* have found him dead?"

"Possibly," said Gardener. He turned to Johnson. "Where does Mrs Franklin live?"

"Further down the street," said Johnson. "Number twenty-six."

"Where is she now?"

"At home with a cup of tea and another constable, he's taking a statement."

"Did she get a good view of the two that were running away?"

"No, sir. She said she was on her way to bingo. When she was about twenty feet away from this house, these two men came tearing out and ran off that way." Johnson turned and pointed to the hall. "By the time she reached the house, they had disappeared around the corner."

"And she didn't know them?" asked Reilly.

"No, too dark, too much distance."

Gardener and Reilly suited and booted and decided to check out the scene.

Walking down the path, they stepped inside, into a narrow, musty-smelling hallway – with peeling paper and rising damp – which had stairs on the left. The paper on the walls was ancient and stained, with cleaner patches, and the walls were chipped, as if paintings had been put up at one time, but there were none now. Gardener glanced upwards. The socket had no bulb, which made things even more dingy.

The carpet was threadbare, also stained, as if no one ever wiped their feet. But if Sutton *was* what people claimed, he wouldn't have cared. Down the hall and past the stairs, Gardener noticed a kitchen. On his right was a door leading into a sparsely furnished living room that smelled as bad as the rest of the house.

There were two armchairs, one facing a TV. The floor was wooden. Once again, the walls had peeling, faded paper, with no pictures up. A glass cabinet stood along one wall and the TV on a stand was perched in the corner nearest the outside.

Roy Sutton was slumped on a metal-framed kitchen chair in his living room. The curtains at the window had been drawn, and a small lamp next to the TV lit the room, but not very well.

The pair of them moved slowly toward Sutton. His arms were tied together behind his back with what appeared to be a similar length of rope that had been used on his half-brother. The hands were also missing.

As with Steven, he had also been attacked with a nail gun. And once again, the twelve nails formed a circular pattern. However, that was where the similarity ended.

"Well, this is different," said Reilly.

Gardener bent down, peering more closely. Roy Sutton did not have two fingers nailed to his chest, pointing to two different numbers. He had four; and those four pointed to three different nails. If the nails represented a clock, the first was pointing toward the number one. Two were pointing at the number seven, and the fourth at the number nine.

"What the hell is this about?" said Reilly.

"A different set of numbers, Sean. What's he trying to tell us now?"

Gardener stepped around the corpse. Similar to the scene in Beeston, Roy Sutton was dressed only in a pair of soiled black underpants, obviously due to his high level of fear. There were other cuts and bruises on the body, with trails of blood running downwards, all of which indicated a level of torture. His throat had also been cut.

Back around the front of the body, Gardener leaned in and scanned the chest, locating the two puncture marks of the Taser, which he pointed out to Reilly.

"Same MO, same man," said his partner.

"Or men," said Gardener, thinking about the two that had been seen running away.

"It's possible there's more than one," said Reilly. "Neither of the Suttons are small men, are they? And if you think about what's been done, maybe it does take more than one."

"Maybe," said Gardener. "Unless whoever is doing this is a pretty big lad himself. After all, he has the Taser to stun, so it probably doesn't matter about the size of the victim."

"The scene is pretty identical, so I think it's safe to assume it's the same killer," said Reilly. "But what about the numbers?"

"I wondered about that," said Gardener. "Why two pointing to seven?"

"Is it a code?" asked Reilly. "We have two at seven, one at one, and one at nine."

"If it *is* a code, it could be anything," said Gardener. "A safe, a padlock. Maybe it's not a code for a lock or a safe, maybe it's a date for when something happened."

Reilly stared on for a minute or so. "If it's a date, there are a few choices – anything from 1779 to 1977."

"God help us if it's the earliest one," said Gardener, studying the rest of the room. He stepped out and into the kitchen, which was a bigger mess than the rooms in the house he'd so far seen. Pots and pans all over the place, stacked high; greasy takeaway cartons. Carrier bags piled up in one corner, dirty washing in another, although he saw no washing machine.

Gardener opened the fridge. There was very little, aside from a mouldy piece of cheese, and the remains of a bottle of milk that resembled the cheese, and a rancid onion. He shut the door quickly because of the smell, it was actually worse than the house.

As he stepped back into the living room, his partner had some envelopes in his hand.

"They're all addressed to Roy Sutton. One looks like a final demand, not sure about the others."

"I think we're done for now, Sean. The similarities between the two murders are far too much to discount a link. We know it's Roy Sutton. We have to work on the assumption that it's the same killer, or at least linked killers, so it's time to call the team."

Chapter Twenty

There might not have been anyone there when Gardener and Reilly had pulled up, but the scene outside was now somewhat different. Crowds had gathered; eight people stood near the hall, with a few more in the opposite direction, further down the street; some were even standing in the cemetery. Most were smoking, huddled inside jackets; despite the cold, they were going to miss nothing. Gardener couldn't imagine scores of police cars being something new to the street.

His own team had arrived, as well as the SOCOs in two vans, an ambulance, and the Home Office pathologist.

Though Gardener was keen to talk to the team, he was also eager to have the SOCOs start their tasks, and for Fitz to assess the body in the living room; he didn't think that would take long.

Once he'd signed the scene over, he gathered the team together and explained exactly what he and Reilly had found. Given the time of night, and the similarities to the scene in Beeston, he wanted to move things along as fast as he could.

"We're pretty sure the victim is Roy Sutton. The neighbour who found him said as much. It's likely there is little or no family, so most of what we find out will hopefully be through the other neighbours."

"I doubt he has many friends," said Reilly, "but you never know."

"The neighbour who found him," asked Bob Anderson, "where does she live?"

"Number twenty-six," said Gardener. "A constable is in there with her so we can avoid that one for now. Sean and I will talk to her as soon as we've finished here."

"We need to find out where he works," said Reilly. "Assuming he actually does, but from what we've heard, it's doubtful."

"Speak to any colleagues and try to ascertain last known movements," said Gardener. "The lady at twenty-six is called Ann Franklin. Drugs have been mentioned. If he *is* mixed up in drugs, I can't imagine anyone will want to speak to us."

"*Is* it a drug-related murder?" asked Colin Sharp.

"You might be forgiven for thinking that," said Gardener. "But we don't think so, we certainly haven't found anything to support that with Steven Sutton."

"The MO is identical to the scene in Beeston," said Reilly, "but with different numbers."

"*Different* numbers?" asked Rawson.

"Which ones?" asked Thornton.

"This time there are four fingers pointing to three different numbers."

"That doesn't add up," said Gates.

"I thought you could count better than that, sir," added Longstaff.

Gardener smiled, and explained the layout of the fingers, explaining that one of those pointing to the number seven was inside the circle, whilst the other was outside.

"Christ," said Gates. "We'd better see what our graph says about that."

"Judging by what the graph said last time," said Gardener. "I don't think it was much help. It's possible we need to concentrate on the meaning of the numbers, as opposed to what they say about the person."

"You're probably right," said Longstaff.

"But by all means see it through, something might stand out," added Gardener. "House-to-house will be important. Some of the people may have been out at the bingo, like Ann Franklin was intending, so maybe we can find out where that was being held; and if it was local, find out everyone who was there and see if we can speak to them, see what they might have seen, especially the people who live down this street."

"I know this place is pretty desolate, but there must be some pubs around here," said Reilly, "not to mention some kind of local shops that we can try when we have a photo."

"That's a point, Sean," said Gardener. "Maybe the SOCOs can pay attention to that, see if there is a photo lying around somewhere. Even the nastiest of people have a photo that means something to them. Hopefully we can use that a little further afield."

"I wonder if he's known in Armley?" asked Rawson, staring at the jail.

"Probably," said Gardener. "I wouldn't be surprised if he's done a stretch. Maybe we should have checked our DNA database for Roy Sutton before now."

"To be fair, sir," said Gates. "It's not as if we had a lot to go on. We only found out he was called Roy last night."

"Did anyone pay a visit here today?" asked Gardener.

"Check with Paul Benson when he comes, sir," said Longstaff. "I'm sure he mentioned something but he didn't find anyone at home."

Gardener nodded. "Check if there is any CCTV in the area. I can't see any, but that doesn't mean it's not here. Some of the houses may have hidden cameras, there're enough bars up at the windows and doors."

Gardener blew into his hands before continuing. "I'll get the SOCOs to check any electronic equipment. A phone will be a certainty, but whether or not he has a computer, or an iPad, I'm not sure."

"We didn't see any," said Reilly.

"Maybe we can cross-check his and Steven Sutton's phone," said Gardener. "It's a faint possibility, but there could be contacts who appear on both."

Longstaff nodded, indicating she was onto it.

"Was a Taser used?" asked Rawson.

Gardener nodded.

"So we still can't rule out an officer."

"No," said Gardener. "It might be one of ours whose son or daughter has suffered at the hands of a drug dealer."

Gardener was keen to move away from that subject and continue with issuing tasks; the politics if an officer was involved would be off the scale.

"Once we can establish last known movements, it'll be the same old story, we'll have more people to interview: shops, pubs, takeaways. Doubt you'll strike lucky at the shops, judging by what we've seen in the fridge."

"It looks like he kept the takeaways in business," added Reilly.

"From what we've seen," said Gardener, "we really believe the crimes are connected. Now we need to find a reason."

The SIO glanced at his watch. "It's late and it won't be easy. Get what we can for tonight, and tomorrow, concentrate on widening the search. I'd like us all back in the incident room within twenty-four hours. Someone out there is ahead of us, and we need to know why. Once the public hear about this one, we'll come in for a rough time. It will be all about police protection, or the lack of it."

Suddenly, Steve Fenton came out of the house and down the steps, calling Gardener.

"There is something we'd like you to see, sir."

"What is it?" asked Gardener.

"The cellar door is locked and there are no keys that we can find. We'd like you to give it the once over before breaking it down – with your permission, of course."

Chapter Twenty-one

Having already disposed of one set of scene suits, Gardener and Reilly now found themselves in fresh ones.

Inside the house, Steve Fenton led them past the living room, towards the kitchen, to the cupboard door under the stairs.

But it wasn't a cupboard.

Gardener glanced inside and saw a set of twisting concrete steps leading down in the direction of the front of the house. Fenton descended first. At the bottom, the room was bigger than Gardener had imagined. It was roughly eight feet by ten, with bare concrete walls, and one window that he'd noticed from the outside. The only light came from a single bulb in a socket in the ceiling, but no shade.

Glancing around, Gardener noticed a few wooden boxes, some sealed, some open – those that were, had bags of white powder inside. Cobwebs had been spun in each of the corners.

Three SOCOs were in the room; one of them faced a door in the back wall, which obviously led to another room that ran under the house somewhere.

Gardener approached the door, which, at some point had been painted blue but had now faded. It was a solid wooden door with a keyhole on the right, and a wrought-iron handle above that.

He turned to Fenton. "You say you haven't found a key?"

"No, but we'd probably have to scour the house to do so, and there might be something important in there that you need to know about, sooner rather than later."

Gardener turned back, closely studying the door and the frame, wondering how long it had been closed, or undisturbed. It was a good fit, he couldn't see any gaps, nor could he feel a draught of any kind. He wasn't too sure but he thought he could see a thin line of sealant around the edges, indicating the fact that it had once been shut and never opened. How long ago was that? he wondered.

"What do you think, Sean?"

His partner peered around the room and then at the door and the frame. "I'd say it's been like this for a while. Place isn't really damp, there's quite a bit of dust around but it's not really been disturbed."

"The door *is* locked, I take it?" Gardener asked Fenton. The SOCO nodded.

"Maybe there's nothing in there," said Reilly. "But if that's the case, why keep it locked?"

"Precisely," said Gardener. He knocked on the door and called out but there was no response; not that he expected one, but you never knew.

He turned and asked one of the SOCOs to go upstairs and ask Fitz to come down.

Once the pathologist had joined them, Gardener explained the situation and had decided that breaking the door down was their only option. They had to see what, if anything, was in the locked room. It could be someone in need of medical attention.

Everyone pulled their masks closer to the faces and Gardener gave the order. Two of the SOCOs had already been outside to one of the vans, returning with enough equipment to do the job quickly.

Two or three pounding blows, the wood cracked and splintered and the lock relented. The door didn't actually open but more or less fell backwards as the top hinge gave way and the one on the frame flew across the room.

Gardener stared on, unable to believe what he was seeing.

"Well that's not something you see every day," said Reilly.

"No," said Fenton. "Most people don't keep a coffin kicking around."

"This just gets better," said Gardener.

"It's an odd thing to buy without a funeral plan," said Fitz.

"Why would you?" asked Gardener.

"What the hell's gone on here?" asked one of the SOCOs.

"Do you think there's someone in it?" asked another.

"I wonder if the neighbours knew?" asked the first.

"Maybe they've all got one."

Gardener stepped into the room for a closer examination. "It isn't an ordinary coffin."

"What do you mean?" asked Reilly.

Fitz joined them. "Coffins do have a certain style that has changed over the years. The size, shape and type of handles could well give you a date within a few decades. Depending on the lining inside you might also be able to date the material."

"Agreed," said Gardener. "But this is home-made. Look at the wood, it's smooth but it looks like floorboard to me – tongue and groove. I'll grant you it's had a coat of lacquer but not recently. The lid isn't held on with screws, or those fancy domed nuts, it's been hammered down with nails."

"There's a difference between stage and prop coffins and real ones," said Fitz, "which are much more sturdy. I'll grant you, this is bit cumbersome. A lot of the manufacturers actually put their maker's mark inside, but like you said, this isn't a proper coffin."

Gardener stood up. "It could be full of drugs. On the other hand, there could be something or someone in there, pertinent to our investigation. We won't know until we open it."

Gardener gave the order.

Chapter Twenty-two

"That's definitely what you'd expect to see in a coffin," said Reilly.

Once the dust had settled, Gardener leaned forward and peered in. The tongue-and-groove floorboarding was a little more prominent on the inside because there was no lining. The wood was of an age that Gardener wouldn't like to guess at, but it didn't resemble modern-day floorboard, backing up the fact that they were staring at an old, undisturbed scene.

Gardener turned. "We now need to treat this as a new crime scene."

He turned back to view the skeleton. Although it was complete, he could not see everything, as some of the clothing remained, though it was now rags.

"Whoever it is," said Reilly, "they were dead when they went in there. The inside of the lid is smooth, no bloodstains."

Gardener glanced at the hands. True enough, the nails were fine, no ragged edges. The right hand was clenched, as if it had arthritis. As for the rest of it, the bones were a strange sort of browny orange colour; the teeth were intact and appeared to be in good condition. Whoever had put the body in here had placed it deliberately, because it was laid out straight, with the arms across the chest cavity. The height clearly said it was an adult.

"Who the hell is this?" asked one of the SOCOs.

"More to the point," said Steve Fenton, "how long has it been in there?"

"I think it's fair to assume," said Gardener, "that's it's been in here as long as the basement door has been sealed, and judging by the dust and what little decor there is, that's quite a while."

"What are the teeth like?" Fitz asked.

"They look fine to me," said Gardener, leaning closer in. "I can't see any dental work, modern or otherwise, but I'm sure you'll be able to tell us more."

"If the teeth are good," replied Fitz, "we might able to ID whoever it is."

"Be a bit of a minefield," said Gardener. "Who is this person? Are they local, or even English?"

"I never said it would be easy," replied Fitz. "It would be a very arduous task for two of your team."

Gardener figured he knew which two. "I realize that, but how much time do we have before the killer strikes again?"

"Is there anyone else in the Sutton family?" asked Reilly.

"There is if you count Kerry," said Gardener.

"There might also be parents left," said Reilly. "We haven't found out yet, have we?"

Gardener stood up. "I'd love to know how long it's been here, and what connection – if any – it has to what we're investigating."

"I'm sticking my neck out here," said Reilly, "but I can't imagine it has nothing to do with our case."

"We could do to see the deeds for the house," said Gardener. "Does Roy Sutton own it, or is it rented? If it's rented, who is the landlord? If he owns it, how long has he been here?"

"With Roy Sutton in his current condition," said Reilly, "that won't help us a great deal."

Gardener nodded. "You're right there, Sean. What a nightmare."

"You can certainly carbon-date the wood for the coffin," said Fitz.

Gardener turned to face him. "We need an action on both, really; the coffin and the skeleton need dating. It would be interesting to see if the dates are similar, or widely different."

Fitz knelt down next to the coffin. "You can also carbon-date bone. And you can tell a lot from how a broken bone has repaired."

"Does the skeleton have any?" asked Gardener.

Fitz paid closer attention, very carefully moving the limbs around. He then leaned in a little closer. "I think there is something in the right hand but I don't want to disturb it until we have it on the table."

After another minute, he said. "I can see what I think would've been bruising around the body."

"How the hell does he do that?" asked Reilly. "It's a skeleton, nothing more than bones, yet he can tell there was bruising."

"You know what he's like," said Gardener. "He has very strange hobbies."

Fitz continued, ignoring them. "We definitely have a broken rib, and what looks like a broken arm that has not been set."

"So the person in here could have been assaulted, or ended up in a fight?" asked Gardener.

"Either of which were nasty," said Fitz.

"I wonder what the other bloke looks like," said Reilly.

"There is also some bruising about the head," said Fitz. "I'm not sure, but it might be a fractured skull."

"Is it possible that would have caused their death?" asked Gardener.

"Very," replied Fitz.

"Is it male or female?" asked Steve Fenton.

Fitz checked around. "Male."

"Can you tell how old he might have been?" asked Reilly.

"Not really," said Fitz. "Not without a proper examination, but at a rough guess I would say between thirty and forty."

"But we're still no better off," said Gardener. "We still have no idea how long he's been in there."

Reilly leaned in. "I don't suppose there is any newspaper under the body, is there?"

Fitz said it was a good point and did his best to check without disturbing the skeleton too much. "Can't see anything."

"That would have been far too easy," said Gardener.

"You can always live in hope," said Reilly.

"I have a number of friends in the trade who might be able to help with the age. They're all old, like me," said

Fitz, glancing at Reilly. "I thought I'd get that in before you did."

"You're fantasizing now," said Reilly. "They can't possibly be as old as you."

Fitz grimaced. "My point is it would be easy enough to have an old undertaker, or a historian to take look at some photos that might help."

"It's worth a try," said Gardener. "The trouble here is we don't know how much manpower and time we need to set aside for this scene. It might have absolutely nothing to do with us."

"We *do* have to find out," said Reilly. "However long it takes."

Gardener nodded. "You also made a good point, why would it be down here if it *wasn't* anything to do with us?"

"The only chance we have," said Fitz, "is to carbon-date everything, even the makeshift coffin."

"Does that take long?" asked Gardener.

"Depends on how much money you have."

"As bad as that?" asked Gardener.

"You mean it depends on how much money Briggs has," said Reilly.

"I've seen DNA samples turned around in twenty-four hours for a searchable database result," said Fitz.

"How much was that?" asked Gardener.

"About fifty thousand," replied Fitz, sheepishly.

"Jaysus," said Reilly.

"But in fairness, the case was similar to this one," said Fitz. "A double murder with the suspect still at large. Carbon-dating is no different. Just a bunch of geeks – sorry – professionals, in a lab who are willing to work weekends, long hours, or bank holidays if you have very deep pockets."

Gardener thought about that. "Well, it is a major line of inquiry, isn't it?" As he said it, he was staring at Reilly.

"Very much so," came the reply.

"Okay," said Gardener. "No matter what the cost, I would like it fast-tracked. Let's say, twenty-four hours."

"Naturally," replied Fitz. "But then it won't be me who's taken out at dawn and shot."

Chapter Twenty-three

The following morning was a cold one. An overnight snowfall had left a fine layer that resembled icing sugar covering the pathways in the market town of Bramfield, but nothing serious. It wasn't settling.

Alan Browne entered his shop from the back room and switched on the heating. Didn't do to leave it on overnight, but he wished he had. He clicked the switch for the radio and the room filled with the sounds of light classical music. Crossing the floor he reached the door, unlocked it, and turned the sign from "closed" to "open".

Before he'd even made it back to the counter, the door opened. Browne wished he hadn't bothered unlocking it now. He liked to settle in properly with a cup of tea, a bacon sandwich, and a newspaper before he dealt with anything as fickle as the public.

But Browne was in luck. It was only Elvis who had stepped in, and he had the most welcoming little white sandwich bags with him.

"Well-done bacon with a bit of brown sauce, just how you like it," he said. "Freshly cooked from that white van behind the police station."

"You are a lifesaver," said the jeweller. "You're early."

"Just covering a job in the town."

"I'll make the tea," said Browne.

When he returned, Elvis was halfway through his sandwich, staring at the magazines littering the counter. "You been burgled, Alan?"

"What?" He glanced at the counter. "Oh, no – been doing some research."

"On what?" Elvis slurped his tea.

"Let me finish this, and I'll tell you something very interesting."

Despite the fact that Elvis had only been halfway through his butty, Alan Browne ingested his so fast that he finished ahead of the journalist.

"Right," said Browne, sorting through the literature, half of which he slid to one side.

"Here it is."

Elvis finished his sandwich, screwed up the paper bag and put it in his pocket, before leaning in closer. "These are old, aren't they?"

Browne glanced at Elvis. "Probably older than you, my friend. Look at this one, 1958. Came out when that chubby Cliff Richard was in the charts with his first record."

"Chubby?" questioned Elvis.

"He *was* back then. At least according to a woman in the snug in *Coronation Street*. Anyway," said Browne, "this is the most interesting one." He slid the copy of the magazine toward Elvis.

"Hey, wait a minute. Isn't that the watch that that bloke brought in the other day, acting all cagey?"

"Certainly is."

Browne pointed out that given that there was only one in existence, he knew very well it had to be the genuine article.

"How do you know it's the only one?" asked Elvis.

"Trust me," replied Browne. "I've been in this game a long time, seen a lot of things, but I've never seen that before – in the flesh, so to speak."

"You sound like you know something about it."

"Oh, I do, my friend. I know a lot about that watch."

Elvis glanced at him, eyes narrowed. "Are you absolutely sure? You know for a fact that it's *that* watch, the one-off?"

"Like I said." Browne moved back a little. "I might not have had it in my hands very long but I clocked everything I needed to know. It had a high jewel count; screw-set jewels, and a micrometer regulator."

"What's one of them?"

"Micrometer regulators were used on higher-quality movements, allowing the owner or a jeweller to make precision adjustments to the oscillation rate of the balance wheel, changing the speed of the watch. It also had a double-sunk dial. No, my friend, that watch was one of the highest quality ever made, and it was done so right here."

"In Bramfield?"

"Not quite, in Leeds."

"By who?"

"It was something to do with William Potts," said Browne, finishing his tea. "William Potts was born in 1809. He was an apprentice to Samuel Thompson, a Darlington clockmaker. When he was twenty-four, Potts moved to Pudsey, near Leeds, to set up his own business. Initially, he was concerned with domestic timepieces. Eventually, he expanded into the manufacture and repair of public clocks.

"He moved the business to Guildford Street in Leeds in 1862, and then opened a workshop for public clocks in nearby Cookridge Street. That was a good move, with large numbers of public clocks being installed both at home and abroad.

"Apparently, there's even one in the station at Bursley Bridge. Queen Victoria granted the company a Royal Warrant in 1897."

"So this watch was made in the 1800s?" asked Elvis.

"No, it's not that old." Browne grabbed the magazine and feverishly read the text for a reminder. "He had sons, who also had sons. This watch was made by a close family relative. His name was Reginald Potts – now deceased. Given his background, the watch was made of the highest quality, using the latest technology available at the time and, in some respects, well ahead of its time. It bore a resemblance to something called the Gotham Gunmetal Railroad Pocket Watch, but it was sufficiently different."

"So how did he come to make it?" asked Elvis. "And why?"

"Rumour has it that Reginald had been approached by the Railway Commission in 1964. He was summoned to make a one-off watch for the railway superintendent of the time. Five months it took him; had to be ready in time for his fiftieth birthday."

"Five months?"

"Well, you have to remember the time period, you couldn't pick things up as easily as you can now. Most of the components had to be sourced from all over the UK and delivered by rail. Anyway, turns out this superintendent didn't have it very long. He died; some even say he was killed."

Elvis had his notepad at the ready. "How?"

"Not sure," said Browne. "An accident involving the railway. The watch was reported stolen, never seen again. And I tend to think that's true, because until the other day, I had never seen it, despite knowing so much about it."

Browne picked up the magazine. "I remembered seeing this publication; knew I still had it." Browne leaned in forward but instead of shouting he had lowered his voice, as if his own shop was bugged. "I would have killed for this watch."

"How much did it cost to make it?"

"I've no idea," replied Browne.

"Do you know what it's worth now?"

"No." Browne leaned back. "There's something dodgy afoot here. You mark my words. No good will come of this."

"Maybe you should call the police, Alan," said Elvis.

Chapter Twenty-four

Given that Roy Sutton's murder had not started being investigated until ten o'clock in the evening, twenty-four hours for a result from DNA and carbon dating was asking a lot. But Fitz had done the next best thing when he'd called Gardener and Reilly at ten in the morning, thirty-six hours later.

They were in his office within the hour. Reilly had poured three coffees. Fitz had even removed a packet of chocolate digestives from his desk drawer, to save the Irishman looting the stock in his filing cabinet.

"I gather you have something for us," said Gardener.

"Something interesting, you could say," replied Fitz, sipping his coffee. "I'm not sure how relevant it might be, or whether it's going to help."

Gardener didn't like the sound of that. He suddenly saw lots of money disappearing into a sinkhole, and his invitation to the firing squad moving ever closer.

"The post-mortem on Roy Sutton revealed pretty much the same results as it did for Steven Sutton," said Fitz, "except for the fact that he was coked up. He had taken amphetamines sometime during the day, possibly late evening. His throat had been cut with a smooth blade by someone who is right-handed, as it was with his half-brother. But there was little doubt in my mind that we were looking for the same killer because of the nails."

"Was it the same pattern?" asked Gardener. "The last nail doing the damage?"

"I'd say so," said Fitz. "Straight through the heart."

"What is this man looking for?" asked Gardener. "He's now tortured and killed two people from the same family. What is he after?"

"Whatever it is," said Fitz, "it doesn't sound like they have it, or had it."

"Steven Sutton certainly didn't have it," said Reilly. "Otherwise, why torture and kill his half-brother?"

"So, whatever it is," said Gardener, "Roy Sutton *might* have had it, and the killer's walked away with it."

"And if he hasn't?" said Reilly.

"Then someone else in that family could be in trouble," said Gardener. "Someone we haven't yet identified."

"I can only think of Kerry," said Reilly.

"Possibly," said Gardener. "Maybe the only reason she escaped was because she was on holiday at the time."

"Have you discovered anything more from the scenes?" asked Fitz.

"Not really," said Gardener. "We've learned a number of things we didn't know, but nothing that really moves us forward. We still don't know a lot about the nail gun that's been used; only that it's old, and likely no longer in production anymore."

"Judging by what we saw in the basement in Armley," said Reilly, "I'd say the nail gun could be as old as that scene."

Gardener updated Fitz on what they knew about the nail gun so far. Even he was beginning to wonder how significant it really was but it could be the key to everything.

"What can you tell us about the skeleton?" Gardener then asked Fitz.

"That *was* interesting," said Fitz. "We've had some results back and we've managed to put an age to it. The teeth revealed a couple of fillings but they were not modern. Two of the ribs were broken, as was the right arm. As I said in the basement, the arm was broken but never reset. And there was definitely a fracture of the skull."

"And in your opinion, he'd been nowhere near a hospital?" asked Reilly.

Fitz shook his head. "None of the bones had been set professionally. I've a good mind to think they were broken before he died, or possibly as a result of."

"It sounds like he'd been involved in a fight of some sort," said Gardener, "that he neither won nor walked away from."

"Maybe," said Fitz.

"How the hell did he end up in a makeshift coffin in a cellar in Armley?" asked Reilly.

"That's down to you two," said Fitz, "assuming there is a connection to your murder case."

"This is bizarre," said Gardener. "What age did you come up with?"

"Well, I said between thirty and forty. The lab people who did the carbon dating had it between the ages of thirty and thirty-two, so I wasn't far out."

"What about the coffin?" asked Reilly.

"The wood appears to be older than the body. That's nearer fifty."

"That suggests that whatever took place, did so sometime in the seventies," said Gardener.

Fitz nodded. "Looks like that."

"So someone's killed this bloke, and then built a coffin and put him in it? Why?" asked Reilly.

"To avoid detection?" offered Gardener.

"But if there were no witnesses, why would you need to put the body in a coffin and keep it for the rest of your life, which is what it sounds like?" said Reilly.

"I agree with what you're saying, Sean," said Gardener, "but there are some strange people out there. If it's been there since the seventies, it's going to take a lot of work to pin this one down. It has to be someone's cold case, and it predates HOLMES."

"Did it even happen locally?" asked Reilly. "It could have happened anywhere. Maybe the person who owned the house at the time had brought it from somewhere else."

"That's really far-fetched," said Gardener.

"And this isn't?" asked Reilly.

He had a point.

"Well before we get carried away," said Fitz, "I found something even more interesting that might put you on the right track – and very possibly give you a local angle."

"Go on," said Gardener, hoping for a miracle.

"Clutched in the right hand of the skeleton was a key. It looked like a safe key to me so I sent my assistant, Richard, into the town to ask if the locksmith could identify it. Apparently, the key was for a particular type of safe, specific to the railways."

"Could he identify it?" asked Gardener.

"Not immediately," replied Fitz. "He said he would look into it and get back to me."

"Still a needle in a haystack," said Gardener.

"But then we had a real stroke of luck," said Fitz. "You sometimes need it in this game. The DNA came back, and we had a hit from the database."

"Serious?" asked Gardener.

Fitz nodded. "If correct, the skeleton is the remains of a man called Jack Walker, whom it was believed went missing within the time frame that we're looking at. It took quite a while to speak to the right person but it *was* a cold case, as you mentioned. I realize things weren't as advanced as they are now, but it appears that they still had a brush and a comb from the man's house, sometime in the 1990s, when they were looking into his disappearance again, and they were able to test it."

"Really?" Gardener asked.

"Here's the interesting bit," said Fitz. "Jack Walker's last known address was a house in Bursley Bridge."

Chapter Twenty-five

It had been another long day, which wasn't unusual with murder investigations. Gardener had the team together, ready to inform them of what Fitz had told him.

Earlier, he had phoned Maurice Cragg in Bramfield, to see if he could enlighten them about a former resident by the name of Jack Walker; he told Cragg what he had discovered, that the man had lived in Bursley Bridge, and appeared to have gone missing sometime in the seventies.

Cragg admitted to knowing the name from somewhere, but that was all. He said he would investigate it thoroughly and call them back when he knew anything.

It took Gardener another thirty minutes to inform the team.

"The most important thing we have to do now is start looking at connections, because Roy and Steven Sutton were related," said Gardener. "So the big question we need to answer is, why have two members of the same family been killed?"

"And are there any more members of that family that we have yet to find?" asked Thornton.

"Didn't you mention the name Patrick Sutton in the last meeting?" asked Anderson. "Is he in the mix as well?"

"Very possibly," said Gardener, glancing at Gates and Longstaff.

Gates nodded. "We spent some time going through the housing records and the electoral roll, and the house does belong to Roy Sutton. It's not rented."

Gardener wasn't surprised, he couldn't imagine anyone wanting to rent the property they had seen – but people did.

"It was left to Roy when his father, Patrick, died in 1999," said Longstaff."

"And there we have an answer to your question, Bob," said Gardener. "How long had Patrick Sutton owned the house?"

Gates checked her notes. "He bought the place in 1969."

"That must mean," said Reilly, "that Patrick Sutton knew about the coffin and who was in it."

"Jack Walker went missing in the seventies," said Gardener. "We don't know the circumstances around that as yet, but we have the oracle on it in Bramfield so I'm very confident he will come up with something."

"Chances are no one found him because he was in the coffin in the cellar in Armley," offered Colin Sharp.

"Certainly looks like he was murdered," said Thornton. "Question is, who did it?"

"Was it Patrick Sutton?" asked Rawson.

"It depends if they knew each other," said Gardener. "Chances are, they did, otherwise why would one of them be dead in the other one's house, especially as he owned it during that time period?"

"We need to know a lot more about both of them," said Reilly. "But if they did know each other, did they end up fighting about something?"

"If they did," said Gates, "what the hell was it?"

"It had to be something serious if it ended with a murder and a cover-up," said Longstaff.

"Maybe it *was* enough to murder someone," said Rawson. "But was it Patrick Sutton who killed Jack Walker?"

"It might even be something as serious as a long-standing family feud between the Suttons and the Walkers?" offered Gardener.

"Feuds that are often serious to families," said Reilly, "are usually something and nothing to other people."

"Whatever it was," said Gardener, "I believe it is connected to our current cases, and it will be well worth our time digging a lot deeper."

"At least you haven't blown all that money for nothing, boss," said Rawson.

Gardener glanced at Rawson. "I should keep your voice down, Dave. I haven't heard anything from DCI Briggs yet, and we have no idea where he's lurking."

The team laughed.

Gardener continued. "Do we have any witness statements for Roy Sutton's last movements?"

"We have something from the night itself," said Edwards. "But it's a bit like it was in Beeston. We can't rely too much on the witness statements because no one wants to talk to the police. However" –he scanned his paperwork – "someone reckons they thought they saw some bloke arrive earlier in the evening. Dressed like a city gent."

"City gent?" said Gardener. "We've seen him again?"

Benson took over, providing the description that the witnesses in Beeston had given them of the man with the bowler hat, case and possibly a long coat or a cloak.

"That's twice he's been seen," said Gardener. "He's definitely a common link. Did anyone see *how* he arrived?"

The answer was negative. The only witness who saw him was a lady called Mary Stuart.

"What time was that?"

"She thinks it was between half six and seven," said Edwards. "She was on her way to bingo."

"She pretty much gave the same description as our dog walker in Beeston," said Benson, "passing him on Hall Lane, which is pretty much around the corner. It was cold and she had her head down and didn't realize she'd passed anyone until he coughed as he went past."

"According to this report," said Rawson, with the sheet of paper in his hand, "a bloke called Rodney Cooke thought he had seen the man going into the house, carrying his bag."

"What time was this?" asked Gardener.

"Similar time, possibly nearer seven."

"Where does Rodney live?" asked Reilly.

"Other end of the street, but he was walking toward Sutton's house, still quite some distance away."

"He wasn't going to bingo as well, was he?" asked Reilly.

"No, the pub. A place called The Executioner's Arms."

"The what?" asked Gardener.

Rawson repeated the name.

"Sounds a lovely place," said Reilly.

"The last known sighting we can pin it down to," said Sharp, "is a neighbour called Paula Priestley who also lives further down the street. She said she saw Roy Sutton filling one of his bins at around six o'clock. She passed by the house, also on her way to the SPAR shop on Armley Road to buy some milk. She said hello, all he did was turn, glance at her and grunt."

"And she never mentioned the man in the bowler?" asked Gardener.

"No," said Sharp.

"If these people are reliable, our man was not around at six, but he was between six-thirty and seven," said Gardener.

"There are also some statements here about Sutton's movements earlier in the day," said Thornton.

"What do we have?" asked Gardener.

"From what we've picked up," said Anderson, "Roy Sutton is mostly a loner, who does not like people knowing his business, so he does not mix with many people."

"Understandable," said Reilly, "judging the state of the house."

"Most of his drug deals are done on street corners," said Thornton. "Sometimes close to where he lives, other times out of town. He's often dealing around the back of the prison, which is where most people have spotted him."

"He was spotted early in the morning behind the prison," said Anderson. "A man called Cliff Poulton who lives a couple of streets away saw him dealing behind the prison and he believes he was with another local drug dealer by the name William Stones."

"Later in the day he was in Starbucks on Canal Street with a coffee and a plateful of crap."

"Who saw him?" asked Gardener.

"One of the counter staff said she served him and another well-known dealer by the name of Pete Roberts, also known to the police."

Gardener delved into the witness statements he had in front of him from the previous night. "We have something here from a woman who saw two people running away from the house around the time the man in the bowler was spotted. Do we have names yet?"

"No, sir," said Edwards.

"So it could be these two. Either way, drag them in and make them talk."

Pens hit notepads.

Sharp added that he had another statement. "Later in the day, the time confirmed as four-thirty, Angie Potter who works in the SPAR shop at the Euro Garage on Armley Road said she had served him with groceries, if that's what you could call it; mostly it was ding meals and garbage, like sausage rolls and doughnuts. She said he was often in, buying the same stuff. Most times he looked shocking – lank long hair, greasy, sticking to his skin, pallid expression, pale skin, bloodshot eyes and, in the last few months, he had put on a fair bit of weight."

"So, from everything we've heard he was alive and dealing earlier in the day. In the shop at four-thirty, and putting out the rubbish around six," said Gardener. "After that, nothing. There's a fair bit going on there but I think we need to scour the area again and try to gain something more from the people who live there. The doctor being the most interesting link we have."

"There might be more in the witness statements yet," said Reilly. "See if we can get the operational support officers on to it."

"Good idea, Sean," noting it on the whiteboard. He felt they were heading in the right direction, and he really wanted to know a little more about the man dressed like a city gent.

Turning back, he asked if anything more had been found on the nail gun.

Anderson nodded. "We know what it is."

"Really?" asked Gardener.

"Yes," said Thornton. "One of the old timers from Jewson in Leeds recognized the shape of the nails. Reckoned they sold them by the pallet-load in the seventies."

"Here we go again," said Reilly. "The seventies."

"It's a powder-actuated nail gun," said Anderson. "Arguably, one of the most dangerous and abused pieces of construction kit ever sold."

"Was it that bad?" asked Gardener.

Thornton nodded. "Apparently. He thinks it's a Ramset J20 powder-actuated nail gun, discontinued now. Made in Australia. He showed us a picture, looks a bit like a bloody sawn-off shotgun. Here, in the UK, you needed a firearms licence."

"How the hell did they sell something like that?" asked Reilly.

"Here's the interesting bit," said Anderson. "Under some peculiar by-law of the Railways Act, it was not required for operators to hold a licence whilst working on railways covered by the Act."

"Railways," said Gardener, thinking about the safe that Fitz had mentioned.

"Yes," said Thornton. "It really was a heavy piece of kit, encased in a large heavy-gauge orange construction case with all sorts of essential components like a selection of nails that were tipped with bright conical-shaped orange plastic caps, and a number of powder discharge bullet-shaped capsules, all of which were colour-coded depending on their charge strength."

"How do you mean?" asked Gardener

"Well," said Anderson, reading from a sheet, "from weakest to strongest, it went as thus: Green was quite tame, good for nailing through two bits of timber, not particularly loud. Yellow, definitely more clout, good for nailing through timber into concrete, getting a little loud when fired. Red – feels like firing a quite powerful pistol, ear defenders definitely necessary especially within a confined space, can go through strips of quite thick metal as well as concrete.

"And then you get the serious one," said Thornton. "White, described as scary powerful with the ability to go through thick metal without much difficulty, very loud, rarely used as, in most cases, the nail will simply go straight through the material and out the other side."

"Christ," said Reilly.

"On the railway," said Anderson, "the gun was predominantly used to affix timber frames into concrete slabs."

"We have another link here, then," said Gardener. "The railway. And Steven Sutton worked for the railway, as did Aaron Butcher."

"And a lot of other people," said Reilly.

"But it was discontinued a long time ago," said Gardener. "What's the likelihood of National Rail in Leeds still having them and using them?"

"Not very high, I would have thought," said Sharp. "If they were discontinued, you probably can't get the nails, or any parts for them."

"True," said Gardener. "But whilst they might not be able to use them, they could still have one."

"So could any other railway," said Reilly.

"Well that's the other problem," said Anderson. "All we have to do now is find out how many were sold, and to who."

"But at least we have the name of a distributor down near London," said Thornton. "Raptor Supplies in Hounslow, Middlesex. They may be able to help."

Gardener nodded. "Great work, lads, keep going with it."

After updating the board with the actions, he asked Sharp and Rawson if there was any news on the rope, or ropes.

"This is becoming really interesting," said Sharp.

"What is?" asked Gardener.

"Why is everything we're uncovering connected to the railways?" asked Rawson.

"I didn't know it was," said Gardener, "until today. Are you going to tell me that you found out something about the rope that is connected?"

"You could say that," replied Sharp. "Those forensic boys know what they're doing. Apart from the fact that the rope bore a number of stains, one of them being diesel, the important stain they identified was a particular brand of grease."

"Which is?" asked Gardener.

"It's called Klüber Perfluoropolyether Grease, otherwise known as Klübertemp GR RT 15," said Rawson, smiling from ear to ear as though he was really proud of himself.

"What the hell is that?" asked Reilly.

"It's a high-temperature, high-performance grease," said Sharp, "which is particularly resistant to oxidation and to chemical agents, and compatible with all types of material over a wide range of temperatures."

"It's fucking expensive," shouted Rawson. "About £225.00 a tube and there's only a hundred grams in it; but they buy it in 12.5kg tubs."

"Who do?" asked Gardener.

"The rail industry."

Gardener glanced at Reilly. "You couldn't write this, could you?"

"I don't know," said Reilly. "They always seem to manage it on the telly."

"What do they use it for?" Gardener asked Sharp.

"Everything, by the sound of it," replied Sharp, reading his notes. "Mainly for metal-metal combinations with medium-fast movements and high loads. It's suitable for the permanent lubrication of sliding guides with high forces and low sliding speeds. Long-life lubrication for assembly and maintenance."

"It's not *just* for railways," said Rawson, "but mostly for them. It's also used in the car industry on cylinder head bolts and guides, car mirror adjustment mechanisms. And this stuff is used as an emergency lubricant for parts of the rotor head of wind power plants."

"So it's widely used," said Gardener.

Rawson nodded.

"But you're saying it's mostly in the rail industry," said Anderson.

"So now we have Steven Sutton, a nail gun, a safe and a grease, all connected to the rail industry," said Reilly.

"The thing is," said Gardener, "this also puts another company, and two more people into the frame."

"Dawson's Engineering," said Reilly.

"And Steven Sutton's friends, Petter and Smith."

"Three if you count Aaron Butcher," added Gates.

Gardener turned his attention to Edwards and Benson. "Didn't you go and see these guys again today?"

"We did," said Benson. "We had quite a good chat with them in their tea breaks. They all appear to be very good friends and the pair of them are still devastated about what happened to Steven Sutton."

"Both have alibis," said Edwards. "Smith and Petter's wives have vouched for them. The thing is, Peter and Smith had a quick pint with Sutton in the club bar after the game, and the Petters and the Smiths all went out for a meal after that. We have the name of the restaurant and they confirmed the booking."

"What about Aaron Butcher?" asked Reilly.

"He also has an alibi," said Benson. "He was with his wife at the White Rose Centre, Christmas shopping, and they have the receipts to prove it."

"We also managed to speak to some of the people around the other areas close to the cemetery and the football ground for witness statements," said Edwards. "No one has reported seeing anything unusual."

Gardener was disappointed; back to square one, but they had learned something positive here. "Paul, Patrick, can you go back to Dawson's, see if they use this grease on anything, have them do a stock check and let me know the outcome?"

"Will do," said Edwards.

"We also managed a few minutes at the Leeds United football ground, sir," said Benson.

"Yes," said Edwards. "The steward we spoke to said he knew Steven Sutton, although he never actually saw him at the ground on Saturday because *he* wasn't working that shift, but he reckoned he would have been there."

"But he says their CCTV is absolutely state-of-the-art," added Benson.

"It has facial recognition," said Edwards.

"How the hell does that work?" asked Reilly. "With so many people?"

"Similar to an airport passport system," said Benson. "When you scan your ticket or your app through the turnstile, there is some kind of camera that clocks your face. If it's not you, it sounds an alarm."

"I still don't see how it works," said Longstaff. "What if someone buys you a ticket but they don't go themselves?"

"Appreciate the question," said Gardener, "but we might be going off-track a bit."

He turned back to Benson. "So we can check if Steven Sutton was in the ground?"

"Yes," said Benson. "And very probably outside, because it operates around the perimeter of the stadium."

"Any word?"

"Not yet. They're checking it for us and they're getting back to us."

"I've just had a thought," said Reilly.

"I thought I could smell burning," said Rawson.

"You'll smell burning in a minute, old son," said Reilly, "it'll be the rubber on the soles of your shoes as I'm chasing you down the corridor."

Even Gardener laughed. "Go on, Sean, enlighten us."

"Maybe the city gent is a Leeds United fan, if we're lucky, maybe we'll see him on the CCTV outside the ground."

"Never thought of that," said Benson.

"It's a good suggestion," said Gardener.

"I agree," said Gates, "but have you any idea how many will have been milling around the ground at that time?"

"Both before and after the game," added Longstaff.

"I never said it would be easy." Gardener smiled. "But it has to be worth looking at. And if this system is as good as they say, it's possible we might be able to pick him out, maybe even get lucky as he goes through the turnstile."

Benson nodded, taking notes. "It has to be worth a try."

Chapter Twenty-six

Gardener studied the whiteboard. "What does that leave us?"

He turned to face the team. "The big one – numbers. We need to discuss this and try to make some headway, or at least make a decision as to what we think it is."

"Before we get on to the numbers," said Gates. "We've been through all of Steven Sutton's electronic equipment and his social media accounts."

"There is nothing untoward anywhere," said Longstaff. "We cannot find a connection anywhere to his half-brother, or anyone called Walker."

"He's a member of the Leeds United supporters club," said Gates. "As well as various Leeds associated groups on Facebook."

"He pretty much spent the entire week, up until his death, talking to his friends and joining in any discussions on the upcoming match," said Longstaff.

Gates added that he only had a small amount of friends, and pretty much all of those paid tribute to what sounded like a really nice guy.

"Did we get in touch with any of them?" asked Gardener. "Perhaps to see how he was during that week?"

"Not so far, sir," said Longstaff. "If his posts were anything to go by, everything sounded fine in his life. He mentioned a couple of times that his wife and son were away for the week."

"So, whoever did this to him," said Anderson, "might be a part of one of those groups and they knew his family were away."

"Very possible," said Gates. Turning to Gardener, she said, "Would you like us to give it a go? Contact some of them and try to get a background on them and him?"

Gardener thought about it. "It's a lot of work, but it's not really something we can ignore. Bob has made a good point."

"It might be worth drafting in some of the operational support officers to chase up on it," said Reilly.

"Okay," said Gardener. "See what you can do."

"If we don't look into it and something comes of it," said Reilly, "we'll be dragged over hot coals."

"He's right," said Gardener. "I know we're talking about Steven, but what about Roy Sutton's phone – anything on there?"

Longstaff shook her head. "We have his phone. There are no contacts that appear on both his and Steven's phone. Roy's number is not on Steven's phone, and Steven's number is not on Roy's phone."

"Probably plenty of drug dealers on there, and people he sells to," said Gates.

"Might be worth a cross reference with narcotics," said Gardener, "see how many they know."

"Will do." Gates nodded.

"As for the numbers from the crime scenes," said Longstaff. "We put everything into the graph, and here's what we found."

She switched on the overhead projector and the following appeared on the screen.

123456789
ABCDEFGHI
JKLMNOPQR
STUVWXYZ

Example:

ROY SUTTON
967132265

22 19
4 1
4+1 = 5

"The only interesting thing is this," said Gates. "If you add up Roy and Sutton, they add up to twenty-two and nineteen, just as his brother's name did. As you can see, the number five now relates to both Suttons."

"But still doesn't tell us a great deal," said Reilly.

"No. We also added up the numbers that the fingers point to on the chest," said Longstaff. "Add one, nine, seven and seven together, it equals twenty-four. Two plus four equals six."

"And what does six give us?" asked Gardener.

"Nothing worth talking about," said Gates.

"I'm beginning to think all this numerology stuff is bollocks," said Reilly.

"I wish you'd stop mincing your words and just say it how it is," said Rawson, which brought a smile to the group.

"I think he's right, ladies," said Gardener. "I'm not sold on the numbers from the graph. Let's assume the nails represent a clock – if they don't, why are there twelve of them?"

"That has to be the most logical solution," said Sharp. "But then, there *are* twelve months in a year."

"It's possible," said Thornton. "But you don't have two Julys, so why two sevens?"

"Doesn't bode well, does it?" said Gardener. "It has to mean something else; we have to work out why the severed fingers are pointing at those numbers in particular. We've already discussed it representing the time and nothing stacks up."

"Does it have anything to do with house numbers?" asked Edwards.

"I wouldn't have thought so," said Gardener. "One of them lived at number forty, and the other lived at forty-two."

"Roy Sutton's could represent a four-digit code of some kind, possibly a padlock or a safe," offered Benson.

"After what we've heard today, Paul," said Gardener, "I'm inclined to go down that line. It seems far too much of a coincidence that the skeleton was clutching a key to a safe specifically used on the railways."

"I'll go with that," said Reilly. "Considering two lines of inquiry have led us down that path."

"I'll chase up Fitz in the morning," said Gardener, "see if anything has come of the key; he had his assistant take it into Leeds to be identified. If we can find out the manufacturer of the safe from the key, they might still be around, and might be able to point us to the local railways that bought them."

He wrote the action on the board.

Turning to face the team, he asked, "If it's nothing to do with any of those, however, then what else could they mean?"

"We've also given that some thought," said Gates, "and we think that the numbers belong to a two-part puzzle."

"How do you mean?" asked Gardener.

"We don't really think that the three and the five on Steven Sutton's chest meant anything on their own."

"But if you add the other four," said Longstaff. "There is a lot more to go at."

"Okay," said Gardener. "We have a total of six numbers." He wrote them down on the board: 1 3 5 7 7 9. "How many possible permutations are there on six numbers?"

Longstaff had her phone out. "Actually, it's not that bad. Only seven hundred and twenty."

"Only," said Gardener.

"To be honest," said Reilly. "I thought there would be more."

"It could still be anything," said Gardener. "Code for a safe, a padlock, a date in history…"

"Could it be the number of a train?" asked Reilly. "Is the killer a railway enthusiast, or a trainspotter?"

"A special train, maybe," said Gardener. "Whichever way we look at it, there is still a lot of work to be done to establish what the numbers mean."

"It's obviously something significant to the killer," said Sharp.

"Agreed," said Rawson. "But what?"

An air of trepidation filled the room, when Colin Sharp suddenly added something. "I wonder if all this fits with something I recently watched on the telly."

"What?" asked Rawson, his partner.

"My wife had gone to bed and I got into this documentary about Bursley Bridge and the railway, and a pocket watch. I was bloody staggered at how much this watch might possibly be worth, because it was the only one ever created by a famous clockmaker here in Leeds."

"Who?" asked Reilly.

"Somebody called Potts."

"When was this?" asked Gardener.

"He started making it in 1964," said Sharp. "Took him five months."

"Five months?" asked Thornton.

"Apparently," said Sharp. "But the watch disappeared in 1966, never to be seen again. Thing is, I'm pretty sure it was made special for a bloke who was a superintendent on the railway, for his birthday. And I'm also pretty bloody sure his name was Walker."

"How sure?" asked Gardener.

"I'd need to check," said Sharp.

"In that case, Colin, I'd like you to chase up the people who made the documentary, and the watch manufacturer. See if they can tell us anything."

Gardener glanced at the board, writing the actions down.

He turned to the team. "I think that about covers things for tonight. We have plenty to be going on with. Does anyone have anything else to add?"

The negative stares said they thought it was all over, until Steve Fenton burst thought the door.

"This looks interesting," said Gardener.

"It is," said Fenton. "We finally checked the contents of the shed in Steven Sutton's garden."

"Oh, yes," said Gardener. "What have you found?"

"We don't know if anything is missing, but Harry the Shard's prints are all over everything."

Chapter Twenty-seven

Phillip glanced at the kitchen wall clock. It was fast approaching eleven in the evening. He picked up his cup of tea and two digestives and took them through into the living room, placing them on the table in the alcove.

As he sat, he removed his glasses and rubbed his eyes. He'd had a tough day, but a very relaxing night in his cinema. Having arrived home a little after seven he'd had a quick shower, cooked himself a meal and then went into his den and chosen a film, one of his favourites.

Cash on Demand was a British black-and-white crime thriller from the Hammer studio in 1961, starring Peter Cushing and André Morell. He remembered reading in one of his collectible magazines that to optimise its £37,000 budget, the film used a limited number of sets: an interior street set, the trading area of a bank, the manager's office, the stairway between office and the vault, and the interior of the vault itself, all under one roof.

The premise was, two days before Christmas, a bogus insurance investigator brazenly conducts a con trick on a bank, largely through forcing the bank manager to believe that his family have been kidnapped. Feeling that he has no choice, the bank manager helps the investigator to steal £93,000 in banknotes from the bank vault, concealing his actions from the rest of the staff.

Phillip loved it because the tension was palpable and more than once he had been on the edge of his seat; no matter how many times he had watched it. The film was a real masterpiece and, he believed, filmed in real time.

Now however, it was time to go to work. He took a digestive, broke it in half, popped it into his mouth and savoured it. He washed it down with a sip of tea, contemplating what, if anything, he felt he could ask the Ouija board.

Since his last session, which wasn't that long ago, he'd spent most of his time trying to work out what the answers to his questions actually meant; when his father had claimed he was trapped.

Trapped where? Phillip had asked. Try as he might, there were no further replies that night.

Phillip had no idea what to make of that, as he ate the other half of the biscuit.

He didn't want to spend too long on the conundrum, but he couldn't give up halfway through. It wasn't like him. Truth was, he couldn't give up until he received what he considered a satisfactory answer.

But what would that be, and when?

Phillip placed the glass on the board and asked a question. "Are you there?"

At first, nothing happened, so he asked again, and the glass moved. Eventually it replied, *yes*.

He asked who was there but there was no reply. With a trembling hand, believing it was his father, Phillip then asked if he was still confined.

The board replied, *no*.

Phillip's heart missed a beat. He stared at the board for some time, wondering. Whilst he was thinking, he broke the other digestive in half and chewed it.

Phillip grew very frustrated very quickly because all further questions were ignored. He put his head in his hands and rested them on the table, sighing. Would he ever reach a conclusion? Would he ever find out what had happened to his father? Why could no one tell him? He wouldn't give up. He firmly believed that more time with the board would eventually give him what he needed; maybe then, he could broach the subject of the heirloom.

Frustrated, he left the table and crossed the living room. If he was lucky, he might still have time to catch the late local news. Then it would be time for bed.

He switched on the TV before taking his cup into the kitchen to wash. He also washed the pots he'd used to make his tea and left them to drain before returning to the living room.

The news anchor was standing outside of a two-up two-down terraced house in Armley, floodlights illuminating his face and the front of the house.

"Police have finally released the details of what must be one of the most gruesome finds they've had for some time here in Armley. Not only was the occupant of the house found brutally murdered, but they discovered a coffin in the basement, with a skeleton inside."

Phillip stood completely frozen to the spot. His knees were weak and his legs wobbled.

He fell back into his armchair, contemplating whether or not there was a connection to what the board had told him, and the coffin having been found in Armley, at the scene of a murder?

The reporter continued. "The police now believe it is the remains of a man by the name of Jack Walker, who disappeared in mysterious circumstances sometime in the 1970s. They would like anyone with any information to come forward."

"Oh, my word, what's going on here?"

Chapter Twenty-eight

Wendy Wilson was clock-watching, which was something new for her. She'd never done it; never had to.

But she had never known Phillip to be late for anything, not an appointment, and certainly not his shift – you could set your watch by him.

The pair of them worked in the ticket office at the railway in Bursley Bridge, having done so for as many years as she could remember.

A queue of people had gathered and she had served each and every one. The morning rush appeared to be over and although she had a number of tasks still to complete, it was time for a cuppa.

The office was a reasonable size and basically all wood. There were two serving hatches, two desks, a number of wooden cabinets with glass doors, a variety of paintings and pictures covering the history of the line and, believe it or not, an old-fashioned fireplace with an open fire – currently in use.

Wendy threw on two more logs and some coal and then retired to another small section at the back, which contained a kitchen, with a toilet next door. As she switched on the kettle, the office door opened and Phillip rushed in, very distracted if his manner was anything to go by.

"Are you okay, Phillip?" asked Wendy, nonetheless very pleased to see him.

"Yes, Mrs Wilson, I'm so sorry I'm late."

Despite the years they had worked together she could never recall him calling her by her Christian name.

Over that time, she had come to respect him immensely. Phillip was not really the kind of man a woman would look at twice; he was stocky and balding, with round, wire-rimmed spectacles. Although his clothes were of good quality – always M&S – they were rather old-fashioned. His manner suited his appearance. He was calm and collected, rarely flapped in a crisis, and always respected the person he was sharing time with. He was probably the calmest person she knew.

So what had gone wrong?

"If you don't mind me saying so," said Wendy, "you really don't look yourself, Phillip. Have you had some bad news?"

"No," he replied. "Just a very bad night's sleep."

"Well don't worry, you're here now. Sit yourself down and I'll make you a nice cup of tea."

It took a few minutes in the kitchen. She and Phillip preferred their tea made in a pot. He couldn't abide people who threw a tea bag into the cup. Once it was made, she slipped some digestives on to a plate and took everything through.

He was sitting at one of the desks, slightly calmer, with a little more colour in his face.

"Now then, get this down you and tell me what's bothering you," she said. Not that she thought he would. Phillip had always been a very private man. He had discussed personal matters with her over the years but it took him time to open up. Maybe it was grief; he *had* recently lost his mother.

"Is it your mother? Is there a problem with the paperwork?"

Phillip grabbed a digestive and broke it into two pieces, popping one half into his mouth. He sipped his tea.

"Nice cup, that," he said. "No, I don't think so. Everything seems to be okay, and in order. It was just a terrible night's sleep. I've pretty much suffered that since I was a boy."

"Oh, I didn't know," replied Wendy. "Do you think it was anything to do with your dad?"

She wasn't sure why she said that. Wendy was trying to make him open up, but the comment seemed to have an effect.

"Maybe," said Phillip. "But my childhood wasn't all it should have been."

"Oh dear."

Phillip glanced up. "Probably not for the reasons you think. My mother worked hard and provided for us. I suspect what you've said had something to do with it. The situation was tough. And because of that, I was an introvert. I rarely lost my temper – kept everything inside."

"How did you get on with other children, and school?" asked Wendy.

He ate the rest of the biscuit. "Well, at school, though I knew the answer to the questions the teachers were asking, I never volunteered it. On the two occasions I did, I paid the price."

"What do you mean?"

"School bullies. All of those children who had fathers, couldn't understand why I didn't, nor could they understand why I didn't know what had happened to mine. I only knew what my mother had told me; that my father had walked out and left us. That prompted further hurtful comments, that my father couldn't possibly have loved us; then they'd say, who would with a face like that? As a result, I was bullied."

"Oh, love, I'm so sorry," said Wendy. "Children can be hurtful, but I'm not sure they meant it."

"But it didn't last long."

"There you are, then."

"I didn't mean it like that. When I was young, I found out how strong I was. I could lift far heavier weights than any of the other children the same age. One day, another pupil called Brian Preston was showing off to the rest of his gang, picking on me after a teacher had left the class for five minutes.

"Preston was tall and gangly with bulging eyes and a swan neck. Someone had once told me that if you had a swan neck you had to be careful, people could knock you out easily. If you had a bull neck, like me, they would have a hell of a job putting you down or laying you out... Preston made light of the fact that I had no father."

Phillip's eyes glazed over, as he appeared to be reliving it. "He called me a bastard, because he'd seen it on a film. We were in the science lab. I remember it having a large, plate glass window. The bullying and name-calling went on for around five minutes, but Preston then made the mistake of picking up a Bunsen burner and singing my hair at the front, before knocking off my glasses and stamping on them. I can still smell that awful odour."

Wendy reached out to him. "You don't have to tell me any more if you don't want to."

He finished the second digestive, and continued as if he hadn't heard her. "That stung, made my eyes water. It really hurt. Wound me up."

He sipped more tea, and stared at Wendy with an expression she couldn't read, like he was alone and completely lost in the world.

"You know, Mrs Wilson, I've always believed that violence is never the answer. One should never resort to violence, but one can only take so much. I felt I needed to do something, to put the matter to bed, so to speak."

"What did you do?"

"Well, I stopped what I was doing, methodically left everything on my desk safe, as safe as it could be, now that I couldn't see a great deal. I walked slowly over to Preston and simply stood in front of him without saying anything; mainly because I was trying to judge everything. I couldn't see, could I?"

Phillip smiled as he said that, allowing Wendy to relax a little, feeling that the old Phillip, the one she knew, was returning somewhat.

"But Preston took things a step further," said Phillip. "He started poking me on my forehead, underneath the singed hair, telling everyone that I was yellow; that I may have walked up but I wasn't going to do anything."

"Did you?" asked Wendy, wondering what it might be.

"He was wrong," said Phillip. "I felt so ashamed of myself afterwards."

"What did you do?" asked Wendy, fearing the worst, as he'd already said that they were in a science lab. God only knows what you could use against someone if you had been pushed too far.

"I hit him," said Phillip. "Only once, mind you."

Suddenly, Wendy started to laugh. It wasn't as bad as she'd expected. "Oh well, I think you'd be allowed one punch, after everything."

"Trouble was," said Phillip, "one was enough. Such was the force, Preston ended up flying through the window."

"Oh my God," said Wendy. "What did you do?"

"Well," said Phillip, as if he was lost again. "Well, I just turned and calmly asked if anyone else wanted the same treatment. Of course, no one did. It took them five minutes to bring Preston round. No one spoke of the incident to the teachers. They simply said they were working and had not seen how it had happened."

"Did it ever happen again, the bullying?"

"No. Never," replied Phillip. "But can you imagine how ashamed of myself I was. Violence is never the answer, even if you want to get your point across."

Wendy stood up and cleared the pots away. "I agree with you, Phillip, but you were pushed; and you were right when you said it's not the answer but like you also said, you can only take so much. Does it still bother you now?"

He stared at her, as if he was the same little boy who had used the violence he quite clearly abhorred, his expression blank, his mouth open and his eyes lifeless.

"Yes, Mrs Wilson, it does. Sometimes it rears up its ugly head and I can't stop thinking about it and I have a really bad night."

"Well what happened last night to make you relive it?"

"I think I rather stupidly watched the news last night."

As if a light had switched on in Wendy's head, she realized what he must have been talking about.

"Do you mean that murder in Armley?"

"Yes."

"What in God's name is going on over there?" She realized she was still standing, so she sat back down. "Not only was there a murder, but the police found a bloody coffin in the cellar of the house? What *is* going on there?"

"I have no idea, Mrs Wilson," said Phillip, removing his glasses and rubbing his face.

"I've never come across anything like it," said Wendy. "I blame the films on the television myself. The stuff they show these days, and even before the watershed."

Phillip never replied.

Wendy leaned forward. "Do you know, only last night there was one on, some kids messing with one of them Ouija boards. Ouija boards, I ask you. I thought they were banned. They bloody well should be, along with nuclear weapons. How dangerous are those things?"

"Weapons, or Ouija boards?" asked Phillip.

"Both," replied Wendy. "If we're not allowed to use nuclear weapons, why have we got them? Why do we spend all that money on them, never to use them? Not that I'm saying we should. All that money could be put into the NHS, or climate control. Something that could *improve* people's lives, not end them."

"Ouija boards are not as bad as you think," said Phillip.

Wendy stopped dead, about to say something but changed her mind. "You're not involved with those things, are you? Surely not, Phillip, not a man as level-headed as you."

Phillip only glanced on.

"Oh, please tell me you don't."

Phillip reached out and put his hand on top of one of hers, something she had never experienced, not from him.

He suddenly explained how he'd been introduced through a friend of the church, and he told her what had happened, and why he was using it.

"Did you know," said Phillip, "after finishing his schooling, the famous author Sax Rohmer worked in odd jobs, but even as a child, he had dreamt of becoming a writer. He was briefly a bank clerk in Threadneedle Street, then a clerk in a gas company, an errand boy at a small local newspaper, and a reporter on the weekly Commercial Intelligence.

"At the age of twenty, Rohmer started his writing career. There's a story, that he consulted, with his wife, a Ouija board as to how he could best make a living. The answer was 'C-H-I-N-A-M-A-N'".

"Never," said Wendy, shocked by an alternative story to something she suspected to be evil. "But that's only one example."

"There are more," said Phillip. "George Wyman and Louis Bradbury were not alone in their attraction to futuristic thinkers. George Wyman decided to contact his dead brother via what we know now as a Ouija board. Young Mark Wyman had died a few years earlier and George felt it would be best to get Mark's feelings on something called the Bradbury contract.

"According to sources as close to the family as Wyman's own daughter, the message received via the planchette was: 'Take the Bradbury Building. It will make you famous.'" He did, and the rest is history.

"Are you sure about these things, Phillip?"

"Of course I am," he replied, removing his hand. "Have you ever known me do something half-heartedly?"

Wendy smiled. "I can't say I have."

She finally stood to take the pots to be washed. "Hey, maybe you should use the spirit board to find out who's been killing these people."

Phillip laughed. "Maybe I should. Then again, maybe the person responsible has been pushed too far, like I was."

Chapter Twenty-nine

Gardener and Reilly had returned to speak to a tearful Kerry Sutton. She had been allowed back into the house and had made a valiant effort to ensure the living room was okay for her and her son to live in. It was clean and comfortable. In the kitchen, Gardener could hear a radio playing. She had made tea for them all.

He had phoned ahead, mentioning that he wanted to come and speak to her. In person, he asked firstly if she knew of anything that had been stolen from the house and, secondly, from the shed.

It turned out that something was missing from the latter, and Kerry was pretty shocked.

"It was something that belonged to Steven."

"What was it, Mrs Sutton?" asked Gardener.

"A watch," said Kerry. "Well, it wasn't so much the watch that I noticed was missing but the tin it was in. And I only noticed because I was looking for the carpet cleaning stuff. That tin was sitting on a shelf above the carpet cleaner."

Reilly wrote that down and then asked if anything else was missing that she knew about.

"No, not that I can see." She took a sip of tea.

"In fact, it wasn't just my husband's. It had been in the family for generations, as I was led to believe."

Gardener asked her to describe the watch, which she did. It appeared to be very close to the one that Sharp had seen in the documentary, leaving him momentarily confused, because the documentary that Sharp had seen had suggested that the watch had belonged to another family called Walker.

"And you haven't discovered that anything else is missing?" asked Gardener.

"No," replied Kerry. "Are you saying that my husband was not only murdered but we'd been burgled as well?"

"We have some information that could lead us to that conclusion," replied Gardener. "We do need to conduct a full investigation."

"Why wasn't I told about this?"

"As I said, Mrs Sutton, we're not entirely sure that has happened yet. Have you any idea of the value of the watch?"

"To be honest, no. From what I remember, my husband said it wasn't worth anything, and it was simply a keepsake as it belonged to his father and his grandfather."

"Do you know where it came from originally?"

"No," said Kerry.

"Is it possible your husband might have been mistaken about the value and moved it somewhere else for safekeeping?"

"It's possible," said Kerry, "but I'm sure he'd have mentioned it, whenever that was."

"What do you actually know about the watch, Kerry, love?" asked Reilly.

"Not a lot," replied Kerry. "I don't know the full story but he told me that there had been some disagreement over it between two families, one of which lived in Bursley Bridge."

"Did he mention what the disagreement was about?"

"From what I can gather, there was a bit of a bust-up about who actually owned it."

"Did he mention who the other family was?" asked Gardener.

"No. You see, that was the thing about Steven. He was a good husband and a good father but he never spoke much about his childhood or his family. And I never pressed it. I was just grateful to have found a man I could trust."

Despite his having been in prison, thought Gardener.

"Seems a little odd, don't you think?" asked Reilly.

"What does?" asked Kerry.

"That he never spoke about his family or his childhood," said Reilly.

"When you come to mention it, yes." She sipped some more tea and then opened up a little about the watch.

"I first came across the watch about a year ago, maybe eighteen months. In an effort to try and tidy up the house and the garden, I reckoned it was time we decorated the place throughout. I wanted us to extend; build upwards, put an extra bedroom in the attic. And I was sick to death of the old shed we had. I suggested we bought a new shed before the old one fell down."

"Bet that went down well," said Reilly.

"Like I said. He was a good husband, and he earned good money at the railway, so he went along with it. Mind you, it was six months later, in the summer, before he finally decided to clear the bloody place out. I helped him – you know what men are like. They won't part with anything because it will always come in useful for something."

That sentence amused Gardener, as he thought of his own father, and very possibly himself. When it came to the restoration of the bike, he had all sorts in glass jars.

Kerry continued, unprompted. "Most – if not all – was rubbish. He had a whole range of odd bits of bloody glass and plastic, gardening equipment that didn't work due to old age or rust, and old paint tins full of more garbage. The easiest thing was to clear out the lot, which is what he did. After I'd asked him."

"I suspect you told him, Kerry, love," said Reilly.

She smiled. "Well, you're probably right, there. I might have asked but I left little room for error. Anyway, I then came across an old, round biscuit tin, about six inches in diameter, similar to the one my grandmother had. That was probably worth a fortune."

"And that had the watch in?" said Gardener.

"Yes. A pocket watch, like the ones they used on the railway. It looked pretty nice, to be honest with you. It could have ended up in a landfill. I gave the tin to Steven and asked him if he knew anything about it."

"What did he say?" asked Gardener.

"He reckoned he'd heard of his father mentioning such a watch, but Steven had never laid eyes on it before. I asked if it was worth anything. He said it wasn't, that his father had kept the watch because it was *his* father's, but they were ten a penny on the railway and worth nothing."

"And you believed him?" asked Gardener.

"He was my husband," said Kerry. "I'd had no reason to doubt him before, and I knew nothing about watches."

"So what happened?" asked Reilly.

"I said if it was worth nothing, that he should get rid of it. But for some reason I can't think of, it ended up back in the new shed; at least, the tin did."

"Do you think your husband had known more than he was letting on?" asked Gardener.

"It's always possible," said Kerry. "But surely to God if there had been any value to the watch, why didn't he sell it?"

"Maybe he did," said Reilly.

"I think he'd have told me if he had," said Kerry.

"Do you have a picture of the watch?" asked Gardener.

Kerry said she didn't. "I can't believe all this is happening. Was my husband hiding something from me?"

"I can't see any reason why he would, Mrs Sutton," said Gardener. "Like you said, if he'd known, he could have given all of you a better life, which leads me to believe he hadn't had it valued."

Kerry grabbed a tissue from a box close to her chair and wiped her eyes. "What the hell is going on? I go away on holiday and come back home to find my husband murdered, and then I find out we've been burgled."

She suddenly stopped talking and her eyes widened.

"Oh, my, God. It isn't just Steven, is it? I haven't really been paying attention to much, but a bloke in Armley's been murdered as well, hasn't he?"

She quickly stood up, walked into the kitchen and returned with a newspaper, pointing to the story. "It was Roy Sutton, wasn't it, Steven's brother?"

Gardener nodded. "Yes, Mrs Sutton."

"Was he burgled as well?"

"We don't know," replied Reilly. "It wasn't easy to tell."

"Why have they both been murdered?" she asked.

"That's what we're trying to find out," said Gardener.

"And you think it has something to do with this watch?"

"We don't know," said Gardener. "But it is possible."

"Why?" asked Kerry.

"We're trying to piece together everything we know," said Gardener. "It's a bit of a jigsaw puzzle at the moment. Can I just ask once again? You are absolutely sure nothing else was taken?"

"No, nothing," said Kerry. "To be fair, once we had the new shed built, Steven was very careful to keep things tidy. Everything still appears to be where it always was."

"It's possible the burglar was disturbed by the murderer," said Reilly. "We're not sure yet if the burglar was an opportunist, or whether or not he actually knew what he was looking for. Or if the burglar and the killer are the same man."

"Maybe it's that bloke who has been stealing all the watches on Leeds railway station," Kerry said.

"Stealing watches?" asked Gardener.

Kerry nodded. "There was a big spread about it in the newspapers recently, asking people to be on their guard because someone was stealing watches at the station."

Gardener suddenly thought of Harry Pinchbeck. When they had first interviewed him, he had said he spent most of his days in the station to keep warm. And they knew for a fact he had been at the Suttons' house on the night in question. Is it possible he stole the watch, and that it had nothing to do with the murder, or murderer?

"Maybe whoever it is knew my Steven," said Kerry, "because he worked there – but why would he kill him, unless he was caught red-handed?"

"What do you mean, caught red-handed?" asked Gardener.

"I meant, did my husband walk in on the burglar, and then the burglar killed him?"

Gardener didn't reply, but that was not what he believed had happened from the information he'd been given. Which led him to consider there had been more than one person and if one of them was Harry the Shard.

"Oh, my God," said Kerry. "Are we safe, me and my son? What if this bastard comes back?"

They were very good questions, thought Gardener. He glanced at his partner, who was obviously wondering the same thing. If the killer had not found what he wanted in either Steven or Roy Sutton's house, would he return here?

"There are a couple of things we can do here, Mrs Sutton," said Gardener. "We can post a police car outside your house for the time being."

"No, I'm not sure I like the idea," said Kerry. "Staying here, that is. I think it might be safer if I stay with my sister. I don't fancy hanging around here even with a copper outside my door."

"We can arrange someone to keep an eye on things there, Mrs Sutton," said Gardener. "And it would give us some peace of mind until we can complete our investigation."

"Do you know anything about Steven's father, Patrick Sutton?" asked Reilly.

Kerry took her time in answering. "Like I said, Steven never talked about family."

"Did the pair of you never meet?"

"We met twice that I can recall. The first time, naturally, was at our wedding. Steven invited his father, but not his half-brother. I could tell there was some tension between us but he seemed nice enough. He was polite, wished us all the best and told us that if we ever needed anything we only had to ask."

"And the second time?" asked Gardener.

Kerry nodded. "Second time was at the shops. We were out at The White Rose Centre one day and we bumped into him. That must have been a couple of years later."

"Didn't you find it strange after those two meetings that you never met again?" asked Gardener.

"I did, and I did ask Steven about it, but like I said, he wouldn't talk about it. As I said, he was my husband. Where we come from, when you get a good one, you keep him, whatever the cost."

Gardener really wanted to know more about the situation but figured he might be fighting a losing battle.

"Do you have any idea what Patrick Sutton did for a living, or how he earned his money?"

"No," said Kerry. "I did wonder if he'd left the house to Roy, because I had heard it mentioned that Patrick lived in Armley and it was near the prison. But that can't have

159

been the reason that Roy and Steven didn't talk, because they weren't talking when we met."

"Do you know when Patrick passed away?"

"Years ago. 1999, maybe, but that's about all I can tell you. I have no idea why or what happened."

"Did you go to the funeral?" asked Gardener.

"Yes, but we didn't stay. I saw someone who resembled Steven, which I took to be Roy, but they never spoke to each other, and Steven never gave him the chance before he whisked us away."

Gardener didn't think there would be a lot of point in pushing Kerry Sutton any further. She had answered all their questions, but as far as Patrick Sutton was concerned, it might prove more fruitful to let his team continue investigating; he was sure he would find out a lot more from them.

Gardener also felt that he and Reilly needed to speak to Maurice Cragg about everything they had learned, to see what he knew about the watch and the names that kept cropping up.

At that point, his mobile started ringing. After excusing himself whilst he took the call, he discovered from David Williams at Leeds Central that they had Harry Pinchbeck in custody.

Chapter Thirty

Back at Leeds Central, Gardener entered the office and nipped over to his filing cabinet. As Reilly walked in, the SIO switched on the kettle and made the drinks before taking a seat.

Gardener took a sip of his tea and then asked, "Is that what this case is all about, an antique watch?"

"It's possible," said Reilly. "We've known people kill for less, but it sounds like this thing is valuable enough to kill for."

"It must be some watch," said Gardener. "If that's the case, it suggests to me that the killer definitely knows about it, he's looking for it, and it's possible that as yet, he still hasn't found it."

"Meaning that he thought the Suttons had it, but they didn't," said Reilly. "Which then means someone else could be for the chop."

"There's a lot at stake," said Gardener. "It sounds like there might be some kind of family feud going on; at least with two names that we know of: Walker and Sutton."

"But there could be more," said Reilly. "Trouble with that is, how far back are we going?" said Reilly. "You know what these things can be like."

"We'd better start with that idiot in the interview room. Let's see how much *he* knows."

"If he's our only hope, we're fucked."

Gardener laughed as the pair of them left the office. Two minutes later, they dropped in on Harry Pinchbeck, whose beauty had not improved since last they saw him. He was dressed in a black leather jacket and jeans. His right leg was going twenty to the dozen and his nervous tic was raging.

"Why am I back here?" he shouted before they had even shut the door."

"We told you we might need to talk to you again," said Gardener, taking his seat.

Reilly also sat. They both placed their drinks on the table.

"Don't I get one?" asked Harry.

"Depends on how truthful you are," said Gardener.

"Which, from where I'm sitting," said Reilly, "doesn't look very likely."

"Look," said Harry, "I told you everything I know last time."

"But that's not quite true, is it?" said Reilly.

"Yes it is, I told you. I had taken nothing."

"From the house," said Gardener.

"That's right. I was disturbed."

"Yes," said Gardener, holding his forehead, as if he was struggling to remember. "You heard the front door slam."

"Yes."

"And you left," said Reilly.

"Yes."

"And went where?" asked Gardener.

"I bloody well told you," said Harry, obviously becoming irritated. "The Chinese."

"Was that via the shed?" asked Gardener.

"The shed?"

"Yes," repeated Gardener. "Did you go into the shed before or after you went into the house?"

"I never went into the shed."

"Let's not play this game again," said Reilly. "We have evidence you went into the shed because we have your prints all over it."

Harry didn't reply.

"What did you take?" asked Gardener.

There was still no reply.

"Okay, Mr Pinchbeck," said Gardener. "If this is how you want to play it, we have far better things to do. Given that we can hold you for twenty-four hours, it could be a while before we return."

The pair of them stood up.

"Okay. Not much," said Harry, before they reached the door.

Gardener turned. "So you *did* take something?"

"Okay, for Christ's sake," said Harry. "Yes, but it was only a tin of biscuits."

"A tin of biscuits?" repeated Reilly, taking his seat.

"Yes, an old one, they were fusty."

Reilly leaned forward. "If you don't level with us, Harry, old son, we're going to lock you up and throw away the key. What was in the tin? Because it sure as hell wasn't biscuits."

Harry appeared to be thinking. He must have known they had him banged to rights, but that if he played his cards right and cooperated there was very little they could hold him on.

"A watch."

"Finally," said Reilly. "What did you do with it?"

"Why?"

"We ask the questions," said Gardener. "What did you do with it?"

He took another elongated break before answering. "I sold it."

"Who to?" asked Reilly.

"I can't remember," said Harry, staring at the ceiling as if he was bored.

"Try again," said Reilly.

"Honestly," shouted Harry, a little too confidently. "I can't remember."

"You don't know the meaning of the word, Mr Pinchbeck."

"It was down the pub, sold it for a drink."

"Which pub?" asked Gardener.

"The Peacock."

Easy one to remember, thought Gardener. He'd used it last time they were questioning him. "When?"

"I don't know."

"One more of them and we're off," said Reilly. "And you can whistle if you want us to come back. And judging by the state of your face that'll be something worth seeing."

"Who did you sell it to?" asked Gardener.

"What do you think I am, an accountant?" Harry said.

"We know what you're going to be soon – incarcerated."

"Rubbish," said Harry. "You have nothing on me, you're just fishing."

Gardener liked it when Harry's confidence grew, it left him wide open. "You think?"

"Is that your final word?" said Reilly.

"Yes, okay, you got me for taking an old biscuit tin with an even older watch," Harry said, "but I didn't kill anyone."

"We don't know that," said Gardener.

"You do."

"We don't. So as far as we're concerned, Mr Pinchbeck, we are going to keep you, read you your rights and charge you with the murder of Steven Sutton." Gardener stood up again. He had no intention of going anywhere but it had the desired effect.

"What?" shouted Harry. "What the fuck are you talking about?"

"You are allowed a phone call," said Gardener, "to your lawyer."

Harry stood up and waved his arms in the air, as if he was directing a jet into the runway. "No, no, wait a minute, this isn't right. I never killed nobody."

"That's a double negative," said Reilly.

"A what?"

"Means you did." Reilly stood up.

"Okay, okay," said Harry. "Wait a minute."

"Why?" Gardener asked.

"I didn't kill anyone."

"Let's sit back down, then," said Gardener. "Who did you sell the watch to?"

"Archie Figgs."

Gardener pushed pen and paper across the table. "Address."

"I don't know."

They stood up.

"Honestly," shouted Harry. "I don't know. I just meet up with him now and again."

"Where?" asked Reilly. "Leeds railway station?"

"Sometimes."

"Is that where you steal watches together?" asked Gardener, having now checked what Kerry Sutton had claimed.

"What are you on about?"

"You said you're always at Leeds Railway station to keep warm," said Gardener. "We know that people are having watches stolen and we know you're a thief."

"Nothing to do with me."

"Just like the watch Steven Sutton had," said Reilly. "That was nothing to do with you, either, was it?"

"No," said Harry. "I took that one, I'm admitting it, but I haven't taken the ones at the station."

"So you took the watch in question and sold it to Archie Figgs," said Gardener. "But you don't know where he lives."

"No."

"Where did you meet this Archie Figgs?" asked Reilly. "To do the deal."

"The café by the canal, at Rodley."

Gardener made a note. "We'll check it out. When did you meet?"

"A couple of days after I took it."

"When?"

"I've just said."

"What time?"

"In the morning."

"How much did you sell it for?" asked Reilly.

"Fifty quid."

"Why him?" asked Gardener.

"He's obsessed with watches," said Harry, finally. "He's your man for the railway station. He's the one taking people's watches. He dresses up and has a clipboard in his hand, starts asking questions, as if he's with a charity, or something. Next thing they know, they're watchless."

"You know all this, how?" said Gardener.

"It's all bloody true, I tell you."

"Yet you don't know where he lives," said Gardener.

"No," replied Harry. "All I know is he lives with his mother."

"His mother?" said Reilly. "How old is he?"

"About fifty."

"What?" said Gardener. "And he still lives with his mother?"

"Well, he reckons *she* lives with *him*."

"What's the difference?"

"You'll have to ask him."

"What's he look like?" asked Reilly.

Harry explained as best he could.

Gardener had most of what he wanted, finally. He decided he would release Harry on bail after he had read him his rights and charged him on two counts: theft, and wasting police time.

Chapter Thirty-one

Elvis – aka Dwayne Rooney – was standing on the platform staring up at the station clock.

"That's the one," said Giles Middleton, the station manager.

As far as Rooney could see, Middleton's name fitted his appearance. He was around sixty years of age. He'd lost most of his hair, had a bulbous nose and wore thin wire-rimmed glasses. To his credit, he was dressed in a black business suit. He was overweight, but for all that his posture was erect – ex-military, maybe. In his hands he had some paperwork, perhaps to try and support his point.

"When was it installed?" asked Rooney.

Middleton puffed out his cheeks. "Before my time, Mr Rooney. Let me have a think. Sometime after the First World War, William's two sons started their own clockmaking business, they both left before 1930. I think it was Charles who installed this in 1933."

Rooney had his notepad in hand, busy writing everything he could. Glancing down the platform he noticed the ticket booth, with a frame outside, a poster advertising the services, timetables of the trains, and a plaque, which he would have to remember to read before he left. There was also a waiting room, a weighbridge, a bench, and some fire buckets.

He snapped a couple of pictures of the station, and then of the clock, which he didn't believe was anything special – simply a big round clock.

"Are Potts still in business?"

"I don't think so, son," said Middleton. "I think they joined the Derby Group in 1935 but what happened after that I don't really know. But they are still a recognized name in the north of England."

"It's not a problem," said Rooney. "I can do some digging around."

If there was one thing he couldn't stand it was sloppy journalism. If you were going to print something, be sure of your facts. It didn't hurt to wait a little longer for the finished article so long as it was right. At least then, no one could sue you.

Although he'd found out some information from Alan Browne, he would definitely need to pay another visit. That man was a walking encyclopaedia.

A woman approached them along the platform, and stopped when she reached them. She was middle-aged, slim, with long auburn hair and a pleasant face, and wearing a station uniform. She carried with her some notes.

"Morning, Mr Middleton."

"Morning, Mrs Wilson." He turned to face Rooney. "This is Mrs Wilson. She works in our ticket office."

The journalist nodded.

"So, you're writing an article," said Middleton to Rooney, "on the railway?"

"Not entirely," replied the journalist. "That will be a part of it but my main interest is the watch."

"The watch?" asked Middleton.

"Yes," said Rooney. "You might recall when I called you the other day, I wanted to talk to you about a particular watch. It was a one-off and was said to look like the Gotham Gunmetal Railway Watch, because that's what colour it was, gunmetal grey."

"Oh, yes," said Middleton. "You did mention something."

"The what?" asked Wendy Wilson.

Rooney explained.

"I remember something about that," she replied. "Wasn't there a documentary on it recently?"

"Apparently," replied Rooney.

"I never saw it," said Middleton, "but I did record it."

"Do you know anything about the watch?" Rooney asked Middleton.

"Very little, I'm afraid," he replied, "other than it was supposed to have been made sometime in the 1960s, before disappearing, never to be seen again. I've certainly never seen it."

"I have," said Rooney.

"You have?" whispered Middleton, as if it was somehow against the law. "When?"

"Last week."

"Last week?" shouted Middleton, suddenly appearing rather excited. "Where?"

"The jeweller's in the town," said Rooney.

"He was selling it?" asked Wendy Wilson.

Middleton touched Rooney's arm. "The jeweller in the town was selling it? Where the hell did he get it? Are you sure it was that one?"

"No," said Rooney. "He wasn't selling it. Some bloke brought it in for a valuation."

"A valuation?" said Middleton.

Rooney was rather amused at how Middleton repeated everything he was saying.

"Where did *he* get it?" Middleton asked Rooney.

"Claims it was in a box of fire-damaged stuff at an auction somewhere in North Yorkshire. Only, Alan Browne knew nothing about the auction, and believe me, Alan Browne misses nothing."

"I can believe that," said Middleton. "But that watch has been missing for ever."

"How much was it worth?" asked Wendy Wilson of Rooney. To Giles Middleton, she said, "How can you put a price on something like that?"

"He couldn't," said Rooney. "He had no idea how much, but he was dead sure it was the real thing. Kept rabbiting on about a high jewel count, and screw-set jewels and even something called a micrometer regulator. I had no idea what he was going about but he knows his stuff."

"Oh, he does," said Middleton. "But he couldn't put a price on it, you say?"

"No," said Rooney. "Like Mrs Wilson said, how could you? Do you know how much it cost to make?"

"No," said Middleton. He put his hands to his face and sat down. "I can't believe it! It's the stuff of legends. I even doubted its existence."

Rooney noticed that the general manager appeared to have paled somewhat.

"Does he still have it?" Middleton asked.

"No," said Rooney. "The bloke took it with him."

"Did you get his name – the man who took it with him?"

"No," replied Rooney. "Do you know the story behind how it went missing?"

"No," said Middleton. "All of this was well before my time. And whilst one takes a bit of an interest in a legend, the story sort of dissolves after a few years, and nobody really talks about it anymore."

"It's okay," said Rooney. "I have the details of the people who made the programme. I know who made the watch. And I know Alan Browne. I'd like to get to the bottom of this thing."

"Why?" asked Middleton.

"Makes for a good story."

"I know a man who might be able to help you," said Wendy.

Rooney's interest piqued. "Who is he, and where is he?"

"Right here," said Wendy. "He works for us."

* * *

How interesting, he thought, as all three moved away from the clock. So, the jeweller in the town had seen it, and he knows something.

He turned to leave the station.

Chapter Thirty-two

The following morning, desk sergeant Maurice Cragg was outside the small police station, sweeping the steps. Normally, the cleaner would do the job, but it was a little icy underfoot and he didn't want her tumbling down the concrete steps.

"Morning, Mr Cragg," shouted a voice.

Cragg stopped and turned, pleasantly surprised to see the local journalist, Dwayne Rooney. "Morning, Elvis, lad. How are you?"

"I'm okay, thanks."

Rooney had a small white carrier bag with him, and judging by the smell it was likely stuffed with bacon sandwiches.

"How's the world of a newspaper reporter?" Cragg asked Elvis.

"Oh, you know," said Rooney. "Been a bit quiet of late. Looks like the local criminals have been behaving themselves."

"Don't speak too soon," said Cragg. "That'll all change in the next week or so, in the run-up to Christmas."

As Cragg glanced around, the little town was springing to life. Most of the shopkeepers were popping in and out, altering displays. Some were cleaning the windows. There were two snack vans at either end of the market square, a good head of steam pouring from both, as breakfasts were underway, with locals already queueing.

"One of them's not for me, is it?" Cragg asked Rooney, staring at the bags.

"No," he replied. "I value your health far too much, Mr Cragg. We don't want to be filling up your arteries with this garbage."

"Whose arteries *are* you filling, apart from yours?"

"Old man Browne over there."

Cragg glanced at the jeweller's. The front door to the shop was open and a young couple was staring into the window. She was tall and slim with long blonde hair. He was short and stocky with trimmed brown hair. She was probably picking out an engagement ring. He was probably panicking.

"How is he?" asked Cragg. "Not seen him for a while."

"His usual self."

"Not changed, then?" asked Cragg.

"Will he ever?" asked Rooney.

"So," said Cragg, "what are you working on?"

"A mystery," said Rooney.

"Sounds interesting," said Cragg, as the young couple walked away from Browne's without venturing inside. Further down the street, he noticed them passing Wendy Wilson, probably on her way to the station.

"It is," said Rooney. "You ever hear about a one-off watch made for a railway superintendent in the sixties, that pretty much went missing shortly after it was made, and was never seen again?"

"Can't say I have," said Cragg, but he couldn't help thinking that it rang a bell. "What do you know about it?"

"Bugger all," said Rooney. "I'm not sure who it was made for, why it disappeared, or when exactly, and why the hell it's causing such a fuss; it even appeared on a TV documentary recently."

"Does sound intriguing," said Cragg. "Did it happen round here?"

Across the street, Wendy Wilson walked into Alan Browne's shop.

"I think so," said Rooney. "That's why I'm going to see his lordship. Some bloke walked in off the street the other day for a valuation of the very watch."

"The one nobody's seen since it went missing?" asked Cragg.

"Aye," said Rooney. "I think there might be an intriguing bit of history to this thing."

"I wish you luck," said Cragg. "Let me know what you find out. And if I hear anything I'll give you a shout."

"Thanks, Mr Cragg."

That was as far as the conversation went. A sudden interruption came in the form of the most blood-curdling scream from inside Alan Browne's shop, if Cragg wasn't mistaken. He'd seen Wendy Wilson go in only seconds ago. It had to be her.

Cragg jumped, and he dropped his sweeping brush, which clattered down the steps, nearly tripping up an old dear, but she'd stopped at the sound of the scream as well.

Rooney dropped his carrier bag and turned his head. "The hell was that?"

"We'd better go and find out," said Cragg.

As they crossed the road, Wendy Wilson exited the shop with her hands around her mouth and her eyes watering, her posture close to collapse.

"Oh, Mr Cragg," she said, when she saw him. "It's awful." She leaned back against the window, taking deep breaths.

Before Cragg entered, he noticed more people running toward the shop, two of them already tending to Wendy Wilson.

He slipped inside, quickly took everything in, and then slipped back out, only to find DI Gardener and DS Reilly walking toward the journalist and the shop.

Chapter Thirty-three

Within fifteen minutes, the building had been secured with crime scene tape both front and back — although it was noted that the back gate and rear door of the property were open, which didn't fill Gardener with any confidence.

Cones created a barrier on the road either side of the shop entrance, with tape wrapped around those as well. Gardener, Reilly and Cragg all wore scene suits, and two uniformed PCs from Bramfield stood outside, with Elvis, making sure no one entered. Wendy Wilson had been taken across the road to the police station for a cup of tea and a statement.

All three entered the shop. Gardener looked around. To be fair, the room didn't really appear as if it had been ransacked. All of the glass cabinets were intact and untouched and it would be hard to work out whether or not there actually had been a burglary.

So what *had* it been?

"Is this how you found it, Maurice?" asked Gardener.

"Yes, sir."

Not that it could have been any different, thought Gardener. He and Reilly had been walking toward the shop as Cragg had come out.

Alan Browne was face down with his head through the glass counter. It must have taken some force because the pane had smashed, with Alan Browne's head having gone completely through, severing what appeared to be his carotid artery. At that point there would have been little chance of saving his life. His head was caught at a strange angle and any attempt to pull him back through would have been as dangerous as leaving him there.

Gardener felt for a pulse but he realized he was wasting his time.

"What the hell's happened here?" asked Reilly.

"I can only assume an argument of some sort," said Gardener.

"Over what?" asked Reilly. "If you have a look around, nothing looks out of place."

"I know," said Gardener. "I'm thinking that this happened sometime during the night. The only reason you would break into a jeweller's late at night is to rob the place. But it certainly doesn't appear that way."

"Something's bound to have been taken," said Reilly, "but you'd need to do a proper stock check."

Maurice Cragg slipped back toward the shop door, examining the lock. "Nothing looks forced, sir. Nothing broken."

"Do you think he left it open?" Reilly asked. "Some chancer pops along after a late-night curry, notices it and decides to have an out-of-hours poke around."

"Browne hears him and comes down," added Gardener, "which is the start of whatever transpired."

"Doesn't sound like Alan Browne to me, sir," said Cragg. "I gather Charles Dickens based *A Christmas Carol* around Browne, only there was no change of heart at the end. Browne was so tight he squeaked when he walked."

"As bad as that," said Reilly. "So it's doubtful he'd forgotten to lock up."

"Doubtful," said Cragg. "Not impossible."

"Did he have late-night openings?" asked Gardener. "In the run-up to Christmas."

"I think he did, but I couldn't tell you which nights," replied Cragg. "He even opened on Sundays."

"How long's he been here?" Gardener asked Cragg.

"Years. It's a family business, but he's the last of the line as far as I'm aware."

Gardener peered into the cabinet for a closer inspection. Although most of the display was covered in congealed blood, there were no empty spaces, suggesting that nothing in the cabinet below Browne was missing.

Gardener stood up and approached other cabinets. No glass had been broken, no doors forced open. He checked the window. A quick survey told him that nothing appeared to be missing there, either.

He turned back to his partner. "What the hell was this about? And when did it happen? The suggestion of forgetting to lock the door and a late-night visitor seems unlikely."

"Unless everyone in this place is honest," offered Reilly.

"Can't be that honest," said Gardener, pointing at Browne. "Otherwise, he wouldn't be there."

"We have our fair share of daft lads in this place, sir," said Cragg, also peering more closely at Browne. "I'm sure you remember Manny Walters."

"Christ," said Reilly. "If Manny had been anywhere near this, the place would be empty."

Gardener glanced at Browne's wrist. "Even *he's* still wearing his watch. Whatever this was, it had nothing to do with a burglary."

Gardener turned to Cragg. "The local rumour mill suggests he was tight, but do you think he might have shelled out for CCTV? I can't see any cameras."

"Give us a minute," said Cragg, turning back to the front door of the shop.

Gardener heard him shout the question to someone in the crowd, a man who resembled a sixties rock star.

Cragg returned. "Elvis reckons he did."

"Elvis," repeated Reilly. "Who's Elvis?"

"Local reporter, a good friend of Browne's," said Cragg. "His real name's Dwayne Rooney."

"I can see why he prefers Elvis."

"Anyway," said Cragg, "Browne does have something." The desk sergeant peered at the door leading into the rear of the premises. "There it is."

Gardener followed the line of Cragg's finger. A small camera was perched above the door but very well concealed, probably giving them a bird's-eye view of the interior.

Gardener approached the door, opened it, and slipped into the back room. Cragg's comment about Charles Dickens hit home. The room was sparse, with two very old armchairs either side of an open fire with a pile of grey ash in the grate. The carpet was threadbare, as if it had been down years. The flowered wallpaper faded. An antique sideboard – the type made from a variety of different woods – stood against the back wall, with a number of silver trinkets scattered across the top. A family photo was pinned to the wall above the fireplace, and a rectangular clock above that, the ticking sound rather loud. Two more doors in the room suggested one led to the outside, while the other went upstairs.

"Is this how he lived?" asked Reilly, "with all that money?"

"Some people do, Sean," said Gardener. "Though Lord knows why."

"He was well known for it," said Cragg. "I've never been this far, but they do say he slept on his money, that his mattress is stuffed with it."

"And look what good it's done him," said Reilly. "If it's true, who's going to get it all now?"

Gardener headed for the sideboard. There were four drawers above two large doors, with locks on. He tried the drawers and found a set of keys. One of them opened the double doors. Inside, on a shelf, sat a rather outdated CCTV system, comprising a DVD recorder, with a small monitor to one side. There were also a couple of DVD+R re-recordable discs. Perhaps they contained older footage.

"What the hell are you meant to see with that?" asked Reilly, pointing at the monitor.

"I bet he never watched it," said Gardener. "Why would he, if he never left the place?"

Within minutes they had it switched on and were going through the footage, which only went back forty-eight hours, suggesting that Browne might have erased anything older.

The footage from the previous night revealed that the shop *was* open late. Browne had been popping in and out of the place quite frequently, suggesting he was busy with something. Sometime around nine in the evening he switched off the lights and proceeded to lock the front door when a hooded figure pushed its way through.

Browne staggered backwards and fell to the floor, quickly raising himself to his feet. The hooded figure then closed and locked the front door. The lighting was dim and the sound was bad so it was nigh-on impossible to make anything out, but the two of them were having an altercation.

"Don't recognize the hooded figure, do you, Maurice?"

Whoever it was, they were not as tall as Browne but very stocky. The coat with the hood was long, covering most of the body.

"No, sir, could be anybody," said Cragg. "Not necessarily anyone from the town."

Gardener watched on as Browne and his assailant appeared to be in the grip of a fierce argument in the middle of the shop, but there were no hand gestures or body movements. It was two people having a verbal exchange. Anyone passing the shop may not have taken a second glance.

Gardener tried to increase the sound but nothing he did was helping.

"He might have had CCTV," said Reilly, "but when did he have it installed? This thing is years old."

"He probably didn't think he needed it, Sean."

Suddenly, the two figures moved. The jeweller quickly ran back around the counter, where the stocky assailant reached out and pulled at Browne's cardigan sleeve. At that point, the jeweller actually slipped backwards, cockled over and went head first into the counter. His head went straight through the glass and even on the small screen, and from the distance the image was being picked up, they could see a stream of blood shoot outwards, filling the cabinet very quickly.

The hooded figure then panicked and actually appeared to be helping Browne, trying without success to free his head; even at that point however, everyone watching realized he was fighting a losing battle. When his head went through the glass, Browne's movements were erratic. At the time he was being helped, his body gestures had slowed somewhat.

The hooded figure put his hands to his head, as if worried. He started scurrying around, as if searching for something to use to help. A phone might have been handy, thought Gardener.

That was in fact the last they saw of the hooded figure for a while, as it went out of camera shot, toward the door leading into the room they were in now.

"That didn't look to me like a premeditated murder," said Reilly.

"I was thinking the same," said Gardener.

"But the conversation grew heated and things took a turn for the worse," said Cragg.

"It looks that way," said Gardener. "If he'd been there to steal something, he would have done. If he'd been there with the intention of murdering the jeweller, I'm sure we'd have seen a weapon."

As they were discussing the situation, they suddenly noticed the hooded figure reappear, stare at Alan Browne's lifeless body, and leave.

But not before Gardener noticed something else.

"What's in the hooded figure's right hand?"

Reilly leaned in close and managed to rewind the footage. They watched again, more closely.

"Looks like a piece of paper," said Cragg.

"I doubt we'll ever find out what's on there," said Gardener.

"Might have been what he was looking for," said Reilly.

"But where did he find it?" asked Gardener. "It must have been in here."

Gardener glanced around. "Okay, let's call the team and the SOCOs, and Fitz, and have this place scoured. I can't imagine there are many prints in this room, so it might be quite easy to check whose they are, if they have a record. We'll take the CCTV system back to the station and see if Gates and Longstaff can do anything with it; see if they can find anything older."

"They might able to do something with the sheet of paper in the hooded figure's hand."

"That would be nice, Sean."

As they left the shop, Cragg turned to Gardener. "I think you should have a word with Elvis before you go. He told me something really interesting this morning that may or may not have a bearing on things."

* * *

An hour later, after Gardener had set his actions in motion, he and Reilly and Cragg were in the back room of the station with Rooney.

The journalist told Gardener everything he had told Cragg.

"That bloody watch again," said Gardener. "It's beginning to look like that thing is at the root of everything."

Gardener turned to Cragg. "Do you know anything about the watch?"

"No," replied Cragg. "I were quite intrigued when Elvis was telling me about it this morning. I'll do some digging for you."

"Can you describe the man who brought it in?" asked Gardener.

"Yes," said Rooney, "I had a pretty good look at him. He was stocky, with black hair. It looked neatly trimmed. He had a black leather jacket and jeans and a flat cap, which is why I couldn't see much of his hair."

That could have been the man in the picture, thought Gardener, but for the bloody hood.

"You didn't get a name?" asked Reilly.

"No," said Rooney."

"Have you seen him before?" asked Gardener.

"No," replied Rooney.

Gardener turned to Cragg. "Sound like anyone you know?"

"No, sir," said Cragg, after some thought.

"Have you ever heard of someone called Archie Figgs?" Gardener asked the desk sergeant.

"No," said Cragg. "But now you come to mention it, the name Figgs is familiar."

"What about you?" Gardener asked Rooney.

"No, never heard of him," said Rooney. "Why do you ask, do you think this bloke with the watch was Archie Figgs?"

"Could be," said Gardener. He went on to explain to Cragg how he had come by the name and what was going on in his world; the two murders, and how the names Walker and Sutton appeared to be intertwined with the elusive watch.

"Harry Pinchbeck?" said Cragg. "Is that waste of space still around?"

"Do you know him?" asked Reilly.

"Everybody knows Harry," said Cragg. "He'd sell his own grandmother if it got him off the hook. He's involved in everything that goes down."

Gardener asked Cragg if he could have a dig around, see if he could pick up anything on the watch, but perhaps more importantly, find out anything he could about Jack Walker's disappearance.

"I wonder if the mysterious Archie Figgs was the hooded figure in the shop," said Gardener.

"Can't see why," said Reilly. "What reason would he have to return? He took the watches with him." He turned to Rooney. "You say the meeting between Browne and the man with the watch was amicable?"

"Very," said Rooney. "It just seemed a bit odd that he left in such a hurry, without waiting for Browne to give him anything."

"Maybe Browne *did* find something and called him back in," said Gardener. "That might explain what the paper was all about."

"Can't see how," said Rooney. "He never gave us any contact details at all. And Browne never mentioned anything else to me."

"What is going on around here?" said Gardener, standing. "Thank you for your cooperation this morning, Mr Rooney. Please stick around, we may need to speak to you again. And I'm sure I don't have to tell you what you've heard this morning is confidential. Please don't mention this to anyone."

"Will do," said the journalist.

Gardener turned to Cragg. "Thank you, Maurice. Looks like you've got yourself into a major mystery with us once again. Once we have the CCTV at the station we'll go through it more closely, and we'll also check the date the mystery man brought the watch in, it might show us something."

"Would you like me to arrange a press release for witnesses?" asked Cragg. "We might get something."

"Please, Maurice. And can you also get every scrap of CCTV from around the town, see if our hooded friend appears anywhere on there?"

Cragg nodded.

Chapter Thirty-four

The Calverley and Rodley railway station, originally called Calverley Bridge Station for the nearby river crossing, opened in 1846, a little after the start of other services on the Leeds and Bradford Railway. It had one island platform, two outer platforms, tracks serving a goods shed, and a loading stage. Sadly, it closed to passengers in 1965, and to freight in 1968, along with the other intermediate stations between Leeds and Shipley, which was all down to the infamous Beeching cuts.

The station building was now a private residence belonging to Maude and Archie Figgs.

As Archie stepped through the front door, he heard the clock in the hall chime, followed by six resounding clangs of the bell. He didn't actually hear anything else, which signalled the fact that his mother Maude was more than likely asleep, following a taxing day in the armchair.

He'd had a tough day at the station, which usually meant he'd had to work a little harder to relieve people of their watches. A really bad day was anything less than five, but he'd managed six. None of them were worth any real money but he would double-check.

Glancing furtively around, making sure Maude wasn't lurking in hidden recesses, he left the hall, walked through the study and then into what he liked to call his secret room, especially as Maude never actually ventured as far as there.

The room was dedicated to a lot of Archie's stuff; mostly his watches, which were kept in a large floor safe that could only be opened with a foot-long key that Archie had hidden in his garden shed, in another safe. The key to that one was kept in a locket around his neck. He wasn't taking any chances. No one was robbing Archie Figgs.

Archie removed the foot-long key from his pocket. He shifted the bits of carpet, opened the safe, removed the watches from his carrier bag and dropped them in, intending to do his research a little later.

Leaving the room, he walked back through the study and into the hall, calling out to his mother, but there was no answer.

"Typical," said Archie. He's out all day earning money, keeping her in the manner to which she had never been accustomed in the early days, and she couldn't even have a meal ready for him when he came in.

"Suppose she's flat out in that fucking chair in front of the fire, roasting her corned-beef legs."

She'd have done nothing all day and as soon as she laid eyes on him she'd complain about all her aches and pains and then expect him to cook tea.

Archie opened the living room door, gingerly. The room was old and past its prime but it was clean. Despite the furniture and the fixtures and fittings being quite ancient, they were in a good condition and very comfortable. The carpet was light green and the curtains had been made to match. A number of oil paintings adorned the walls and a grandfather clock stood against one wall.

The first surprise he found was that Maude was not slumped in the chair at all; she wasn't even in the room. The fire was lit, staving off the cold air outside.

Archie then groaned, because the second thing he found was no surprise. The floor was covered in newspaper.

"Oh, for fuck sake, Ma, can't you leave the paper in one fucking piece for once?"

Maude's use of the newspaper really annoyed Archie. He always brought one home but very rarely had the chance to read it before she did. She'd ask him to do the cooking, or to pop out for fish and chips, while she made a lunge for the paper.

Maude's time-honoured fashion was to seat herself in her favourite chair by the fire, and literally consume the bloody thing, page by page, which she then threw, *page by page*, onto the floor after reading. By the time Archie had the chance to read it, he had to put it back together, by which time he had usually lost interest.

He suddenly heard the clanging of pots and pans and plates and cutlery.

Archie stood up, listening. "Fucking hell, is she ill? Don't tell me she's finally cooked a meal."

Archie's only living relative was Maude, his mother. He was an only child – no surprise there. His father died many years back from pneumonia, which he probably only did in an effort to escape Maude. Before he died, Charley shared a lot of his knowledge about watches with Archie, and gave him some old ones that he managed to keep from Maude because she disapproved.

Maude gave Archie some grief. She ordered him around, often had him fetching and carrying and cooking, yet still called him lazy and stupid. Archie was not allowed to sit at the table with his cap on – woe betide him if he ever forgot – and he had to wash his hands and face before eating.

A sudden bellow from the kitchen rendered Archie's legs useless. "Come on, boy, get yourself in here, your meal's ready."

Archie nearly fainted. Maude? Cooking a meal?

Although he couldn't see her, she quite clearly knew he was there. "Don't you be spending all your time looking at them watches. They won't earn you no money, boy."

"How do you think we manage to live, you dozy cow?" muttered Archie.

"What did you say, boy?"

"Now," he shouted, "I'm coming now."

When he'd finished reconstructing the newspaper he dropped it on the armchair in front of the fire, threw on another couple of logs with some more coal and crept into the kitchen.

Maude came into view as he entered, placing his tea on the table – steak and kidney pie, chips and peas. A tea tray had already been set out with a teapot inside a cosy, cups, milk and sugar.

Maude resembled a rather large haystack in a dress, with silver hair cut short like a man, a waxy, pale face that appeared to have been moulded from plasticine, and big square teeth. She wore long flowery dresses that ended in a pair of large flat feet, a bit like ET in the film.

Maude moved very slowly back to the countertop to retrieve her own meal. She couldn't move fast, or carry much, on account of the large ivory-headed cane she used to support herself. Archie wasn't sure it was needed but it gave her an excuse to order him around, claiming she couldn't do stuff.

Archie laid eyes on his mountain of food and shouted his usual phrase, "Attack and destroy." He took his seat.

That was a major mistake, as she slammed the ivory-headed cane down on to the tabletop, nearly splitting it in half.

"Wash your hands, boy. Don't you sit at my table with dirty hands."

Archie jumped so fast and so high he nearly cracked his head on the ceiling.

He washed and dried his hands at the sink and took his seat at the table again.

Maude slammed her walking stick on the table yet again, causing the cutlery to jump, and Archie almost to have heart failure.

"Are you trying to wind me up, boy? Remove your hat."

Before Archie did, she actually raised the cane and with one quick swipe, knocked it off. She's too fucking handy with that thing, thought Archie. He was also thinking that one more mistake and he'd be a dead man.

"Next time," shouted Maude, "it's your head that will feel the wrath of my cane. Now eat your food before it goes cold."

Archie pulled a face that luckily Maude didn't notice.

"Give it a rest," said Archie.

"Pardon, boy," said Maude, quickly adjusting her hearing aid.

"Test, Mam," he said. "Just testing."

"I'll test you, boy. What have you been doing today?" asked Maude, in a lighter tone.

"I've been busy, Ma."

"Ma," repeated Maude. "Ma. What kind of a word is that? American, I shouldn't wonder, from all these films you watch. Call me mother."

Archie said nothing, simply rammed a load of chips into his mouth in an effort not to talk, because you weren't allowed to talk with your mouth full either.

"Busy doing what?" she asked. "Earning money, I hope." She suddenly stared at him. "You'll do to remember that the devil makes work for idle hands, boy."

Is that so? thought Archie. You should be run off your fucking feet, then. In fact, the only thing Maude had run recently was a bath, and that wasn't very often.

She never really waited for an answer before continuing. "I'll need some things picking up from the shops tomorrow. We're running low on some items for the kitchen and the bathroom, and you can do a food shop while you're at it. And fetch a newspaper."

Archie nodded, shovelling in another mouthful of food. He had to admit it was good. Maude rarely cooked but when she made an effort it *was* worth eating. She was good to him in some ways, though he was fucked if he could remember what and when.

"And because you're doing all that, I'll give you some extra money for your favourite sweets. You'll have earned it, boy."

How old did she think he was? Six?

"Have you seen the newspaper today?" said Maude, pouring both of them a cup of tea.

Chance would be a fine thing, thought Archie.

"You're not safe in your own bed these days."

"You should be," muttered Archie. "No fucker would touch you."

"Pardon, boy," shouted Maude, adjusting her hearing aid yet again. "Don't mutter. What did you say?"

"Too true, Mam," said Archie, glancing up. "Too true. Why? What's happened?"

"There's all sorts going on around here," said Maude, sipping her tea. "Muggings, attacks, murders. There's been two murders only recently. One in Armley and one in Beeston. Don't you read?" Before Archie answered, she continued. "And then that poor jeweller in Bramfield has been murdered."

Archie stopped eating. "Jeweller? In Bramfield?"

"That's what I said."

"Which one?"

"Browne, I think his name was."

Archie felt the rumble in his stomach. He'd heard nothing about Alan Browne being murdered. She probably had the name wrong.

"The article made mention of a mystery watch involved, that everyone is looking for. Police reckon they want to talk to a man who might know something about the watch."

Archie nearly fainted. It had to be Alan Browne.

"Did, er, did they say anything else?"

"Such as?" demanded Maude.

"Did they say who the man was?"

"No. Reckon he's as big a mystery as the watch, but all these murders might be connected to it."

Archie put his knife and fork down, his appetite quickly waning.

He suddenly wondered who was killing all the people, and why, and if it *was* connected to the watch.

More to the point, thought Archie, did the murderer know he had it?

Chapter Thirty-five

Early the following morning, Gardener and Reilly pulled into the market square in Bramfield and parked the car at the side of the station. Gardener jumped out and glanced over at Alan Browne's shop, which was still under police protection but there was only one scenes of crime van outside. He figured there might be some news by the end of the day.

"I'm not so sure they're going to find much," said Reilly.

"I don't think they will, Sean," replied Gardener. "The few minutes of footage that we watched was pretty limited. Whoever the suspect was, he was wearing a hood to make sure we didn't see him."

"Maybe Maurice will have had some luck pulling up the CCTV from around the town."

"You'd like to think so," said Gardener. "I'm not so hopeful with that hood. If he was as careful around the town as he was in the shop, we'll have our work cut out."

Reilly turned and faced the police station. "It must be some watch if that's what's really at the centre of the investigation."

"In some respects, Sean, I hope it is. At least we're not wasting our time now."

As they entered the station via the front door, activity was relatively quiet. A radio could be heard from the back room but no phones were ringing and no one was in the reception area.

Cragg slipped into view. "Kettle's just boiled."

"Can't fault him," said Reilly.

Once they were settled in the back room, Gardener asked Cragg what he had for them.

"I think you'll be quite pleased," replied Cragg. "It took nearly all day and most of the night, mind, tracing back through old paper records."

"You must have found something positive," said Gardener, sipping his tea, noticing his partner had already consumed a Kit-Kat.

"I had a breakthrough last night, about eight o'clock. I've managed to find the man who worked the original cases in the seventies."

"Find him as in still alive?" asked Gardener.

"Yes," said Cragg. "And I've even had a word with him."

"Where does he live?" asked Reilly.

"Not far," said Cragg. "His name's Andrew Mortimer. The Mortimers have retired to a village called Kirkham."

"Where is that?" asked Gardener, eager to speak to someone who might be able to fill them in on all the missing details.

"When you go from here," said Cragg, "take the A64 for a few miles until you come to a road sign advertising Kirkham Priory. Take the left turn and keep going. Go over a railway crossing and a stone bridge. A few yards further on you come across the ruins of a small abbey and the Mortimers have a cottage just opposite."

"That's brilliant, Maurice," said Gardener.

"Did he tell you much?" asked Reilly, unwrapping another chocolate bar.

"No," said Cragg. "But he's going to swat up on it before you get there. Apparently, he still has some notes he made at the time. Cold cases bug him."

"Cases?" questioned Gardener.

"Yes," said Cragg. "I gather there's more than one person connected to this case, and the watch."

"Interesting," said Gardener, glancing at his partner.

"Anyway," said Cragg. "He can tell you more about it than anyone else can, mainly because he's the only senior detective still alive. Apparently, Jack Walker worked for the railway station in Bursley Bridge."

"Did he really?" asked Reilly. "Makes sense if this one-off watch is supposed to be a pocket watch. Weren't they mainly associated with railways?"

"It might also make a lot of sense," said Gardener, "when you consider other evidence we have is also pointing to the railway."

"In that case, you might find another bit of information I uncovered as very interesting."

"You have been busy," said Gardener.

"You know me, sir, I like a challenge. Anyway, a visit to the station in Bursley Bridge is in order. They have a man who works for them called Phillip Walker. Now that can't be a coincidence."

"Unlikely," said Reilly. "How is he related to Jack? Or is he?"

"I haven't had enough time to do any digging on this one but Andrew Mortimer believes it might be Jack's son."

"And he works for the railway too?" asked Gardener.

"Appears that way," said Cragg.

"Okay, Maurice," said Gardener. "You've certainly done a good job for us." He glanced at his partner. "I think we'd better start with Andrew Mortimer."

Both men rose and made their way out of the station. In the lobby, Gardener turned back to Cragg.

"Thanks, Maurice, we'll keep you posted on this. One more question. Has the name Figgs come back to you?"

"Not really, no," said Cragg. "Not in so many words."

"We haven't found anything either, but we have two of the team on him," said Gardener. "What did you mean, not in so many words?"

"Well, the name Figgs did ring a bit of a bell," said Cragg. "So, I had a good think. The only person I know by that name is a woman called Maude. She lives in Calverley somewhere, but I'm not sure where."

"It's not exactly a common name," said Gardener, "so there could be a connection. How do you know her?"

"Mainly on shoplifting charges," said Cragg. "But that was years ago. I'm not sure she'd still be alive. I certainly don't know of her ever having had a family."

"Okay," said Gardener. "It's worth a follow-up. If she's been done for shoplifting, she'll have a record and she'll be on the system. We might get lucky."

As they were leaving, Reilly said, "Do you know what gets me?"

"Go on," replied Gardener.

"How did the bloke who invented the watch, or the clock, actually know what time it was?"

Gardener glanced at his partner and smiled. "Only *you* could ask that question."

Chapter Thirty-six

Maurice Cragg had been spot on with his directions, and the pair of them found the Mortimers' cottage quickly and easily. Reilly parked the car in the small car park near the ruins of the abbey opposite.

As they crossed the road, the front door opened and a lady immediately introduced herself as Andrew's wife, Masie.

She was plump, and would have been at home in a large farmhouse kitchen. Masie had grey hair, tied up in a bun, and glasses perched on a round button nose. She wore a long, flower-patterned dress with a pinafore.

Gardener and Reilly displayed their warrant cards but she immediately waved them away. "I know what a policeman looks like after all these years. Come on through."

She led them down a comfortable hall that finished in a nice warm kitchen with an island in the middle and an Aga along one wall.

"He's been looking forward to it," said Masie. "Gives him a break from gardening, not that there's much to do this time of year."

She then opened a door at the side of the kitchen, which took them into a richly decorated study. The ceiling had roof beams in dark oak and most of the furniture around the place was the same colour or shade of wood, including a desk and a filing cabinet and a couple of ordinary cabinets.

Andrew Mortimer rose from his desk to greet them. Gardener thought he had weathered well for his seventy-four years. He was shorter than Gardener, slim, with white hair, glasses, and a smooth complexion.

"How lovely to meet you both," said Mortimer. "And how bloody exciting it is to find you might be working a case that I started on fifty years ago."

Gardener and Reilly shook hands and Mortimer asked them both to sit in the comfortable chairs available, with a small glass-topped table in-between.

"Right," said Masie. "I'm going to make some tea and leave you men to it. I'm sure you have a lot to talk about."

Mortimer sat and immediately said, "I like your hat. Where did you get it?"

Gardener was in the process of removing it. "My late wife."

"Oh, I'm so sorry," said Mortimer. "There's probably an awful story attached to it but I won't ask, out of respect."

Gardener nodded, thinking how comfortable the chairs were despite their obvious age.

Masie returned with a tray containing tea and scones, which she placed on the table. That would keep his partner happy for a while, thought Gardener.

The SIO poured tea for everyone and sat back, as did Mortimer.

"I've thought a lot about this case over the years. It was a real puzzler. I kept a bit of a diary, you know, because the case went cold; and then became more intriguing as time passed. I remember it well. Jack just went missing."

"You never found any trace of him at all?" asked Gardener. "No clues?"

"No. But I gather you have."

"In a manner of speaking," said Gardener, before relating what they had so far found and what had led them to his door.

"This is interesting. I *can* tell you that this case starts further back than the seventies, though."

"How far back?" asked Gardener, although he had an idea from the snippets he'd heard.

"Mid-sixties," said Mortimer. "It could go further back than that but I don't have any proof. In fact, what I am going to tell you, I have no real proof of. Between us, my colleagues and I took names and places and dates, and all we could do was make an educated guess."

"I'm sure you know more than we do, Andrew," said Reilly. "So tell us anyway."

"This feud has gone on for years," said Mortimer. "One of those family things that has never really died by the sound of it."

Mortimer picked up and leafed through his diary, which was basically an old A4 notebook that had weathered the years almost as well as he had.

"I'm going to start with Jed Walker, Jack's father, because he's the one I know most about. It was his death we were investigating. He was born in Bursley Bridge in 1915. Following his schooling he did his National Service. When demobbed, he joined the railway, which, at that time, was the LNER in Bursley Bridge.

"He started at the bottom like you always do, in railway maintenance. He covered tasks like railway lubricator, signal maintainer and track inspector, before moving on to plate laying. I don't understand these jobs, but then, I didn't need to.

"Over the next ten years he did everything from structural engineer to lighting engineer, and electronic equipment engineer, before moving into the station environment to cover turnstiles, escalators, lifts, lighting, and telephone systems."

"He was certainly an experienced man, then," said Gardener.

"Definitely," said Mortimer. "And all those years of experience paid off when he made the position of superintendent in 1965. He was fifty. For that, he received a special watch that had been commissioned for him."

"This was the watch that seems to be causing all the trouble," said Reilly, before adding, "These scones are amazing."

"Thank you," said Mortimer. "She makes them herself, to her mother's recipe, and that, I believe, came from *her* mother."

"Can't fault them," said Reilly. "Neither can I understand why you're so slim if your dear wife can bake like this."

Mortimer smiled. "Anyway, the watch. Yes, this is the one that's causing all the trouble. I don't know too much about it, except that it was a one-off made by the company William Potts. I'm not sure who made it, but it took about five months, and back then, cost an arm and a leg. About two hundred pounds, I believe."

"I wonder what that would be in today's money," said Gardener.

"I shudder to think," said Mortimer. "Or what it could be worth now, considering what's going on. Jed actually died less than a year later, in a mysterious train accident. A goods locomotive derailed on the main line between Beck Hole and Whitby, after the unit had collided with an old Bedford truck sitting across the track."

"What the hell was a truck doing across the track?" asked Reilly, buttering his second scone.

"I'll come to that," said Mortimer. "I *can* tell you that no one knew who put the truck there."

"Did you eventually trace the owner?" asked Gardener.

"Yes," said Mortimer. "It belonged to an old farmer in the area, by the name of Watkins, who, to be fair, had reported it stolen the previous week. It was investigated but never retrieved. The locomotive derailed approximately sixty metres in front of the Grosmont Tunnel, originally known as Horse Tunnel, which had been upgraded to steam locomotion in the 1840s to accommodate trains.

"The loco tipped over onto the adjacent track, which ran towards the south. An official report appeared after the accident, stating that a ganger, Billy Trotter, the man in charge of a group of labourers, found Walker lying in the six-foot way on the main line about thirty yards from the tunnel."

"I take it he was dead," said Reilly.

"I'm afraid so," said Mortimer. "His head was severed from his body, which they eventually found twenty yards further away. An inquest was conducted the following week, and a decision was reached that while the train was in motion, one of the doors had swung open suddenly, due to a faulty latch. The collision then caused him to fall out onto the adjoining railway line. Other body damage suggested that he must have gone under the train and been dragged down the line before it came to a halt."

"Any idea why he was on the train?" asked Gardener.

"It was a new one being brought into service, and he'd been invited to go on the maiden run."

"So presumably someone had told him about the faulty door and he was checking it," said Gardener.

"That's about the size of it," said Mortimer. "I remember interviewing the conductor, a man called William West, who had been alerted by a passenger about the door. He happened to be with Jed at the time, and Jed said *he* would look into it."

"The conductor didn't go with him?" asked Reilly.

Mortimer shook his head. "Might have been better if he had."

"So there was no evidence of anything happening other than the fact that he fell from the train while it was in motion?" said Gardener.

"That's all we could find, but naturally we were not happy that the truck had been left on the line. We never ever found out who was responsible. It didn't sit right with us, but we checked out every lead, followed up on every bit of information, but couldn't find anything untoward."

"Did you have any suspicions?" asked Gardener.

"Some," replied Mortimer, finishing his tea. "We had an idea of why it had been stolen, and why it was on the line. This is where we come to the Suttons and the possible start of the feud."

Gardener sat back.

"Cyril Sutton was born in Bramfield, three years before Jed Walker," said Mortimer. "On the day that the Titanic sank – rather memorable. I need to give you a bit of background so you know how it all ties in. Cyril was one of seven children. Food and money were scarce. He rarely went to school, and his father rarely went home; he was either out with the local gangs on the rob, or down at the pub spending whatever housekeeping he had.

"Cyril's mother held down two jobs in an effort to try and keep the family together, and often relied on handouts from *her* family when she fell pregnant and was unable to work. From around the age of seven, Cyril was forever being chastised by the local police for stealing anything he could lay his hands on – pushbikes, prams, other people's property, and whatever he could fit in his pockets at the local shops."

"He sounds a good 'un," said Reilly.

"You've not heard the half of it," said Mortimer. "When he was fourteen, Cyril was sent to borstal for GBH. He had been caught stealing by one of the residents of the village and a fight broke out. The man ended up in hospital, and Cyril was sent for correction.

"He didn't spend a lot of time there, and when he came out, a little after his sixteenth birthday, one of Cyril's older brothers managed to secure him a place on the railway – the LNER in Bursley Bridge. To be fair, he settled, and managed to become a valued member of staff. Maybe borstal had done him some good. But Cyril Sutton never rose to the heights that Jed Walker did, and for some reason, always resented that. He had a real chip on his shoulder, which is why I say the feud may have started before this, but I can't tell you why, because no one ever told us what went on between them."

"But you think something obviously had," said Gardener.

"Apparently Cyril often claimed that Jed curried favour by sucking up to the bosses, which was why he was over compensated with much better jobs and salary, not to mention a special watch to mark his fiftieth birthday and his promotion. When Jed became super, Cyril claimed that Jed picked on him by giving him jobs that no one else would tackle, tasks that rarely – if ever – included any overtime.

"Cyril resented that and ended up reverting to his old ways. He went on the rob, but by now, the cache was bigger – motor vehicles in particular – in order to rob post offices and banks. Though we could never prove it, we definitely thought it was Cyril who stole the farmer's truck and left it on the line, knowing that Jed was aboard that train."

"I sense there's a lot more to this train derailment, Mr Mortimer," said Gardener.

"That's what we thought," said Mortimer. "Sometime later, another gang member claimed that Cyril was also on the train. Apart from carrying goods, it was being used as a bullion train. He said Cyril somehow knew this, and he and his gang were aboard, monitoring all the movements, despite the risk of what could happen.

"What I am going to tell you now is all supposition because I have no proof. We thought it more than possible that, at the relevant time, Cyril opened the door of the goods carriage and let it swing around, and very possibly damaged the lock. It must have been a dream come true for Cyril when Jed Walker was given a message about the door being open and finally appeared.

"When Jed came to inspect, the moment must have been perfect, because that was when the train must have crashed into the truck. Jed probably reacted. We think that Cyril then appeared and perhaps pushed him, before taking cover. Once the train had overturned and settled, Cyril and the gang managed to grab the loot and escape, unhurt, into a nearby field where another truck or van was waiting to collect them.

"We found tyre tracks, but you have to realize we didn't have the technology available then to get anything concrete."

Mortimer quickly checked his diary.

"Of course, we found out a little later that Jed's watch was missing."

"Missing?" questioned Gardener. "You think Cyril Sutton took it?"

"Quite possibly," said Mortimer. "Nothing was pinned on him because he had alibis. We suspected they were rubbish because they mostly came from his family, or his criminal fraternity."

"He would have been taking a hell of risk, though, wouldn't he?" asked Reilly. "If he did derail the train, he could have been killed himself."

Mortimer nodded. "I agree. But it would have paid off, wouldn't it?"

"What do they say?" asked Gardener. "Fortune favours the brave."

"It certainly does," said Mortimer. "And if the story is true, there can't have been anyone braver than Cyril and his gang that night. None of them were injured, which was a pity. An injury just might have helped us prove they were on it."

"Christ," said Reilly. "This takes come believing."

"So where does Jack Walker tie into all of this?" asked Gardener. "He obviously does. He's bound to have found something out."

Mortimer's expression was apologetic. "I really don't know a lot about Jack. I know he was born in Bursley Bridge to a family and a country still recovering from the war. Being in a rural setting they had fared better. People stuck together more, looked out for each other, grew food for themselves, shared rations.

"His childhood was pretty normal. He eventually followed in his father's footsteps and applied for a position with the railway. At that time, the Bursley Bridge railway was part of the British Rail network. He even worked with his father for a while, from what I can gather, but the bizarre railway accident in which he lost his father pretty much terrorized him. He was absolutely convinced he knew who was responsible."

"But he had no evidence," said Gardener.

"No, just a lifetime of bad blood," said Mortimer.

"So how did he take it?" asked Reilly.

"Badly," said Mortimer. "For a while he turned to drink, behaved badly. His work suffered. He publicly blamed the Suttons more than once but eventually he had to accept that neither we, nor he, could prove anything. But something strange did happen a little while before he disappeared."

"What?" asked Gardener, leaning forward.

"It's hearsay. Once again, there's no evidence that this happened the way I heard it."

"I understand that," said Gardener.

"Following some station maintenance one evening, the local rumour mill put it about that Jack Walker was approached by a reporter who had been covering a completely different story, when he had managed to unearth something very interesting that he felt was worth a further investigation."

"Something to do with what had happened to his father?" asked Reilly.

Mortimer nodded. "I only found out about this a couple of years after Jack disappeared. But I looked into it.

A reporter, a school friend of Jack's named David Saunders, suggested that he and Jack should pop out for a drink. David claimed he had uncovered what had really happened on the night of his father's death.

"The information had come from an old lag in Armley who said he'd been involved that night, as well as in a number of other robberies, partnering Cyril Sutton. The old lag felt he had nothing to lose; he was banged up for life, covering for Sutton. Now he was dying and willing to trade information for an early release. Saunders had all the proof he needed, and he told Jack something that no one else could possibly have known, about his father's watch."

"There it is again," said Reilly, "the infamous watch. What did he tell him?"

"As far as I'm aware, he described it," said Mortimer. "The old lag in Armley had told the reporter all about the watch. As it was a one-off, very few people knew anything about it. But Jack did."

"So it's fair to assume that Jack Walker went after Cyril Sutton?" asked Gardener.

"I would say so," replied Mortimer. "I found a newspaper report, only a small column, mind, covering Cyril's death. Apparently, it was accidental. I checked into it a bit further and it seems as if Cyril had mixed up his meds. What you will find interesting is this: The delivery man pulled up to the house and searched the van for the package. Some bloke with two shopping bags of groceries appeared. He asked the driver if they were for his dad, nodding to the front door. The driver agreed, dropping the meds in one of the carrier bags, because he was running late."

"And do we know who the man was?" asked Reilly, "as if we couldn't guess."

"From the description we had," said Mortimer, "we think it was Jack Walker. But there was no CCTV and no proof. And, as I said, by the time I had found out, Jack had already disappeared."

"Do you know anything about his disappearance?" asked Gardener. "Did the police find anything they could go on?"

"I'm afraid I don't know much," said Mortimer. "I did hear that the night before Jack disappeared, he and his wife had had a massive argument *about* the watch."

"So, he *did* have the watch," said Gardener."

Mortimer nodded. "It would seem so."

"Suggesting he must have had a hand in Cyril Sutton's death," said Reilly.

"Yes," said Mortimer. "Anyway, Brenda, Jack's wife, felt it should be in a bank for safekeeping, particularly if it *was* worth that much. She was heavily pregnant and did not need the worry. As she was staying with her mother for a week in a caravan in Filey, she suggested he get on with it."

"He obviously didn't," said Reilly.

Mortimer shook his head. "It was unlikely. The next day, Jack had disappeared, and so too had the watch, leading her to believe that maybe he was not the man she had first thought; that he did not agree with her, that the watch meant more to him than she did, and somehow, he had chosen to leave instead. Neither Jack nor the watch were ever seen again."

"And the police couldn't find any evidence of anything happening?" asked Gardener.

"Not that I heard," said Mortimer. "The next morning, a heavily pregnant Brenda returned home from Filey. She discovered an empty house and immediately reported it as very odd to the police. They came round, checked out everything and put out a missing person's report, with a description and a photo. All avenues were checked: rail stations, taxi firms, buses, airports, but Jack was never ever found, and the case went unsolved."

"And the watch was missing?" asked Reilly.

Mortimer nodded.

"But we now know different," said Reilly. "Perhaps he was made to go missing, and maybe whoever did it wanted the watch."

"Patrick Sutton was Cyril's son," said Mortimer. "He was a bad one, just like his father. But once again, the police, namely me, because it was where I started, could prove absolutely nothing. He wasn't seen anywhere near Jack Walker at any time, so once again, they have no idea what really happened."

"This is absolutely bizarre," said Gardener.

"Isn't it?"

"Do you know that Jack had a son?" asked Gardener.

"I did hear about Brenda giving birth," said Mortimer. "Everything was fine despite what had happened, but I never heard anything else."

"She called the boy Phillip," said Reilly. "Have you ever heard anything about him?"

Mortimer shook his head. "No, I'm afraid not. I left Leeds shortly after that incident and I never came back to Bramfield. Lost touch with everyone."

"You don't know a Maurice Cragg, then?" asked Reilly.

"No," said Mortimer. "But I have heard of him."

That made them all laugh.

"I think we might have taken up enough of your time, Mr Mortimer," said Gardener. "Is there anything else you can think of?"

Mortimer thought long and hard, if his expression was anything to go by. "I don't think so. I've told you what I know, and what I suspect. I just hope it helps."

"You've certainly filled in some blanks, so you have," said Reilly.

"It's not likely any of Cyril's gang are still alive, is it?" asked Gardener.

"I seriously doubt it," said Mortimer. "And if they are, I doubt they'd be of sound mind enough to tell you anything."

Gardener leaned forward and grabbed his hat, but before leaving he asked another question. "Can you let us have the dates that all of these people either died, or went missing?"

Mortimer scanned his diary and wrote them down before passing the details to Reilly.

Chapter Thirty-seven

When you were stuck in the middle of a murder investigation, the days were long, and the nights felt even longer, thought Gardener whilst studying the whiteboards. The current case had taken them from Beeston to Armley to Bramfield and Bursley Bridge, with the possibility of Whitby looming, should they need to investigate the cold cases in more depth.

Following their interview with Mortimer, Gardener had summoned the team to an early evening incident room meeting. Reilly had been up to his usual tricks and had somehow commandeered some food from a local bakery to go with the tea and coffee the station were providing.

When everyone was seated, he told them about the meeting with Andrew Mortimer, and how the ex-policeman had managed to fill in some of the blanks.

"If we follow the trail," said Gardener, "we can see it starts with Jed Walker. He was killed because of the derailment of the train."

"So did Cyril Sutton cleverly manage to pull off the perfect murder and make it look like an accident?" said Bob Anderson.

Gardener nodded. "That's what Mortimer thought. Trouble is, no evidence."

"Sometimes, you don't need much," said Thornton. "A good copper's instinct will tell you what you need to know."

"Trouble is, Frank," replied Gardener, "you can't arrest, charge, or take someone to court on a copper's instinct."

"More's the pity," said Sharp.

"Bloody dangerous game to play," said Rawson. "Silly bugger could have killed himself and half his gang."

"That's what Mortimer said," added Reilly.

Gardener continued. His team were not saying anything Mortimer had not said. "The trail then moved on to Cyril Sutton, who appeared to die of an overdose due to a mix up in his meds, which may have been done deliberately."

"Once again," said Sharp, "no evidence, but a copper's nose and logic put Jack Walker, Jed's son, in the frame."

"It obviously *wasn't* a mix-up of meds," said Gates. "I'd like to know how long he'd been on them."

"If it was a recent prescription, you could be forgiven for making a mistake," said Longstaff. "If he'd been taking them ages, there's no way he would have messed them up. Sounds to me like Jack Walker sorted Cyril Sutton out for killing *his* father."

"I agree," said Gardener. "Still, no real evidence."

"Maybe not," said Benson. "But Jack must have taken the watch back, because it wasn't found amongst Cyril's possessions."

"You see, that's the problem with all of this," said Gardener. "What happened seems logical, but we have nothing to back it up."

"And no bloody watch, seemingly," said Gates. "I'd love to see this thing when it finally makes an appearance."

"Wouldn't we all," said Reilly.

"If it ever does," said Gardener.

"What do you mean, sir?" asked Edwards.

"We still don't know who has it."

"Or who wants it," added Reilly.

"We only know someone – the reporter, Dwayne Rooney – who believes he has seen it recently," said Gardener. "In the hands of someone – namely Archie Figgs – that no one has ever heard of, or is able to find. According to what we have, Archie Figgs does not exist. No one of that name draws benefits, or pays tax; doesn't appear to have a bank account – very possibly does not exist according to the authorities. He's not on the system at all."

"You don't think Harry Pinchbeck has made it up, do you?" said Thornton. "That *he* still has the watch?"

"If he has," said Gardener, "he'd better watch his step, hadn't he? Because someone out there wants it bad enough to kill for. It's only going to be a matter of time before they find him."

"Maybe we should bring him back in again," said Reilly.

"Maybe," said Gardener. "So, let's get back to the trail. We've now caught up to Jack Walker. If he *did* kill Cyril Sutton and take back the watch, then someone knew about it and finally caught up with him. Jack disappeared but we now know he was killed. That someone had to be Patrick Sutton, he must have been responsible, otherwise, why would Jack Walker have ended up in a coffin in a house that used to belong to Patrick Sutton?"

"And Mortimer didn't know anything about Patrick Sutton?" asked Edwards.

"Not a great deal," said Gardener. "Have *we* discovered anything about him?"

"Only bits," said Sharp. "We know he was born in 1946 and, like his father, Cyril, he turned out be a bit of a rogue. From the records we've been able to dig up, and the few people we could talk to, Patrick grew up in a world of violence, and soon found himself on the road to ruin. He didn't appear to have any interest in women in his early years, only in making himself money. He fell in with a bad lot and disappeared from the Leeds area for a while when he was sixteen."

"We don't know where he went?" asked Reilly.

"Couldn't find anything," said Rawson. "We do know he returned when he was eighteen to look after his father, who by then had heart problems. Following Cyril's death, Patrick returned to his life of drugs. That's when the boys in blue took a keener interest – they pulled him in a couple of times."

"There was talk of him finding a girlfriend, who managed to straighten him out a little," said Sharp. "Enough to get him off drugs. Her name was Tilly Clark."

"Did you find her?" asked Gardener.

"No," said Rawson.

Gardener made notes on the whiteboards. He turned and continued. "Do we know what happened to Patrick?"

"He passed away in 1999," said Rawson. "That's when he left the house to Roy in his will."

"No mention of the watch?" asked Gardener.

"Not from what we can see," said Sharp.

"Might be fair to assume, then," said Gardener, "that he left the house to Roy, and gave the watch to Steven."

"On the face of it," said Longstaff, "that hardly seems like a fair trade, unless you knew the real value of the watch."

"I think that sums it up nicely, Julie," said Gardener. "Did Roy Sutton know the true value of the watch?"

"Possibly," said Reilly. "Maybe that's why there was a rift between them."

"Why should there be?" said Benson. "Roy Sutton had the house."

"Maybe it was Steven who started the rift," said Gardener. "After all, he would have known Roy was given the house, while all he got was a watch."

"Possible," said Anderson. "But then again, they were half-brothers. Maybe they just weren't close anyway."

"It can happen that way with families," said Thornton.

Eager to move on, Gardener continued. "Now we're in current times. Steven and Roy Sutton have both been killed, leaving us to concentrate our efforts on a man called Phillip Walker, as he appears to be the last of the line."

Before launching in a brainstorming session about Phillip, he continued with his summary, which he felt was important. Everyone had to know where they were up to.

"At the centre of this little mystery is a watch that went missing shortly after it was made, never to be seen again until quite recently, when someone took it to Alan Browne for a valuation. That someone appears to be called Archie Figgs, whom I will come back to. We've been told that Archie bought the watch from Harry Pinchbeck. Judging by the description we've been given, it wasn't Harry Pinchbeck who went to see Alan Browne for the valuation, in case we're wondering if Harry and Archie are one and the same."

"But now Alan Browne has been killed," said Anderson.

Gardener nodded. "Studying the CCTV that we've all seen, does the fracas in the shop have something to do with the recent reappearance of the watch?"

"It must," said Benson. "If whoever it was in the shop believed that Alan Browne had it."

Gardener nodded. "Or is all of this connected to two drug dealers, names of Pete Roberts and Cliff Poulton, the two possible people seen running from Roy Sutton's house? Have we anything more on those two?"

Paul Benson shuffled some papers around. "We've spoken to Cliff Poulton. He bought stuff from Sutton, but he didn't kill him."

"Does he have an alibi?" asked Reilly.

"Yes," said Edwards. "On the night of Roy Sutton's death, he was being held in a police cell here in Leeds."

"That's about as good as it gets," said Reilly.

"Roberts is still a mystery," said Benson. "We haven't found him yet. From what we've heard, though, Roberts controls all of them. He has a history of violence, but there is no evidence that he knew or had anything to do with Steven Sutton – only Roy."

"When was he last seen?" asked Gardener.

"The nearest anyone can pin it down to is the night before Steven Sutton was killed," said Benson. "In the Peacock pub opposite Leeds United's ground."

"So he *could* be responsible for both murders," said Gardener. "Is Pete Roberts our elusive killer? Keep looking."

"Here's another random question," said Reilly. "Does Roberts have any connection to Phillip Walker?"

"Not that we could find," said Edwards.

"Where does Phillip Walker fit into all of this?" asked Gardener. "Is he looking for the watch, or does he actually have it? Does someone else want it bad enough to kill for? Is he likely to be next?"

"Or is he controlling it all?" asked Reilly.

"But if Phillip Walker *has* killed the Suttons," asked Gates, "why? He couldn't know for definite that Patrick Sutton was responsible for his father's disappearance."

"The fact that Jack Walker's remains were found in a coffin in Roy Sutton's basement only came to light after Roy had been killed," said Longstaff. "Steven was killed first."

"Phillip's father, Jack, disappeared before Phillip had even been born," said Thornton. "How much could Phillip really know?"

"Good point," said Gardener. "But people have a way of finding things out, especially if they want something bad enough."

"If Phillip *had* found out when he was growing up," said Edwards, "why wouldn't he have killed Patrick then instead of waiting to kill his sons now?"

"Yes," said Sharp, "Jack Walker's remains would almost certainly have been found then."

"More good points," said Gardener. "All of which make you wonder whether Phillip Walker is a suspect or a victim."

"Either way," said Reilly, "we need to find him and talk to him."

"I agree," said Gardener. "Sean and I did pop over to the railway station after we'd been to see Mortimer, but it was Walker's day off. We didn't find him at home, either."

"He does exist, then?" asked Anderson.

"And he is who he says he is?" asked Thornton.

"What do you mean?" asked Gardener.

"Is he known as Phillip Walker by some people, and Archie Figgs by others?"

"I wouldn't have thought so," said Gardener. "If he was Archie Figgs, he would have the watch. If that's what this is all about, the murders of Roy Sutton and Alan Browne probably wouldn't have happened."

"We have a photo of Phillip Walker here, from the railway station website," said Reilly, "and he is nothing like Archie Figgs was described to us."

Reilly passed the photo to Gardener and he put it on the whiteboard. When he turned, he said, "We do have to consider that the Suttons are connected to drugs, and known to all the dealers. It's possible their deaths *are* drug-related, and the watch going missing might be a coincidence."

A few of the team groaned. The boss throwing another spanner in the works was not something they appreciated.

Gardener changed subjects. "Further topics to nail down – sorry about the pun but I may as well use that as a start. The nail gun."

"The station at Bursley Bridge had them, bought in the seventies," said Thornton. "And you're not going to believe who actually bought them."

Gardener immediately clicked and asked, "He didn't?"

"Yes" – Anderson nodded – "of all people, Jack Walker."

"Christ," said Reilly. "That's ironic. Did they only buy the one?"

"No," said Thornton. "They bought three."

"Do they still have them?" asked Reilly.

"They do as a matter of fact," said Anderson. "It took a while to locate them but they were all in some random goods shed, not far from where the town used to have a trout farm. Didn't look as if they had been used for a while."

"What does that mean, then?" asked Edwards.

"It means we have to keep searching until we find one that should be somewhere, but isn't," said Gardener. "Keep going."

He turned to Sharp and Rawson and asked about the grease and the rope.

"Pretty much the same thing," said Sharp. "Dawson's Engineering, National Rail in Leeds, and a number of other local stations, including Bursley Bridge, all use the grease found on the rope."

"We've taken samples," said Rawson, "but I don't see how it's going to help us."

"Not yet, maybe," said Gardener. "However, if forensics can match a particular batch of grease to the ropes we have, it might tell us where and when it was bought. We can hope. Keep pestering."

He threw another question out. "Anyone manage to find out anything on this strange little safe? If we have, does it match our key?"

Longstaff said she knew what the safe was, but it was going to be very difficult to pin down.

"Railways all over the UK had purchased them," said Gates, "but we finally found out for definite that Bursley Bridge also bought them."

"And they have five altogether," added Longstaff.

"I don't suppose we managed to get there and check all five, did we?" asked Gardener. "Seeing as how Bursley Bridge railway is playing such a big part in everything."

"We did," said Gates. "But only three of them remain, and all are still in use."

"But our key doesn't fit any," said Longstaff.

"Where are the other two?" asked Gardener.

"They have no idea," said Gates. "It *was* a long time ago."

"Jack Walker probably owned one of them," said Reilly. "Maybe that's where he kept the watch."

"Good point, Sean," said Gardener. "But think about it. The key Jack had was gripped in his hand, suggesting that the killer may not have known anything about where he had the watch. If Patrick Sutton had made Jack Walker unlock the safe and give him the watch, why would the key still be gripped in Jack's right hand?"

"Unless Sutton put it there to make it look like Jack *was* protecting something," said Sharp.

"We'll probably never know," said Gardener. "Because Jack disappeared, or that's how it was made to look. The detectives examining the scene were looking for a missing person, they were not investigating a murder. Which it wasn't, until *we* found him. The mention of the railway, however, now gives us yet a further connection to Phillip Walker. Does he actually know anything about his father's disappearance, or in fact, the whole story? In which case, he might well be our man."

"Is Walker looking for the killer himself?" asked Reilly.

"I hope not," said Gardener. "The killer is one dangerous man. I think we have to assume that Phillip Walker knows something, and that maybe he *is* looking for the watch. Colin, you find out anything more about it?"

"Nothing we don't already know, unless you count having a picture of it." As he said that he glanced at Gates, referring to the earlier comment.

"You have a picture?" she asked.

Sharp passed it over to Gardener. "I can't tell you a great deal but there is one very popular connection to it."

"Tell us what you can," said Gardener.

"We caught up with one of the Potts family in Leeds," said Rawson. "John Potts, and he remembered it being made. He dug the picture out for us. It was actually designed and made by John's grandfather, Reginald; started in late 1964, finished in early 1965. The Railway Commission had asked for something special, and that's what Reggie wanted to give them, a one-off. Parts had to be shipped in from all over the UK."

"Why so special?" asked Gardener. "Admittedly, the man it was made for was fifty, and he was a superintendent, but he wasn't retiring."

"John Potts didn't know," said Sharp. "To the Potts it was a commission, and it cost something in the region of two hundred pounds. They called it the PRS watch – a Potts Railroad Special."

"Here's the interesting thing," said Rawson, "John Potts told us that we were not the only people who have been asking about it."

"I imagine the TV company must have been one, they made the documentary," said Gardener. "So who else has been asking?"

"After checking his records," said Sharp, "Potts told us he had recently been contacted by a collector, who wanted to authenticate the existence of the watch."

"Who?" asked Gardener.

"Phillip Walker," replied Sharp.

Chapter Thirty-eight

"When?" Gardener asked. A strange feeling ran through his body. The more the railway and Walker were being mentioned, the less he liked it.

"A few weeks back," said Sharp. "After the documentary had aired."

"And before Steven Sutton died," added Rawson.

"That statement lends some credence to Phillip Walker being the man we want to talk to," said Gardener, "and that he didn't have the watch then."

"He didn't then," said Edwards, "but he might have now."

"So he could well be our killer," offered Reilly.

"Possibly not," said Thornton. "If he has it, he didn't get it from Alan Browne."

"Maybe not," said Gardener, "but we still don't know what that altercation was actually about – may have nothing at all to do with the watch. And we might never know, because the sound on the CCTV was ropey, and Alan Browne is dead."

"So the man we want *could* still be Phillip Walker," said Benson.

"*If* that was Walker in Browne's shop," said Gardener, "he *would* be responsible for the jeweller's murder, but it didn't appear to be premeditated, it was more accidental."

"But the Suttons' deaths weren't accidental," said Reilly.

Gardener thought about it. The argument was convincing. Either way, they needed to find the man.

"We did try to find Phillip Walker when we visited the station this afternoon," said Gardener, "but he wasn't there; nor was he at home, nor had anyone at the station seen him recently."

"So no one knew where Phillip Walker was?" asked Gates.

"What does that mean?" asked Longstaff.

"It means *we* have to find him, Julie," said Gardener. "One way or another, we have to find him. As things are progressing, I'm leaning on the side of Phillip Walker being our killer. Follow the line of the feud, he's the only one left. It's only natural he's going to want the watch back."

"But is he prepared to kill for it?" asked Reilly.

"That's what we need to find out," said Gardener. "Until we find him, we won't know."

Gardener updated the whiteboard, with the emphasis on Phillip Walker.

He turned. "*Is* there anything to report on Alan Browne's murder?"

"As far as the note in the suspect's hand goes," said Gates, "not a lot."

"It doesn't matter how much we blow up the picture," said Longstaff, "we simply cannot see what is on that paper."

"But we did notice one thing," said Gates. "It really looks like he's wearing gloves."

"So he had some sort of intention when he went into the shop," said Thornton.

"And it's my guess he had a look around the back room," said Gardener. "As far as I can tell, he wasn't in the room too long. Did he know where to look for what he wanted?"

"It's possible," said Gates. "We think he knew where the CCTV was."

"The CCTV showed him entering the shop," said Longstaff. "There was no CCTV at the rear of the premises."

"So we have no idea what happened in there," said Gates.

"Also," added Longstaff, "Alan Browne's antiquated equipment only had two days' worth of CCTV, anything before that had been erased."

"And it's possible that the lack of additional discs is because the killer made them disappear," said Gates, "took them with him."

"Either way that means that there is no remaining footage of the elusive Archie Figgs, who had popped in for a valuation," said Gardener.

A knock on the door interrupted the meeting. David Williams entered with a report. "Thought you might like to see this, sir. The SOCOs have finished up at Alan Browne's shop."

"Nice timing, David," said Gardener. "They find anything of note?"

"Yes," replied Williams. "The suspect's hoodie dumped in the dustbin around the back of the shop, which means his appearance, on leaving, had changed."

Gardener glanced at Gates and Longstaff. "Wasn't he still wearing the hoodie when he left through the front door?"

"Yes," said Gates.

"Looks like he knew the area well," said Reilly. "He's planned what he wanted to do, walked out of the front door, around the back, and dumped the hoodie."

"And perhaps had a change of clothes somewhere else," said Sharp.

"Probably the public toilets near the church," said Gardener. "That *is* only a stone's throw from the shop and the police station."

"Which also renders our search of the CCTV from Bramfield a waste of time," said Longstaff. "We've been looking for a hoodie, but the suspect was no longer wearing that gear."

A collective sigh rose around the room as Gardener thanked Williams for his information. Instead of leaving, Williams took a seat.

Gardener changed subjects. "We've mentioned Archie Figgs a lot. Have we anything to report? Who is *he*, killer or victim?"

His team was negative. No one had anything.

"Maybe we should speak to that reporter, Rooney," said Gardener. "Have an artist sketch a photofit of Archie Figgs, then we can release it to the press."

"He must be somewhere," said Reilly, "even if that is not his real name."

"Surely he can't be that elusive," said Rawson. "Hasn't he been connected to a spate of watch thefts on Leeds station?"

"According to Harry Pinchbeck," said Gardener.

"Maybe a couple of us can hang around there," said Thornton. "He should be easy to pick up."

"Sounds like a plan, Frank," said Gardener. "There's also something else we can do."

"What's that?" asked Anderson.

"We had a possible lead from Maurice Cragg in Bramfield. The only person he knew called Figgs was a lady called Maude, whose last known address was somewhere in Calverley."

"When was that?" asked Benson.

"To be fair," said Gardener, "it was years ago. She had a record for shoplifting charges so if we go back far enough we might come across the address. If we're lucky, she might still be there. Someone check it out."

After updating the board, Gardener asked if anyone had anything else.

"I do, sir," said Williams.

"Go on," said Gardener.

"A couple of your lads have been over to Elland Road and requested some footage from their state-of-the-art CCTV for the day of the first murder. It's just come through."

Williams glanced at Gates and Longstaff. "If I could ask your IT experts to work their magic on the computer, maybe we can all watch it."

"That's good news," said Gardener.

As they were getting the files onto the computer, Gardener added the information Andrew Mortimer had given them that morning to the whiteboard, including the dates that each of the Walkers and Suttons were either murdered or disappeared.

When the footage was ready, Gates and Longstaff fed it through the overhead projector to give everyone a good view.

"Apparently," said Williams, "this stuff is so good, it can pick up every seat in the ground. It does this throughout the match and puts names to faces."

"Is that legal?" asked Anderson.

"I've no idea," said Williams. "I'm not going to question it."

After absorbing the footage, they suddenly realized ten minutes in that it had picked up an empty seat. After watching the rest of the scan, they soon discovered that it was the only empty seat in the ground.

Gardener realized what an overwhelming task he would have if he wanted to know the names and addresses of everyone in the ground that day, but he didn't perhaps *need* to know that. He only wanted to know who hadn't turned up. Could it be the elusive city gent that some witnesses had reported seeing?

He checked his watch. It was late. "Do you think there is anyone still at the ground?"

"I doubt it," said Edwards, scanning his phone for the number.

Gardener rang it but it remained unanswered.

"Does anyone know someone at the ground who is high up?" asked Gardener. "Someone who could get us an answer to our question, like now?"

"I do," said Williams.

"Who do you know?"

"The chairman," said Williams. "He's a friend of mine."

Gardener exhaled a sigh of relief. Sometimes, you needed a bit of luck. He explained to Williams what he wanted.

Williams made not one, but three calls, until he located the very person he needed, who was willing to tap into the CCTV system in the ground and answer their question.

Finally, Williams had it. He thanked the man and cut the call.

"You won't believe this," said Williams. "The ticket for the empty seat belongs to a man called Phillip Walker."

Gardener held up his hands. "Here he is again. Phillip Walker."

"So, if he had a ticket and he didn't go to the game," said Reilly, "where the hell was he?"

Gardener didn't answer immediately. Instead, he studied the boards in silence for a few minutes.

Eventually, he turned and stared at Gates and Longstaff. He explained where Phillip Walker worked. He then asked them to follow any digital trails for train and football tickets associated to Phillip Walker.

Furthermore, he asked if David Williams could arrange a press release and a photo of the man.

In the middle of his actions, Longstaff suddenly shouted. "Oh my God!"

Gardener stopped talking and glanced in her direction. "What's wrong, Julie?"

"The number, sir," she said. "On the whiteboards."

"What about them?" Gardener asked.

"Look at them." She pointed.

"Come and show us," said Gardener.

At the front she pointed to the fourth whiteboard. "In the last meeting, you put these numbers, 135779, on the board."

Gardener watched her as she took a pen for the whiteboard.

"Today, you've put down some more dates, which includes the date that Jack Walker disappeared: 3 May 1977."

She started drawing on the board. "If we rearrange those numbers, change them around a little bit, you'll see that the numbers we have match the date of Jack Walker's disappearance. Especially if you put dashes in the right place – 3-5-1977."

Pleased with herself, she glanced at Gardener.

"The numbers to which the fingers were pointing to on both of the Suttons," said Gardener.

Addressing the whole team, he said, "I want everyone on Walker."

Chapter Thirty-nine

Early the following morning, Archie Figgs was passing the Queens Hotel in Leeds, on his way to the railway station when his mobile rang.

He momentarily ignored it because he had spotted two policemen at the taxi ranks, showing photos and asking questions.

Something had gone off.

As he entered the station, he fished his phone out of the inside of his jacket pocket.

Unknown number.

That was the eighth call he'd had from an unknown number in the space of an hour. What the hell was going on? Was it the same person? No doubt some bastard canvassing for solar panels, or wanting to fit a smart meter. Both of them could fuck off as far as Archie was concerned.

Inside the station were more policemen with photos, talking to businesses and passengers alike. Whatever was happening, it made Archie feel uneasy. Perhaps he ought to abort today's mission.

The phone continued to ring, diverting Archie's attention again.

On the other hand, if it *was* the same person, maybe it really was legit. One of Archie's comrades could have passed his number on. But wouldn't he have told Archie to expect a call?

Archie really didn't like answering his phone to people he didn't know. You never knew what they were going to tie you into. It might even be one of those overseas crank calls where, the minute you answered, they began charging you. Not that they'd achieve much. As far as he knew there was only four or five pounds left on it.

The phone was still ringing.

A commuter suddenly passed him and turned and glared at him. "Aren't you going to answer that?"

"What's it to you?" said Archie. "It's my phone."

The man was tall, built like a beanpole, with little or no weight, silver hair and glasses to match, wearing a dark grey suit and carrying a briefcase.

"I don't know how you can ignore it," said the man. "What if it's urgent?"

"Still my phone, whether it's urgent or not."

The phone stopped.

"Guess we'll never know," said the man.

Well you certainly won't, will you, nosey bastard, thought Archie. Instead, he simply smiled.

As the man turned and entered the station, the phone rang again. Forgetting where he was, Archie suddenly answered and could have cut his tongue out.

"Mr Figgs?" enquired a strange-sounding voice, like marbles rattling around in an empty can.

"Who is this?" asked Archie.

"I believe you are in possession of an expensive watch."

Come straight to the point, why don't you, thought Archie. "Might be," he replied.

An announcement over the station tannoy about a recent cancellation to London drowned out anything else the man said.

"Sorry about that," said Archie. "What was you saying?"

"I said, please let's not mess about, Mr Figgs, do you have the watch or don't you?"

It obviously wasn't a crank, thought Archie, very intrigued all the same. "Tell me who you are."

"Walker," replied the man. "Phillip Walker."

The name rang a bell but Archie's brain was on a go-slow. He chose not to reply; make the man sweat.

"Now, please tell me," said Walker. "Are you in possession of the PRS Pocket Watch, or not?"

Archie had to admit, the man had manners, and manners maketh man. "Why do you want to know?"

"So you are?" said Walker, confidently.

Archie chose to sit himself on one of the chairs outside a café. A waitress glanced at him as if he was something she'd trodden in. Archie turned and ignored her.

"Obviously," he replied. "But like I've said, why do *you* want it?"

"I'm a collector, Mr Figgs. It's the only one in the world like it, and it was my grandfather's. Is that enough for you?"

It was as far as Archie was concerned. That's why the name rang a bell. It was time to talk turkey; talk Archie's language. "How much are you willing to pay?"

"How much do you want?"

Archie's legs wobbled. It's a good job he was seated. Was he serious? "It's a one-off, you know."

"I've just told *you* that," said Walker. "Let's not mess around any longer. Name your price."

Name your price, thought Archie. Name your fucking price. Could be interesting. Archie was thinking 50k, so he said as much.

"That's very reasonable, Mr Figgs. Cash?"

Archie's heart missed a beat, causing near heart failure. "Do you have that much?" replied Archie, in a voice that didn't actually sound like his.

"Of course I have," said Walker. "Otherwise, there would be little point in this conversation."

There was quite a pause before Walker resumed. "If there's one thing you will learn about me, Mr Figgs, it's that I am very serious, I do not waste people's time, and I always see a job through to the end."

"Suits me," said Archie.

"Good. Do you know Bursley Bridge?"

"Yes."

"The station on Park Street."

"Yes."

"Catch the next train," said Walker. "When you exit the station, turn left and go straight on to Undercliffe. Follow that to Newbridge Road."

Archie was thinking. "To where the trout farm used to be?"

"Yes," replied Walker. "Take a left there and you'll see a National Rail goods shed to the left of the car park. I'll meet you there."

"How will I know you?" asked Archie.

"I'll know *you*, Mr Figgs."

Before Archie could reply, the phone went dead. Archie held it at arm's length and stared at the screen, making sure. He checked the memory but then realized it was an unknown number, which meant he couldn't return the call.

Was Walker serious? Would he really pay him fifty thousand pounds in cash? It was a lot of money; but then again, it was a lot of watch.

He glanced at the timetable. The next train to Bursley Bridge left in fifteen minutes, and only took about half an hour to reach the small town.

Archie thought a little bit more. Should he? What was the point of having the watch if he wasn't going to sell it? Maybe that would be a good plan with his other watches; they were not worth as much. But the PRS Pocket Watch was a different thing altogether.

There was every chance it would go up in value, especially if a collector knew for definite it was out there.

What the hell was he talking about, *if* they knew? Of course they knew. People were dying. He'd read the papers. People were being killed all over the place and it appears they were dying for that watch.

Archie suddenly wondered if they were dying because Phillip Walker was killing them. Or was someone else killing them? Will Walker die after he's bought it? It's possible. But if Archie keeps it, *he* might die. Fuck that, time to get rid.

Before leaving for his train, Archie was approached by one of the officers canvassing the station. A big bastard with a big head, black hair and beard and moustache, not someone Archie wanted to argue with. He quickly glanced at the picture on offer and said that he couldn't ever remember seeing the man. He was given the usual spiel: if he did, please phone or visit the station.

Archie put his phone in his pocket and turned, suddenly thinking about the voice on the other end of the line. Who the fuck was he talking to with a voice like that? Dr Phibes?

* * *

Archie's train ran a little late, which was no surprise. That was National Rail for you. Bastards were striking all over the place because they wanted more money, and they couldn't even make the trains run to schedule anyway.

An hour later, Archie left the station in Bursley Bridge and did exactly as instructed, arriving at his destination twenty minutes after that. Luckily, it was mild, and walking was pleasant.

The sign for the old trout farm came into view and when Archie rounded the corner, he saw the car park and a rather huge building, which Walker had called the goods shed. He had no idea why, unless of course it *was* an old one. The building was an imposing corrugated steel unit with windows that were much higher than most people.

Standing outside was a man dressed like a city gent. He wore a brown overcoat with a bowler hat, and he carried a Gladstone bag at his side. He was pretty stocky, with round, wire-rimmed spectacles.

Very professional, thought Archie. If he wasn't a city gent, he could pass for Jack the Ripper.

"Mr Walker?" said Archie.

The man nodded and turned toward a door in the building.

After unlocking the shed, he invited Archie inside. The shed was cavernous with steel shelving layered throughout. The ceiling was pretty high so there must have been a forklift to reach the top.

"Christ," said Archie, his voice reverberating all around. "What does a watch collector want with a place like this?"

The man ushered him inside an office, which was pretty much to the right of the front door they had entered by. He placed his case on the desk and removed his bowler hat.

"You are Phillip Walker?" Archie asked him.

"Please, take a seat."

It had to be, he thought. There couldn't be two people that sounded like a castrated dalek.

Archie didn't sit. He preferred to stand. Although he had his back to the door, if things turned nasty, he could still leave quite quickly. You could never be sure.

"What's with the voice?" asked Archie, trying to break the tension. "I thought it was one of those things you use on a phone to disguise it."

Walker smiled. "Childhood accident, I'm afraid. They couldn't do much in those days, so now I have to live with it."

"Christ, must have been painful."

"It wasn't one of my better moments, or memories," said Walker, opening his case. "Anyway, down to business."

Archie had seen one of those cases before. He'd even sold one or two. They were the business and they weren't cheap. If he wasn't mistaken it was a Tassia Executive leather pilot case. Maybe he wasn't a collector of watches after all. Those cases had pockets all over the place, a small, zipped compartment on the underside of the lid, three pen loops, side pockets with hook and loop closures on both sides. You could certainly store fifty grand in there.

"The watch, Mr Figgs?"

"The watch?" repeated Archie.

"Yes, Mr Figgs, the watch," said Walker. "That *is* why you're here."

Archie suddenly noticed the building was as silent as the grave. He didn't like it. Something wasn't right.

"Oh, the watch," said Archie. "Well, there's a little problem, see."

"Problem?" inquired Walker.

Archie leaned forward and laughed, a nervous laughter. "You don't think I walk around with something like that in my pocket, do you? Anyone could mug me. I had to be sure this was genuine."

"Oh, dear, Mr Figgs. I'm a very busy man, please don't tell me you've wasted my time."

"Oh, no," said Archie. "I just wanted to make sure all this was genuine."

"And why wouldn't it be?" said Walker. "It was me who called you, remember."

"Yes, about that," said Archie.

Walker opened and reached into the case.

Guess the man is serious, thought Archie.

If he'd been expecting money he couldn't have been more mistaken.

Archie didn't even have time to register what was in Walker's hand before his lights extinguished completely.

* * *

When Archie finally came round, he had no idea where the hell he was. At first, all he knew was that it was dark. As his vision came more into focus, he realized he was in a corner.

The second thing he registered was the pain. Why was he in so much fucking pain? His arms were killing him and there was untold pressure on his thumbs.

That was when Archie realized he was hanging by them; as he stared upwards, they appeared to be much bigger than normal.

"What the fuck?" groaned Archie.

Apart from the pain, he was freezing. Glancing downwards he noticed he was wearing only his boxer shorts.

Archie suddenly wet himself. What in God's name was happening?

"Hey," Archie screamed.

"There's no need to shout," said Walker. "I'm not deaf."

Archie jumped, swung round, the pain quite acute and most horrendous. Tears rolled from his eyes.

He came face to face with the man who held him captive, sitting in a chair, having removed his overcoat; drinking tea and eating digestives, as if they were attending a fucking picnic. They might have been for all Archie knew, at Hanging Rock.

"What the fuck is going on here? What have you done to me?" asked Archie.

"One simple job, Mr Figgs," said Walker. "That was all I asked. Had you done that, you would have walked out of here with fifty thousand pounds in your pocket."

"Like that would have happened," retorted Archie, still swinging, and still in pain.

"I told you on the phone, I am a man of my word."

Archie's chest stung like a bastard. A vision of a gun of some kind came into his mind.

"Have you fucking tasered me?"

"I do so abhor violence, Mr Figgs," said Walker. "But sometimes, one finds it necessary in order to get what one wants."

Archie suddenly stopped talking and started thinking. "It's you, isn't it?"

"What's me?" asked the little man, finishing his digestives.

"You've been going round killing people."

"I wouldn't have had to," said Walker. "If only they'd listened, and taken the deal you were offered."

"You're fucking mad."

"I know," said Walker. "But you're incapacitated and I'm not, which makes things worse for you than me. Now I want what is rightfully mine, what belongs to my family. It was stolen from my grandfather and God only knows what's happened to it since, but you have it and I want it."

Archie grew very indignant, or brave, or fucking stupid – he didn't really know. "You're not having it."

"I wouldn't count on that," said Walker.

"I wouldn't sell you that watch if my life depended on it."

"I rather thought it did, Mr Figgs."

He's got a point, thought Archie.

"Anyway, Mr Figgs, you have no need to worry on that score."

"Why?" asked Archie.

"It isn't just your life that depends on the watch."

"What do you mean by that?"

Walker stood up, removed his overcoat from the back of the chair. "I know where you live."

Archie was nearly sick with fear.

"I can see that's struck a chord," said Walker, fastening up the coat. "So I'm going to pop over and see your mother, Maude."

"Don't you fucking touch her," shouted Archie, swinging round, ignoring the pain in his thumbs – but it wasn't easy.

Walker strolled over to Archie and held him still. "Who's going to stop me, Mr Figgs? You?"

Archie waited a few seconds and then said, "You're bluffing."

Walker turned and walked away. "I might be, Mr Figgs, but can you take the risk?"

"No," shouted Archie. "You can't do that. She's old. She doesn't know anything about the watch; she doesn't know where it is."

Walker was some distance from Archie now, still walking very slowly. As he continued, he laughed.

"We'll find out, shall we, Mr Figgs."

Chapter Forty

The day had been a busy one but with little in the way of results so far. Phillip Walker was nowhere to be seen, leaving Gardener to ponder whether or not he really was a suspect, or a victim. He'd had officers out all day, most of them in Leeds, and two at Bursley Bridge. Both had reported that he was not at the station nor was he at home.

As Reilly walked into the incident room with two drinks, he was followed by Sharp and Rawson.

"We've got something, boss," said Rawson.

Sharp fished out his notes. "On the day that Steven Sutton was murdered we have positive sightings of Walker."

"Where?" asked Gardener.

"A cab driver picked him up from the station."

"Where did he take him?" asked Reilly.

"You'll like this," said Sharp. "Elland Road."

"The ground?" said Gardener, glancing at Reilly. "Maybe he *was* intending to go to the match."

"I doubt it, boss," said Reilly. "I reckon the ticket was a cover."

"What time did he drop him off?" asked Gardener.

"Just after lunch," said Rawson. "About twelve-fifteen."

"Did he see where Walker went after he left the cab?" asked Reilly.

"No," said Sharp. "Driver was straight off to another fare."

"Had he ever seen him before?" asked Gardener.

"No."

"Has he seen him since?"

"No," said Sharp.

"How did he pay?" asked Gardener.

"Cash."

"I bet he doesn't have it now," said Reilly.

"Correct," replied Sharp.

"How was he dressed?" asked Gardener.

"Overcoat, bowler hat, and carrying a case," said Rawson.

"That's another black mark against him," said Reilly.

"Can the driver remember any of the conversation?" asked Gardener.

"Very little. He did talk about the match."

"How did he catch the cab?" asked Reilly. "Did he book, or flag it down, or simply jump in at the station?"

"Came out of the station and jumped in," said Rawson.

"Does the driver have CCTV in the cab?"

"No," said Sharp. "You'd think he would, these days."

"Doesn't really matter," said Reilly. "It must be him."

"Did the driver pick him up again after the match?" asked Gardener.

"Yes," said Sharp. "And here's the interesting thing, it was around ten o'clock. He went back to the train station in Leeds."

"Didn't happen to say where he was going from there, did he?" asked Reilly.

"No," said Rawson. "He just went into the station."

"Did he say much on the way back?"

"As a matter of fact, he did," said Sharp, "and there was a bit of a discrepancy with Phillip's story, which later made the driver wonder if he was mixed up about something."

"Go on," said Gardener.

"Phillip told him about a player who was given a red card and sent off, but when the driver talked to a friend a couple of days later, who was also at the match, that was disputed. He says no one was sent off."

Gardener glanced at Reilly. "Chinks beginning to show in the armour."

As he said that, his mobile rang. He reached into his pocket and pulled it out. "It's Julie."

He answered and put it on speakerphone.

"Got something on Walker for you, boss."

"We're all ears, Julie."

"The Elland Road café, not far from the ground. It seems like our man was in there on the day, before the match started. A waitress remembers a small, quiet man dressed in an overcoat, and bowler hat with expensive shoes. She thought he may have been a city gent, or a professional of some sort due to the small bag he carried with him, but he never opened it."

All or nothing, thought Gardener. "How long was he in there?"

"Long enough to eat and drink something. She clearly remembers he ordered a pot of Earl Grey tea with a smoked salmon and cream cheese sandwich."

"What?" shouted Reilly. "In Elland Road?"

Longstaff laughed, so did Gates in the background, before shouting that she had had the same and it was very nice.

"The waitress did notice that he had a very slight limp, but that could have been something he'd done recently," said Longstaff. "Although no one else who'd seen him reported that."

"So he could have put it on," said Reilly.

"I wouldn't have thought so," said Gardener. "It was bound to get him noticed."

"What time did he go in and what time did he leave?"

"He went in at about one, and left a little after two."

"Did she see where he went?"

"No, she was too busy with other customers. She never actually saw him leave."

"Did he say anything when he was in the café?"

"He did. She says for the most part he was reading his paper," said Longstaff. "But when they did talk, he said he was on his way to London."

"London?" said Reilly. "Not the game?"

"No," said Longstaff. "He never once mentioned the game. Said he lived locally and he was on his way to the train station in Leeds to catch the afternoon train to London. He was staying there for the weekend."

"Did you manage to check through any digital trails for train and match tickets?" Gardener asked Longstaff.

"Not yet, sir," said Longstaff. "It is on the list but we've been out with the photos most of the day."

"Okay," said Gardener. "We'll make that a priority when you get back. Was he alone or with anyone?"

"Alone."

"Did he speak to anyone else, perhaps on a mobile phone?"

"Not that she noticed."

"Can she remember how he paid?" asked Sharp.

"Cash."

"Any CCTV?"

"Afraid not. They've never had any trouble and never felt the need."

Gardener realized he didn't really have much more he could ask. At least everything they had said had been positive. He cut the call and collated all the info and started to fill out the whiteboard.

Anderson and Thornton entered the room.

Gardener turned.

Anderson didn't waste any time. "The day of Roy Sutton's death we have a positive from a taxi driver. He recognized the photos we had."

"Another one?" said Gardener, explaining what the rest of the team had come up with.

"A bloke called Tom Earl dropped Walker off outside the prison," said Thornton. "He said he was visiting a sick relative, who didn't have long to live."

Gardener went through a whole series of similar questions to the ones he'd asked everyone else, which pretty much sealed Walker's fate, putting him at the scenes of both murders on the relevant day at the relevant times.

But still, no one had seen him so far today.

Gardener asked Reilly to call Bursley Bridge railway station to check if he had been seen. The answer came back negative.

As they had Walker's mobile number, they called that as well, which went to answerphone.

Gardener sat down a took a sip of tea, which was now cold. "So, where is he?"

"Gone to ground," said Reilly. "Maybe he knows we're on to him."

"Sounds like it," said Gardener. "But where the hell is that likely to be?"

Gardener stood up and studied the whiteboards but he couldn't really see anything that stood out.

He turned back. "I think tomorrow morning we'll collectively drop in at the railway station and have a search around. I'll speak to DCI Briggs about warrants, and I want someone at his cottage. I'll also ask Briggs if there is a way we can gain entry without his permission."

As Gardener was talking, desk sergeant David Williams strolled through the door. "I've had a call from a lady called Maude Figgs. Apparently, she'd very concerned about her son, Archie. He's gone missing, and she is struggling to look after herself."

Victim or suspect? thought Gardener. He was sure now which one.

Chapter Forty-one

Early the following morning, Reilly pulled the pool car into the Market Place car park in Bramfield, adjacent to the police station. As they both jumped out, Gardener glanced over at Alan Browne's shop. The place was locked and closed, with a notice in the window that he couldn't read from where he was. He had heard nothing more from the SOCOs, so they couldn't have found anything else that might help to identify who the man in the hood was.

They took the steps two at a time. As they entered the building, Cragg was in the lobby, on the phone. To his right, Gardener noticed the cleaner doing a spot of dusting, and a fresh citrus smell hung in the air.

Gardener and Reilly nodded to Cragg and slipped into the room behind. The kettle was coming to the boil and

Reilly didn't wait to be asked. As he finished making the drinks, Cragg entered the room.

"Morning, sir," he said to Gardener. "Morning, Mr Reilly. What brings you lads here?"

"A bit of an update, Maurice," said Gardener. He went on to explain what they had found out the previous evening, which had ended with a phone call from Maude Figgs.

"She is still around, then?" asked Cragg, surprised.

"It would seem so," said Gardener.

"What did she want?"

"Her son," said Reilly. "Apparently, Archie's gone missing."

"Has he now?" asked Cragg. "She has one, then?"

"She does," said Reilly.

"Where is she living now?"

Gardener told him, and then updated him a little more on what Maude had told his officers. She had sent Archie out for some shopping early yesterday morning and had seen absolutely nothing of him up to the time she had called them in the evening. Nor had she heard anything.

Gardener had sent Benson and Edwards to see her. They had grilled Maude and were very surprised how little she knew about Archie and his movements; she had no idea where he worked, but he brought money in, so he had to work somewhere. She didn't know his mobile number, or even if he had one; and there were a whole host of other questions she couldn't really answer.

"Didn't want to, more like," said Cragg. "Maude Figgs has always been a law unto herself. She'd tie any officer up in knots – even the best. Sounds like Archie is a chip off the old block."

"Does seem strange," said Gardener. "What's also strange is that we can't find him anywhere: not the electoral roll, no tax records, no PAYE, no National Insurance number... nothing."

"What did she say about that?" asked Cragg.

"Very little," said Reilly. "Apparently she acted dumb."

"Another trick of hers," said Cragg. "Dumb is the last thing *she* is."

Gardener produced a photo of Archie Figgs and asked Cragg if he knew him.

Cragg stared at it for quite some time. "Well, I don't know him, but I can tell you this much: I've seen him, and recently; not sure where."

A PC popped her head around the corner. "There's a Mr Rooney to see you, sir," she said to Cragg.

"Show him in, Gloria."

Rooney entered the room. "You've come just at the right time, lad."

"Why's that?" replied the journalist.

Cragg passed over the photo of Archie Figgs. "Do you recognize him?"

"I do," said Rooney. "This is the bloke who visited Alan Browne to have that watch valued. Is this Archie Figgs, then?"

"It is," said Gardener.

"Where did you find this?" asked the journalist.

"His mother," said Reilly. "He's gone missing."

"Missing?" said Rooney. "There's a bit of a pattern going on here, isn't there? And it's all down to that watch."

"Looks like it," said Gardener.

"People appear to be dying for it," said Rooney, glancing at the photo of Archie Figgs. "He had it, and now he's gone missing. Did his mother have the watch, then?"

"Knows nothing about it," said Gardener.

"Or so she claims," said Cragg.

"You think she might?" Gardener asked Cragg.

"I wouldn't put anything past Maude Figgs," replied Cragg. "She's probably done away with Archie and now she's on her way to sell it."

All four men laughed, despite how serious it was.

"What about this Phillip Walker?" asked Cragg. "Have we found him yet?"

"No," said Gardener. "He appears to have gone missing as well."

"Jesus," said Rooney. "I don't think I want to find this watch anymore. That Maude better watch out if she has it."

Gardener told Cragg everything they had discovered about Walker and the fact that they really wanted to talk to him, but as yet had been unable to find him. They didn't believe that Walker was being held captive; they believed he was their number-one suspect.

"Did you manage to find out anything about his tickets from National Rail?" asked Cragg.

"We're on our way there now," said Gardener. "We know that he bought tickets for London on both days that the Suttons were murdered, but whether he reached London or not is another matter. National Rail said they would cooperate fully if we went along to the station in Bursley Bridge, where he purchased them."

"Where does it leave you if Walker did reach London?" asked Rooney.

"That's something we'd rather not think about for the moment, Mr Rooney," replied Gardener.

"What have you done so far?" asked Cragg.

"Two of my lads are back at the station. We've put out an APB on Walker and Figgs, and I've asked them to alert all the taxi companies, bus stations, train stations, and the airports. I've also asked Gates and Longstaff to keep an eye on Maude Figgs, even though there is a neighbour with her."

"That should be interesting," said Cragg. "And if Walker's not at home?"

"We do have a number of options," replied Gardener. "A Section 18 will let us enter the property if we think someone's life is at risk, or to prevent the property being destroyed. Or if we suspect there is information that could lead to his whereabouts, or evidence of an offence."

"Briggs also said that if he'd been at the property recently, a Section 32 will allow us to enter and search for anything he's discarded or secreted in relation to the suspected offence."

"Sounds like you've got it covered," said Cragg.

"Oh, we're going in," said Reilly. "One way or another."

"Is it okay if I join you?" asked Rooney.

"We can't stop you going to the station, Mr Rooney," said Gardener. "But if anything kicks off, I would advise that you leave it to us to deal with. And remember what I told you last time – keep all of this to yourself."

Rooney nodded. "Okay. I just thought if it did, I might be able to help."

Cragg laughed. "I wouldn't if I were you, Elvis, lad." He then stared at Reilly. "If anything kicks off and *he's* in the middle of it, you'd be well advised to steer clear. At least that way we'll have one less casualty."

Chapter Forty-two

A short time later, Gardener and Reilly were at the railway station in Bursley Bridge. As they headed for the ticket office, Gardener noticed Rooney on the platform, either in search of Phillip Walker, Archie Figgs or a good story – or all three. In the time it took to reach Bursley Bridge from Bramfield, Gardener made phone calls to other members of his team to meet him at the railway station.

They showed their warrants cards to Wendy Wilson at the ticket hatch window and she let them into the small cosy room, where they were surprised to find Janice

Portman from Beeston. She had a rather pale expression and was sitting clasping a cup of tea.

"Mrs Portman," said Gardener. "I'm surprised to see you here. Are you okay?"

She nodded.

"She's had a bit of a nasty shock," said Wendy Wilson. "Well, we all have, to tell the truth."

"Why? What's happened?" asked Gardener. He and Reilly were still standing near the door, relishing the heat in the small room.

"Why don't you tell the officers, love?" said Wendy to Janice.

"It was such a shock, Mr Gardener," said Janice.

"What was?"

"Hearing his voice like that again."

Gardener glanced at his partner.

"Whose voice, Janice, love?" asked Reilly.

"Him as killed poor Steven Sutton," replied Janice, sipping her tea. "I said I'd never heard a voice like it before, and I never wanted to hear it again. My knees went all weak and I came over all funny, like?"

Gardener thought back to the night that Steven Sutton was killed in Beeston, and he remembered Janice Portman's statement that she had heard a very unusual voice coming from the upstairs room.

"And you've heard the voice again?" asked Gardener. "Here, today?"

Janice nodded.

"Did you see the person to whom the voice belonged?"

"No," she said.

"What she heard, Mr Gardener," said Wendy Wilson, "was a station announcement, which had been recorded some time back. We have a lot of announcements that don't need to be live – promotions, that kind of thing."

"And you think the voice on the announcement was the same as the one you heard the night Steven Sutton was killed in Beeston?" asked Gardener.

"No doubt about it," said Janice.

"Can we hear it?" asked Gardener.

Wendy nodded, slipped over to the ticket hatch and pressed a button on an amplifier. They listened to the promotion.

"Oh, dear, God," said Janice. "I'd really rather not hear it again."

"Jesus," said Reilly. "How do you describe a sound like that?"

"It's him, Detective Gardener," said Janice. "I'd know that voice anywhere. It's definitely him."

"Who is it?" Gardener asked Wendy.

"He works here. It's Phillip Walker."

"Have you seen him today?"

"No," said Wendy. "It's most unusual. I've never known him be late for his shift, and I've never known him take time off when he shouldn't. It's so out of character."

She stopped talking, and her expression said she was thinking, and then she said, "Apart from once, a few days back. He was late for his shift, and he didn't look his usual self."

"Did he say why?" asked Reilly.

"He said it was a bad night's sleep, and that he had suffered with his sleep for years because of school bullies."

"I can hardly see that being the reason now," said Reilly.

"No, but we talked. I'll tell you exactly when it was. That same night as when they announced on the telly that a skeleton had been found in a house in Armley, at the scene of a murder."

"Jack Walker," said Gardener.

"Walker?" repeated Wendy. "I never watch the news, it's so depressing these days. Was that skeleton a relation of Phillip's?"

"His father," said Gardener.

"The one who went missing all those years ago?"

"That's the one."

"That might explain it," said Wendy.

"Explain what?" asked Gardener.

She told the two detectives all about Phillip's session with the Ouija board and trying to find his father. She mentioned the school bullying incident and the excessive strength that he believed he had.

"Ouija boards?" said Gardener.

"Yes," said Wendy. "I couldn't believe he'd said it."

"What the hell was he doing with Ouija boards?" asked Reilly.

"He said he'd been introduced years ago to the spirit board by friends from church. He said it wasn't all bad and he thought he could use it to find his father."

Gardener wasn't keen on what he was hearing.

"Didn't work, did it?" asked Reilly.

"Maybe it did," said Gardener. "Only he used his father as an excuse. It would make more sense if he was using the board to find the watch, if he so believed."

"Hasn't found that, either, has he?" said Reilly.

"He might have done by now," replied Gardener. He then asked Wendy Wilson to continue with what she was telling them.

She told them why his voice was so unusual. "He told me that it was down to a childhood accident involving his pushbike. He'd been riding around in very slippery conditions when he came off the bike and skidded into a fence pole that had been knocked over the previous week by a car."

"Ooh my word," said Janice, as if she was now beginning to feel sorry for him.

"The pole stuck in his neck and very nearly destroyed his voice box. He now talks with a definite rasp to the voice, as if he permanently has a frog in his throat. No amount of surgery has ever been able to correct that over the years and he has basically had to live with it.

"It may well be a reason for him being single. Phillip hates the sound of his own voice, so he believes others will as well, which is why he is very shy around the opposite sex."

"I think *I* would be, with a voice like that," said Janice. "The poor man, he's not had it easy, has he?"

"Maybe not, Mrs Portman," said Gardener. "Neither have a lot of people, but they don't turn to murder."

"Sounds like he's determined to get that watch one way or another," said Reilly.

"He's a very determined man," said Wendy. "If he does something he'll see it through to the end. Or if he wants something, he will get it."

At that point the door opened and Giles Middleton, the station manager, appeared. There was instant recognition between him and Gardener.

"Oh, not you two again," said Middleton. "The last time you were at my station you left it in a right mess."

"To be fair, Mr Middleton," said Gardener, "we were actually trying to clean up the mess."

Middleton appeared to soften slightly. "I'll give you that. You have a job to do and it's one I wouldn't like myself. So, what's going on here?"

Gardener explained.

"Phillip Walker, a murderer?" asked Middleton.

"We don't know that yet," said Gardener. "We do need some information from you that will help the investigation."

"We'll do what we can to help. What do you need to know?"

Gardener told them what he knew of Walker's movements on the days of both murders. He asked Wendy Wilson to check those dates to see if Phillip Walker was at work.

Sitting at her desk, she checked the computer. "No."

"Can you check if there were any train tickets registered to him for those days?"

More tapping, before she said, "Yes, he purchased tickets to London. On both days he had one connection, at Leeds."

"Did he reach London?"

The answer to that question took a little longer to find, and involved a phone call. Eventually, she replaced the receiver, tapped a few more keys, and said, "No, he only went as far as Leeds."

Gardener glanced at Reilly. "I think we have everything we need."

"What are you going to do now?" asked Middleton.

Gardener turned to Wendy Wilson. "You've definitely not seen him this morning?"

"No," she replied.

"But he should be here?"

"Yes."

"When did you last see him?

"The day before yesterday," she replied.

"Okay," said Gardener. "I'm going to leave two of my officers here, PCs Benson and Edwards. They can search the station and, should he make an appearance, they can apprehend him."

"I can't believe this," said Wendy Wilson. "I just can't believe Phillip Walker has murdered those people. He's such a gentle man."

"Even the best of us have a snapping point, Mrs Wilson," said Gardener. "Perhaps all this business with the watch was his."

"I'm struggling with it," said Middleton. "He's pretty much been here all his life and we've never had a cross word. He's always been willing to go the extra mile to help." He stared at Gardener. "We'll do all we can to help. But I'll tell you this much, I do hope you're wrong, and that it's someone else."

Gardener couldn't see how that was possible, given all they knew.

"All I ask, Mr Middleton, is that if he does show, please do not try to apprehend him in any way. Simply go and find my officers, who will deal with the situation."

"Where are you going now?" asked Middleton.

"To his house," said Gardener. "Though I doubt we'll find him."

"Probably not," said Middleton. "If he's not there, try the goods sheds about a mile from the station, near the trout farm."

"What does the goods shed have to do with him?" asked Reilly.

"I'm not entirely sure what happened," said Middelton. "I think we were going to knock it down years ago for extra car parking spaces, but Phillip bought it for storage. You might find him there."

Chapter Forty-three

Gardener and Reilly left the ticket office and performed one circuit of the platform first, making sure that Walker wasn't hiding anywhere. Before leaving Gardener updated Benson and Edwards, asking them to continue searching.

As the detective exited the station, he caught sight of Anderson, Thornton, Rawson and Sharp, waiting for him. He told them they were heading across the road to one of the cottages.

The town was relatively quiet, with little traffic or pedestrians to hinder their movement. They arrived five minutes later. Despite the time of year, Gardener thought Walker's garden was well maintained, with a trimmed hedge, a well-cut lawn and a number of potted plants.

Before approaching the front door, he turned to address the team. "Frank, Bob, can you go to the rear of the property for me, please? Make sure he's not around the back, or using it as an escape route."

As they left, Gardener knocked on the front door of the cottage and waited.

"I can't imagine he's here, boss," said Reilly.

"You're probably right, Sean."

Gardener knocked again. Reilly stepped along the path in front of the cottage and peered in through the front window.

"Anything?" asked Gardener.

"Nets are too thick to see through."

Sharp and Rawson were staring at the upstairs windows. "No movement," said Sharp.

Gardener noticed a couple of the nets moving in the cottage windows on either side, and a couple of people had stopped by the front gate. Within half an hour it would be all over the town.

Gardener had both a mobile and landline number for Walker. When he called, the mobile went to answer machine, and the landline continued to ring, which he could hear from outside.

Anderson and Thornton reappeared. "Nothing at the back, sir," said Anderson.

"Okay, do you want to bring the car up and grab the enforcer?"

Both officers had worked with Gardener long enough not to question his motives, so they both did exactly as he asked.

Five minutes later, Rawson had the battering ram in his hand. The law required Gardener to shout that he was coming in, so he did. He then nodded to Rawson. The door caved in after the second attempt.

On entering, he felt the warmth of the room, immediately spotting the Parkray central heating unit. Walker had been here recently. A hi-fi unit stood in one corner, with a table and four chairs in a small alcove at the back of the room. On the table was a Ouija board.

"Looks like he's been busy, already," said Reilly.

"Do you believe in all this shit?" Rawson asked Gardener.

"Not really," replied Gardener. "But *he* must."

Gardener and Reilly gave the place a once-over. With no one home, he then asked Anderson and Thornton to instigate a thorough search.

Outside, he took Reilly, Rawson and Sharp in search of the goods shed. They found it within minutes, exactly where Middleton said it was, near the old trout farm. It was a large, corrugated building with high windows and what appeared to be an impenetrable front door.

Gardener asked Sharp and Rawson to go around the building once to see if there was an easy entry.

When they left, Reilly grabbed the padlock on the outside of the door. "He's not going to be here, is he?"

"Probably not," said Gardener. "He's going to make us work for it if we want him."

They waited for Sharp and Rawson to return.

"Anything?" asked Gardener.

"There's no way in," said Rawson, "but I think someone's in there."

"What makes you think that?"

"I heard something," said Sharp, "so we stacked up some pallets near a window. I'm pretty sure we could see someone."

"Trouble is, he looked like he was swinging on a rope," said Sharp.

"Oh, Christ," said Gardener. "That could be Archie Figgs."

Gardener studied the door. Without cutting gear they were snookered. It was too well constructed.

He asked Reilly to phone the fire service, stipulating that he wanted someone round with cutting gear immediately.

One engine arrived within ten minutes, blue lights blazing, sirens blaring. Five minutes later they were inside the building.

Inside and to the right was an office but it was empty. As Gardener stepped out they heard a weak voice calling for help.

"Where did that come from?" asked Rawson.

"The back," said Reilly, immediately setting off.

"Do you still need us?" asked the fire chief, a tall man, solidly built with a face like granite.

"Maybe," said Gardener. "If you could just hang around."

Gardener followed Reilly, with Sharp and Rawson in pursuit. They scrambled through pathways beside the tall shelving with very little on it, arriving in an area that had a table and a couple of chairs. An empty cup stood on top.

Gardener glanced past the table to a man swinging on a rope, wearing only a pair of boxer shorts, and groaning.

"What the fuck?" asked the fire chief.

Gardener walked past the table. "Mr Figgs?"

"I wish I wasn't," said the man.

"Don't worry, Mr Figgs, we'll get you down."

Reilly grabbed a chair and put it near Archie. Rawson found a ladder and climbed up. When Reilly had his arms around the unfortunate man, slackening the rope, Rawson produced a penknife and cut through it.

Archie bellowed out.

Sharp and Reilly took his weight and lowered him to the floor, before dragging him across to a chair near the table.

Archie rested his elbows on the table. "The bastard," he said, wincing. "Look at my fucking thumbs."

Gardener took the chair at the opposite side of the table.

"I know you," shouted Rawson, staring at Archie. "I spoke to you at the station the other day. Showed you a photo."

"I wish I'd listened," he said.

"We've been looking for you, Mr Figgs," said Gardener.

"I wish you'd found me before he did, I might have thumbs instead of fucking marrows."

Gardener glanced at Sharp and asked him to call an ambulance.

"Who did this to you, Mr Figgs?"

"That lunatic, Walker."

"Why are you here?" asked Gardener.

"The watch. He rang me up, said he was a collector. Offered me fifty grand."

"Does he have the watch with him now?" asked Reilly.

"You don't think I was daft enough to bring it with me, do you?"

"So *you* still have it?" asked Gardener.

"Yes," said Figgs. "Do you think I could have a drink or something? I'm fucking parched. Been up here all night."

Rawson scurried back down the corridor, before returning with a bottle of orange juice. "There was a fridge in the office." He unscrewed the cap and placed it on the table in front of Archie, who made a move and then nearly screamed the place down as he tried to hold it.

Fortunately, Rawson had also brought a straw.

"Mr Figgs," said Gardener, "can you tell me everything, please? From the moment he contacted you till now."

Archie drank half the bottle of orange juice, waited a few minutes, and then filled them in.

Apparently, Walker was dressed like a 'posh nob'. Archie told them about his 'Jack the Ripper case'. "All his shit was in it."

"What do you mean?" asked Gardener.

"They're big cases them things," said Archie. "He had all sorts in it – a rope, a Taser." Archie glanced at his chest. "Fucking tasered me, twice. Look at those marks. It's illegal, that is. He wants locking up, that mad bastard. He even had a nail gun in it. He used that on the Suttons when he killed them, and he killed Alan Browne."

"Did he tell you all of this?" asked Gardener.

"Of course he did," shouted Archie. "How else would I know? He was trying to frighten me. Fucking worked, as well. He was fucking fuming about what happened to his dad. Now he's blaming me for some reason."

"Why is he blaming you?" asked Gardener.

"No idea," said Archie. "Where is he now?"

Gardener heard a siren and saw blue lights outside the building. The ambulance pulled up.

"Oh my fucking thumbs," said Archie. "Look what he's done to me. I'll never be able to use them again. Where is he now?"

"We haven't found him yet, Mr Figgs."

"Haven't found him?" shouted Archie, staring at Gardener. "You mean that freak is still out there? He's not fucking human. He can't be, have you heard his voice? It sounds like he's swallowed a tin of ball bearings. Marge Simpson on steroids."

"We will find him," said Gardener.

The two medics arrived on the scene. Reilly went over to talk to them.

"Oh, Jesus," shouted Archie.

"It's okay, Mr Figgs," said Gardener. "We'll take you to the hospital and have your thumbs seen to."

"I didn't mean that," shouted Archie. "While he's still out there, my mother is in danger. You have to go and find her. He could do anything. She's old. She can't protect herself against him."

"Don't worry, Mr Figgs," said Gardener. "Two of our officers are outside your mum's house now. If he goes anywhere near, he won't reach your mother."

"I bloody well hope not," said Archie. "You need to make sure she's okay."

Gardener stood up. "We will." He called the medics over and let them tend to Archie.

After a few minutes, one of them said he would fetch a stretcher, but Archie insisted he could walk. He didn't want anyone wasting time. He needed to go and see his mother. She'd be worried.

As the medics helped him, Archie turned. "She's all I've got, officer. Don't let that idiot do anything to her."

When he'd gone, Gardener asked Rawson and Sharp to search the goods shed for anything they could use as evidence against Walker. He and Reilly were going over to Calverley.

Outside, Gardener called Gates. She answered after the second ring. "How is everything?"

"All quiet," said Gates.

"You've not seen anything of Walker?"

"Not so far."

"Have you checked on Mrs Figgs?"

"I'm just going over, boss. I'm dying to use the loo."

Chapter Forty-four

Maude was settled in her armchair in front of the fire, listening to *The Archers* on the old radio, whilst also trying to read the paper. She had most of it in her hands, the rest covered the floor in front of her, and to the side, with one sheet around the back of the chair. The fire had been banked up and she found the crackling of the logs comforting.

Maude couldn't really concentrate on the newspaper. She had Archie on her mind. It wasn't like him to go missing. Despite her harsh treatment of him, he was good to her. He was the breadwinner – not that she really knew *how* he made his money, but he did. He did the shopping, a lot of the cooking, some of the cleaning, and he was thoughtful. That said, she felt she had to keep him in his place. After all, what were mothers for?

A sudden knocking sound diverted her attention. The front door opened and a voice called out as she lowered the newspaper.

Maude saw the female detective called Gates appear in the doorway to the living room.

"Hello, Maude, love. Sarah Gates." She flashed her warrant card. "Are you okay?"

"I'm not so bad, thanks, dear," replied Maude. "Have you heard anything of Archie?"

"Yes, Maude, they've just found him."

"Where was he?"

"I don't have the full details, yet," said Gates. "But my boss has been talking to him and he seems okay, but he's on his way to hospital."

"Hospital," shouted Maude. "What's happened to him? And where the hell has he been all night?"

"I don't think anything's happened," said Gates. "It's just standard procedure. They just want to check him over."

"But if nothing's happened, why do they want to check him over?"

"As I said, Maude, love, standard procedure," replied Gates. "He's been out all night and from what I can gather it was not in a hotel, so they want to make sure he's okay before they allow him home. He asked about you."

"Okay, love," replied Maude, wondering if she was hiding something.

"Apart from that," said Gates, "I popped in to see if I could use your loo. I'm bursting."

Maude laughed. "Of course you can, dear. Up the stairs, first door on the left. Is your friend outside with you?"

"Yes, but she's okay."

"Would you both like some tea?"

"I'm sure Julie would love one, and I wouldn't say no. Would you like me to make it when I come down?"

"Don't be daft. You go and use the toilet and I'll sort it out. And I might have a packet of cakes to go with the tea."

"Where's your neighbour, Maude?" asked Gates. "The one who was keeping an eye on you?"

"She's nipped off to do a bit of shopping. She's picking up one or two items for me. I asked her to get two large custards, our Archie's favourite."

Gates nodded and disappeared up the stairs.

Maude raised the newspaper, checked a couple more things, and then thought about making a move, when she heard a noise in front of her.

"That was quick," she said, lowering the paper, which she then dropped. "Who the hell are you? A doctor?"

The man in front of her was small and bespectacled, wearing an overcoat and a bowler hat. He carried what Maude took to be a Gladstone bag.

"I'm not a doctor," replied the man.

Maude winced. His voice sounded like a meat grinder. It went right through her.

She grabbed the arms of her chair. "Well, whoever you are, you can't just barge into my house like this."

Whoever he was, thought Maude, he could be in trouble shortly, especially as the police were in the house. "If you're from benefits trying to catch me out, you're wasting your time."

"I'm not from the benefits office, either." He lowered his bag on to the chair opposite and opened it up but did not reach inside.

Maude pointed a warning finger at him, feisty as ever. "If you're trying to sell me double glazing or solar panels you'd still be wasting your time. I don't have money for that kind of thing."

"If you'd like to shut up and allow me two minutes of your time, I'll tell you exactly why I'm here."

"Is that right?" answered Maude. "Who the hell are *you* to tell *me* what to do in *my* house?"

"I won't beat about the bush. I have Archie."

A sudden chill ran through her. Had Archie been abducted and subjected to God knows what, the man in front of her being responsible?

But he didn't have Archie now, did he? Gates had told her otherwise. She decided to play along, play for time. "Archie?"

The small man glanced at the ceiling and back again. "Your son?"

"Oh, him," said Maude, sitting forward. "Well you can bloody well keep that lazy good for nothing. I sent him to the shops yesterday and he hasn't been back. He doesn't care, that's his trouble. I've not been hard enough on him. Look at the state of this place. He never lifts a finger to clean up or anything, idle layabout. You think I want him back?"

The small man's eyes widened.

She'd show *him* who he was dealing with. "So, if you have him, what are you doing here?"

"We have a small business matter to settle."

"We do?" said Maude, wondering where the hell the policewoman was.

"Yes."

"Any business you have in this house is with Archie, not me. And seeing as you have him, perhaps you can go and ask him if he has what you want, boy," said Maude, raising herself out of the seat. "And when you've concluded your business, perhaps you can send him to the shops so he can get my shopping."

"I don't believe I'm hearing this," said the man, reaching into his bag.

Maude was fully on her feet now. "What business do you have with him?"

"He has something of mine," he replied, drawing his hand out of the bag.

"What?" asked Maude.

"He has a watch that belongs to me, my family."

"Your family?" said Maude.

"I'm not in the habit of repeating myself."

"I wondered when you'd show up, Mr Walker," said a voice from behind the man.

He turned to face Gates. "Who are you?"

Gates had her warrant card in her hand. "DS Sarah Gates, and I would advise you to think very carefully about your next move."

"Oh, I have," said Walker, and withdrew his hand fully from the bag.

Maude couldn't quite see what was going on but thought he had pulled out a gun.

With no warning whatsoever, Walker aimed the gun at Gates and pulled the trigger. Two wires shot out as if fired from a canon, catching the female officer in the chest. She hit the floor immediately – out cold.

Walker calmly reached back into the bag, before turning to face Maude, with another of the guns.

She had one hand in front of her and the other behind her back. "What the hell have you done?"

"The watch," said Walker. "Where is it?"

"What watch?" said Maude. "What the hell are you talking about? There's no watch here. And what have you done to her?"

Walker didn't bother asking a second time, he simply fired the Taser at Maude. The two wires hit her square in the chest but they had no effect whatsoever, leaving her to wonder what the hell he was using and why had it knocked out the police woman.

Walker's eyes grew like saucers. He stared at Maude, lowered his eyes to the gun and then back at Maude.

Fatal mistake.

By the time he was staring at Maude again, she was ready for him. "Bit old to be playing with toys, aren't you, boy?"

She brought her ivory-headed walking stick from behind her back and swung it with everything she had.

Chapter Forty-five

Reilly pulled the pool car into the small car park opposite what used to be the Calverley and Rodley railway station, next to the other pool car, which had only Julie Longstaff sitting in it, checking her phone.

Gardener jumped out and noticed an island platform, two outer platforms, and some tracks; a large warehouse complex that resembled a goods shed, and the station building, which he knew belonged to Maude and Archie.

Longstaff stepped out of the car. "I didn't expect to see you."

"We haven't located Walker yet," said Gardener.

"You found Archie Figgs, though, didn't you?" asked Longstaff.

"Yes," said Reilly, explaining how they had found him.

Gardener said he had left Anderson and Thornton at Walker's house, and Sharp and Rawson at the goods shed where they found Archie, which apparently belonged to Walker; Edwards and Benson were at the railway station.

"Have you seen any action here?" asked Gardener, staring at the station house.

"Not so far," said Longstaff.

"No sign of Walker?"

"No."

"Where's Sarah?"

"She nipped across to see Maude, and to use the loo."

"How long's she been gone?" asked Reilly.

Julie glanced at her phone. "Well now you come to mention it, quite a while. Maybe they're gassing, or making a cuppa, which would be lovely."

Gardener glanced at the house. He didn't like it.

"And maybe it's not as cosy as you make it sound," said Reilly.

"What do you mean?" asked Longstaff.

"Like I said, Julie," said Gardener. "We haven't found Walker, yet."

"You don't think he's here," said Longstaff. "We haven't seen anyone."

"There'll be more than one way into that place," said Reilly.

"Come on," said Gardener. "Let's go."

All three of them used the overhead tunnel that led to the other side of the tracks, their footsteps reverberating all over the place. At the bottom of the stairs, Gardener opened a gate and walked up the front path, listening all the while.

They slipped in through the open front door and the first thing Gardener saw was Gates on her back, out cold.

"Jesus," he said.

As he approached Gates and the door into the living room, he heard a sudden dull thud and the man they had been searching for, whom they knew had to be Phillip Walker, lurched to his right and almost fell into a roaring fire.

His right arm cracked up against the brick fireplace, which deflected the direction he was going in, sending him further to his right and onto the floor. At the same time, he dropped a Taser.

Standing over him was Maude with an ivory-headed walking stick raised and ready for another crack at the man.

"It's okay, Mrs Figgs," said Gardener, his warrant card in the air. "I'll take it from here."

Maude Figgs glanced at him and made a valiant effort to try and drop the cane behind her back, which brought a

256

smile to Gardener's lips, as he thought of how Maurice Cragg had summed her up.

Longstaff immediately stooped to Gates' side, checking for a pulse, before reaching for her phone.

Reilly landed onto Walker like a ton weight, holding him to the floor with one knee.

To give Walker his credit, for a man who been cracked by that cane, he wasn't out. But Gardener had not seen exactly where it had landed.

Maude Figgs sat back down in her armchair, breathing heavily, which Gardener suspected was for his benefit.

"Come on, sunshine," said Reilly, pulling Walker to his feet and producing a pair of handcuffs.

"What the hell are you doing?" said Walker.

Gardener noticed Longstaff on her phone, calling for an ambulance. "Is she okay?"

"She has a pulse," said Longstaff, "but it's not brilliant."

Gardener glanced at the floor and saw two Tasers. He immediately called Rawson and Sharp and told them to stop their search of the goods shed and to come over to where they were.

Gardener finished the call and glanced at the small bespectacled man that his partner had now handcuffed.

"Phillip Walker?" he asked.

"Get these cuffs off me."

"Sorry, Mr Walker. We can't do that."

Walker suddenly slammed backwards into Reilly, who fell back toward the fireplace.

Walker turned, as if he thought he could escape.

Reilly only went down on one knee, but that helped him slide forward, straight into Walker, who tipped over and crashed into the floor.

On his feet quickly, Reilly grabbed Walker by the scruff of his neck and hauled him to his feet.

"Try that again, sunshine, and you won't be walking out of this house," said Reilly through gritted teeth. "Do you understand me?"

"This is police brutality," shouted Walker.

Reilly spun him round to face Gardener. "That will be the least of your worries, Mr Walker." He then read him his rights, which included three counts of murder, one of attempted murder, one of assault on a police officer with an illegal weapon, and torture with intent to harm.

He glanced at Reilly. "Take him through to the hallway, Sean, and stay with him till Dave and Colin get here. They can take him to the station."

"What about my shoulder?" Walker asked.

"What about it?" Gardener asked.

"I think she's broken it," said Walker, staring at Maude.

"I've no idea what he's talking about," she shouted. "He broke into my house, threatened me, and attacked one of your officers. It was lucky for me that he lost his balance when he turned round, and fell over. If you hadn't arrived, he might have killed me."

Gardener turned to Walker. "I'm sorry, Mr Walker, I didn't see anything, apart from my officer on the floor."

Gardener glanced around. To be fair, he couldn't see Maude's cane anywhere.

"Take him away, Sean."

Gardener turned to Maude. "Are you okay?"

"Yes, officer," she replied. "A bit breathless, a little shook up. It's not everyday someone breaks in and tells you they have your son. It fair frightened me, I can tell you."

The ambulance arrived quickly and the medics came through the front door. By now, Gates had come round but she was still a little drowsy.

"Would you like to go in the ambulance with my officer?" Gardener asked Maude.

"Don't be daft, love," she replied. "I'm made of tougher stuff than that."

A few quick checks on Gates and the medics took her to the hospital, with Longstaff accompanying her.

Rawson and Sharp had arrived and Gardener asked them both to take Walker to the station, where Gardener and Reilly would eventually interview him, in the presence of a solicitor no doubt.

Maude insisted she was fine. She even made them the cup of tea she had promised Gates. The pair of them explained that they had found Archie and why Walker had abducted him, and asked her about the watch.

"Watch?" repeated Maude. "There is no watch – that I know of. I have no idea what you're talking about."

They explained more about the watch, showing her a picture. "Are you sure you haven't seen anything like this around here?" asked Gardener.

"I haven't, officer," she replied. "I know our Archie likes watches and he has one or two in his study, but to be honest, he's a bit of a dreamer. He doesn't know as much about watches as he'd like to think. I really doubt that he has what you're after. Where the hell would he get it?"

Gardener explained what they believed had happened and where he had bought it.

"Big nose, Harry." Maude laughed. "You don't want to go believing that daft twat. He's another like our Archie, lives in cloud cuckoo land most of the time. No, officer, there's no watch like that one round here. But you see that room over there?" Maude pointed.

Gardener nodded.

"That's our Archie's study. You have my permission to give it a thorough search. Take what you like, but you'll find nothing like that here."

The pair of them finished their tea and took her up on the offer. They spent about thirty minutes digging around but their search revealed nothing.

Back in the living room, Gardener checked once more that Maude was okay and asked if they could send a couple of officers around to keep an eye on her until Archie arrived, and to perhaps make another search.

Maude was more than happy.

Outside and back at their car, Reilly turned to Gardener. "She's a canny old lass, that one."

"I think you're right, Sean," he replied. "And furthermore, I think she may have even got the better of us."

Chapter Forty-six

Two Days Later

Gardener was in the garage. Christopher Cross was playing in the background. The Bonneville stood in front of him, renovated and polished and ready for action. Spook the cat was lounged in one corner of the garage, in a box with a blanket. She was one of the few connections to his late wife Sarah that he still had.

With a cup of tea in his hand, he admired his handiwork, relishing his first Saturday off in quite some time. Both he and Reilly had interviewed Phillip Walker twice, in the presence of his solicitor, David Macintosh. Walker hadn't said a great deal, he admitted to nothing, and delivered evasive answers. It wouldn't do him much good, Gardener and his partner had him banged to rights; everyone knew it. He would serve more than one life sentence.

He rattled on about the elusive watch, but as no one could find it, there was very little to go on. They were waiting for Archie Figgs to be released from hospital so they could talk to him, and so far, any search for Harry Pinchbeck had proved fruitless. He had disappeared – for now.

Gardener figured that by tomorrow, at the latest, DCI Briggs would want Walker charged with murder.

"You can't stay there all day looking at it," said his father, Malcolm, standing behind him.

Gardener turned. "You're right, I suppose."

"No excuse, it's finished. Time to see if this legendary bike is all you thought it would be."

"You first," said Gardener, placing his cup on a nearby bench.

"What do you mean?" asked Malcolm.

"I want you to have the honour of the first ride."

Malcolm's expression was one of embarrassment. "I couldn't, son, it's your bike."

"I know, but I've made my decision, and I'm sure Sarah would have been happy with it."

Gardener reached up to a shelf and pulled down a helmet. "Go on, you know a lot more about these things than me."

"Oh I get it," said Malcolm, taking the helmet. "You just don't want to be on it if it breaks down."

They both laughed but his father accepted the offer, took the bike off the stand, wheeled it outside, started it, and set off. He turned left out of the drive and took a long country road from Churchaven, towards Leeds.

Gardener had to admit, the machine sounded healthy and throaty.

He reached out and picked up his phone, calling Vanessa Chambers. She answered on the second ring. "I've been wondering where you were."

"Busy, as always," said Gardener.

"Did you get your man?"

"I did."

"Excellent. Care to tell me about it?"

"Over lunch," said Gardener.

"Sounds good to me."

"I'll pick you up in half an hour? Or thereabouts."

"I'll be waiting," said Vanessa. "You *do* know where I live?"

"I have a rough idea."

They both laughed, so she finally gave him directions. His father returned a few minutes later, killed the engine, put the bike on the stand and removed his helmet.

"Brilliant job," he said. "Handles well, sounds good, rides like a dream. And now, it's all yours."

Gardener reached upwards and pulled down his leather jacket from a peg and an extra helmet.

"Are you going where I think you're going?" asked Malcolm.

"Why not?" said Gardener.

"In that case, enjoy yourselves."

Gardener put his helmet on, connected the other to the bike, jumped on, started it, and took the opposite route to the one his father had taken.

He arrived at Vanessa's cottage roughly on time. She lived on Chevin End Road in Menston, not far from The Chevin pub. He pulled into a circular drive, drove up to the cottage that had a garage on the left, and a well in the front garden.

As he removed his helmet she came running out. "Oh, my God, I didn't realize you were on the bike."

"Do you want me to drive back and get the car?"

She laughed. "You dare."

Gardener stood up, cradling the bike between his legs, whilst Vanessa undid the spare helmet from the carrier.

"I can't wait for this," she said. "Where are we going?"

"I was thinking of something light," said Gardener. "I know a great little café on the side of the canal at Rodley."

"Suits me."

He started the bike. She zipped up her leather jacket and placed the helmet over her head. She then jumped on and wrapped her arms around him.

It had been a long time since a woman had done that. It felt right. He told her to hold on and they set off.

Epilogue

Archie had managed to beg a lift from the hospital to the old station house at Calverley.

The last couple of days had left him livid. First and foremost, the fact that he was now on the system. He had a name, a National Insurance number, all of which was logged and connected to his date of birth and current address, and Christ knows how many other things.

He'd have to be normal now, declare his earnings, pay tax, and do all the other shit normal people did.

Phillip Walker was number one on his hit list. What a bastard he turned out to be. Stringing Archie up by his fucking thumbs and leaving him overnight. At the hospital, the nurses and the doctors all had expressions that left Archie fearful that he would never have the full use of his thumbs ever again. They were still painful and the size of fat sausages, and he couldn't use them. Because they had been dislocated, the doctors almost had to break them to re-set them, something that made Archie's eyes water and his mouth run away with him.

The police had been to see him, and taken a statement. They had told Archie that his mother was fine; no doubt she wouldn't be when she realized he had no shopping for her. Apparently, according to the police, his mother had been an absolute legend. Had it not been for her, they may never have caught Walker.

What the fuck did she do, fall on him? Archie figured that whatever she did, it would have involved that bastard cane. Archie hoped she'd stoved Walker's head in.

He thanked the bloke for his lift, walked across the car park, up the stairs and through the tunnel to the front gate. Despite being December, it was reasonably mild. He stopped at the gate, staring at the latch, wondering which fingers to use to perform such a delicate operation.

What an absolute pain in the shitter. He couldn't eat properly, he couldn't dress himself, or tie his shoelaces. Trying to sleep was a laugh a minute. God forbid he rolled over in bed. That had happened the first night in hospital and he woke up the whole ward. He'd needed two nurses to roll him back over because he couldn't put any pressure on the thumbs, so he couldn't actually lift himself up and roll back. Very few people slept that night. He was still on pain medication.

Archie chose his middle finger to undo the latch. He slipped down the path, wondering what kind of mood Maude would be in.

The front door wasn't locked so Archie went straight into the hall and then the living room. The fire was crackling nicely but that was the only thing he recognized.

As he glanced around, the whole room had changed. Not so much in the layout of the furniture, but everything was clean – spotless in fact. All furniture had been dusted and polished and smelled of citrus. The curtains had been cleaned; the nets were new. The carpet had also been cleaned and he could see all the colours in it.

The old radio remained, playing some instrumental song at a low volume. He recognized it but the title failed him. In the kitchen, he could hear the chinking of cutlery. Surely Maude wasn't cooking. He glanced back into the hall, which had the same level of cleanliness.

Archie thought he was in the wrong house, until he heard her.

"Where's my shopping, boy?"

Oh, fuck, not again, thought Archie.

He turned. Maude had left the kitchen and was standing in front of him. He almost didn't recognize her.

She was wearing a long black, sleeveless dress. He stared down at her feet and her shoes were new, and delicate, for her. She'd had her hair done. It was still reasonably short but cut and shaped in a very modern, feminine style.

What the fuck had happened? Archie was a little stuck for words.

"Come here, boy," said Maude. She reached out and grabbed Archie and pulled him close.

Maude grabbed his head and gave him a great, slobbering kiss. "How are you, my love? I have missed you."

Archie freed his face. "Are you really my mother?"

"What do you think, you daft beggar? Of course, I'm your mother."

"What the hell's happened?"

"Things have changed around here, Archibald."

Oh, Jesus, my Sunday name, thought Archie. And then another, apocalyptic thought hit him. Maude said things had changed. And they had. And so had she. Everything was different.

Archie pulled back from her. "Just give me a minute."

He left the living room and rushed out to his shed, which was empty. Archie glanced around in a state of panic. Where was his stuff, most importantly, the key to the study safe?

He left the shed and ran back into his study. He kicked the rug out of the way, and there in the recess in the floor was an open safe – an empty one.

"Oh, fuck," said Archie. "What the hell has she done?"

He scurried back into the living room. "What's happened, Ma? Are you ill?"

"What do you mean, what's happened?" She was now sitting in her favourite chair near the fire.

"Everything's changed."

"I know it has, love," said Maude. "And not before time. I was sick to death of the mess around here. Day in, day out, same old drudge."

Maude leaned forward. "If my brush with death has taught me anything, Archibald, it is that life is for living, and that's what we're going to do."

"Your brush with death?" repeated Archie. "What are you on about?"

Maude sat back and clutched her chest. "Oh, you have no idea. That man broke into the house and came charging into the living room. I was here by myself, you know. You weren't here."

"I know, I was in the fucking hospital."

"Language, Archibald," she chided him.

"Sorry, Ma. But where is everything?"

"All gone, my love. I was fed up with clutter. You couldn't move in this bloody place for clutter and junk. I got rid of all of it."

"All of it?" Archie's knees weakened.

"Yes," she said. "All of it. It was time to do something with my life, so I had a massive clear-out. Everything went to the charity shop in Bramfield. They came and collected the lot, and when they had, I paid a team of cleaners to give it the once-over. They finished this morning. Looks lovely, doesn't it?"

"What about my stuff, ma?"

"Well," said Maude, elongating the word, smiling at him, flashing big square teeth like a cartoon horse. "You have to admit, most of your stuff *was* junk, wasn't it. And do you know, I feel a lot better for it. Yesterday, when the cleaners were here, I took myself off to Rodley, met up with Dora and persuaded her we needed a day out together. And what a day out we had. We had our hair done, and we had dinner in a café. We thoroughly enjoyed ourselves. We're going to do it again soon."

Archie couldn't believe what he was hearing. He thought his head had been put through a blender. Most of the watches he didn't care about, but the bloody railroad pocket watch...

Archie spotted Maude's cane. It took everything he had not to pick it up and smash her face in.

"Right, Archibald, you go and wash your hands and we'll have a nice cup of tea and your favourite, a piece of custard."

"Ma," said Archie, with as much patience as he could possibly muster, "which charity shop in Bramfield?"

"Cancer Research," answered Maude, lifting herself out of the chair. "The one in Market Place."

Maude left the room and went into the kitchen. Archie left the room and went out of the front door, almost killing himself in the process. He tripped and rolled and landed in the front garden – face up, luckily.

He managed to lift himself to his feet and ran through the tunnel to the car park and quickly jumped on a local bus.

Half an hour later he was in the shop in Bramfield, which, luckily for Archie, had only one browsing customer. The assistant behind the counter was tall and skinny and had lank black hair. She wore a black shirt and jeans and a name badge in green, which said her name was Anna. She also had glasses and bucked teeth and appeared to be very slow at her job.

Archie inquired about the watches they had picked up from a house in Calverley within the last few days.

"Oh those," said Anna. "Yes, there were some lovely watches."

"Where are they now?"

"Over there," said Anna, pointing to the right-hand wall. He scurried over and returned to the counter within seconds.

"That's not all of them."

"No, we sold three or four," said Anna, who was now starting to irritate the life out of Archie.

"What about the rest?"

"Well, here's the funny thing. Our Mr Brough, who collected them, is an expert on timepieces. And he said a few of them were valuable, especially something called a railroad pocket watch. I had no idea what he was talking about."

Archie could have cried.

"What's Mr Brough done with them?"

"They're all in London now."

"London?" cried Archie. "Why the fuck are they in London?"

Anna stared at him. "I'm not sure I like your attitude."

I don't like your fucking face, thought Archie, but we all have a cross to bear. "I'm sorry. I'm just out of hospital."

"Oh, I'm sorry, you must be a little stressed."

"The watches?" asked Archie, very stressed.

"Oh, yes," said Anna. "Gone to Christie's to be auctioned. We did tell the lady we got them off, and she was so happy that she was able to help. Said her mother and father had died of cancer and she couldn't think of a better cause. Anyway, Christie's said, when the watches sold, they would make a healthy donation to the charity, and also give the kind old lady who gave them to us a bit for herself."

Archie's knees buckled. Fucking Christie's. He'd never see them again. He'd never know what it was like to be rich. All his life, his mother had messed things up for him, and she was still fucking doing it!

Archie never said a word. He simply left the shop, stepping out into Market Place. The sky was blue, the temperature was mild, people were happy.

His life was complete fucking bollocks. Couldn't be any worse.

"Archie Figgs?" inquired a voice.

Archie glanced upwards. There were two of them. One was average size, thinning on top, with a widow's peak. The other was a mountain of a man, with a beard and a moustache, dressed in an ill-fitting suit. They were coppers. He could smell coppers a mile away. He recognized the big one, who had approached him at the railway station in Leeds only last week, with a picture of that deranged lunatic who had taken Archie's life to hell and back. If he ever saw that Walker again…

"DS Rawson, Leeds Central." He held out his warrant card.

"Look," said Archie. "I've told you everything I know about that nutjob, Walker. There's nothing left to add."

"That's not why we want to talk to you," said the other one.

"Well, what do you want? I'm not really in the mood at the moment."

"Can you accompany us to the station, please, Mr Figgs? We would like to question you about the theft of an electric bike and some watches from the railway station in Leeds."

Archie threw his hands in the air. He'd left the bike behind the police station in Bramfield recently, and it had been nicked.

Only it probably hadn't, thought Archie. He glanced over at the station. On the steps leading to the building was the moon-faced desk sergeant.

He was staring at Archie, grinning, holding up his thumbs.

Acknowledgments

It's been said many times before, and will be again, I'm sure. No author ever writes a book on his own. I'd like to offer my thanks to two professional people, who also happen to be great friends, Darrin Knight and Bob Armitage. I would also like to extend those thanks to my publisher and a fantastic editorial team.

If you enjoyed this book, please let others know by leaving a quick review on Amazon. Also, if you spot anything untoward in the paperback, get in touch. We strive for the best quality and appreciate reader feedback.

editor@thebookfolks.com

www.thebookfolks.com

ALSO AVAILABLE

If you enjoyed IMPALED, the eleventh book, check out the others in the series:

IMPURITY – *Book 1*

Someone is out for revenge. A grotto worker is murdered in the lead up to Christmas. He won't be the first. Can DI Gardener stop the killer, or is he saving his biggest gift till last?

IMPERFECTION – *Book 2*

When theatre-goers are treated to the gruesome spectacle of an actor's lifeless body hanging on the stage, DI Stewart Gardener is called in to investigate. Is the killer still in the audience? A lockdown is set in motion but it is soon apparent that the murderer is able to come and go unnoticed. Identifying and capturing the culprit will mean establishing the motive for their crimes, but perhaps not before more victims meet their fate.

IMPLANT – *Book 3*

A small Yorkshire town is beset by a series of cruel murders. The victims are tortured in bizarre ways. The killer leaves a message with each crime – a playing card from an obscure board game. DI Gardener launches a manhunt but it will only be by figuring out the murderer's motive that they can bring him to justice.

IMPRESSION – *Book 4*

Police are stumped by the case of a missing five-year-old girl until her photograph turns up under the body of a murdered woman. It is the first lead they have and is quickly followed by the discovery of another body connected to the case. Can DI Stewart Gardener find the connection between the individuals before the abducted child becomes another statistic?

IMPOSITION – *Book 5*

When a woman's battered body is reported to police by her husband, it looks like a bungled robbery. But the investigation begins to turn up disturbing links with past crimes. They are dealing with a killer who is expert at concealing his identity. Will they get to him before a vigilante set on revenge?

IMPOSTURE – *Book 6*

When a hit and run claims the lives of two people, DI Gardener begins to realize it was not a random incident. But when he begins to track down the elusive suspects he discovers that a vigilante is getting to them first. Can the detective work out the mystery before more lives are lost?

IMPASSIVE – *Book 7*

A publisher racked with debts is found strung up in a ruined Yorkshire abbey. Has a disgruntled author taken their revenge? DI Stewart Gardener is on the case but maybe a hypnotist has the key to the puzzle. Can the cop muster his team to work some magic and catch a cunning killer?

IMPIOUS – *Book 8*

It could be detectives Gardener and Reilly's most disturbing case yet when a body with head, limbs and torso assembled from different victims is discovered. Alongside this grotesque being is a cryptic message and a chess piece. A killer wants to take the cops on a journey. And force their hand.

IMPLICATION – *Book 9*

When a body is found in a burned-out car, DI Stewart Gardener quickly establishes that a murder has been concealed. But with a missing person case and a spate of robberies occupying the force, he will struggle to identify the victim. When the investigations overlap, he'll have to work out which of the suspects is implicated in which crime.

IMPUNITY – *Book 10*

After a young woman passes out and dies, the medical examiner makes a grim discovery. Someone had surgically removed her kidneys. Detective Stewart Gardener must find a killer evil enough to think of such a cruel act, let alone have the gall to carry it out. It looks like revenge is a motive, but what had the victim, by all accounts a kind and friendly girl, done to anyone?

All FREE with Kindle Unlimited and available in paperback!

www.thebookfolks.com

Other titles of interest

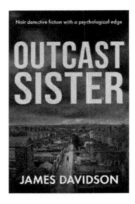

OUTCAST SISTER by James Davidson

London detective Eleanor Rose is lured back to her home city of Liverpool by Daniel, an ex-boyfriend and colleague who's in danger. But when she retraces his steps to a grim housing estate, he's nowhere to be found. Has she walked into some kind of trap? Is Rose ready to confront the demons she finds there?

THE STORM KILLINGS by Iain Henn

As tornado season gets under way, the FBI's advanced
computer system highlights an anomaly in the casualties. It
looks like someone is using the chaos caused by the
weather as cover to kill unsuspecting women in their
homes. Special Agent Ilona Farris heads into the eye of the
storm to catch them in the act.

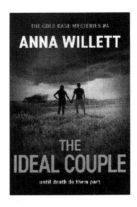

THE IDEAL COUPLE by Anna Willett

Detective Veronika Pope heads to an old mining town in
Western Australia, tasked with the cold case of a couple
who went missing there some three years previously.
Everyone in the town seems to be hiding something and
she gets few leads. But the more she probes, the more
cracks appear, and if she can avoid falling into one, just
maybe she can get closure for the couple's family.

All FREE with Kindle Unlimited and available in paperback!

www.thebookfolks.com

Printed in Great Britain
by Amazon